THE SEA OF TREES

Books by Yannick Murphy

Stories in Another Language

The Sea of Trees

THE SEA OF TREES

YANNICK MURPHY

HOUGHTON MIFFLIN COMPANY

BOSTON   NEW YORK   1997

For information about permission to reproduce selections from this book,
write to Permissions, Houghton Mifflin Company, 215 Park Avenue South,
New York, New York 10003.

For information about this and other Houghton Mifflin trade and reference
books and multimedia products, visit The Bookstore at Houghton Mifflin
on the World Wide Web at http://www.hmco.com/trade/.

Library of Congress Cataloging-in-Publication Data
Murphy, Yannick.
    The sea of trees / Yannick Murphy.
      p.   cm.
    ISBN 0-395-85012-6
    I. Title.
PS3563.U7635Y43   1997
813'.54 — dc21   96-49692
                            CIP

Printed in the United States of America

QUM 10 9 8 7 6 5 4 3 2 1

Book design by Melodie Wertelet

The author wishes to thank Georges and Anne Borchardt, Gerald Freund, the Whiting Foundation, the National Endowment for the Arts, the MacDowell Colony, the Chesterfield Film Writers' Project and the Sewanee Writers' Conference for their support.

THE SEA OF TREES

THE JAPANESE CAME WHEN I WAS IN THE GREAT ROOM standing on my mother's feet and she was dancing me around the symboled borders of the oriental carpet. At the symbol for fire they took me from her, but my mother still danced. They pushed us out the door. Outside there was a forest. The Japanese called it the Sea of Trees. My mother said she was dancing with my father. The Japanese followed behind us, holding their sabers at their sides.

We talked about my birthday. I was asking for a noodle stew. My mother danced around me on the path, saying that if there were flour I would have it. One short Japanese was told to pull up his saber, it was hitting on the ground. The trees were tall, my mother let her head drop back and she looked up. The Japanese looked too. My mother danced in circles with her head back and her arms held out.

"I am dancing with your father," she said.

...

On my birthday we had grass from the marsh. Pulling up the grass, we found a man floating on the water. Do you know him? everyone said, passing him on down. Others washing by the marsh took hold of the cuff of his pants and pulled him closer.

"No," they said, and passed him down again.

Crickets hopped on his face and my mother waved her hand over him. Someone tried to get his shirt off, but he was too bloated and no one could free it from his floating arms. We took his buttons, though, turning them around and around. As we twisted the buttons loose his legs brushed the grass we were pulling up for my birthday dinner.

"You can grow on these," my mother said, and pulled the longest blades of grass and put them in her shirt.

My amah cooked the grass in water with an onion. My mother danced around the pot, her arms crossed, her feet moving slowly, I thought she was cold.

"This is Indian," she said, meaning her dancing.

My amah gave me the first bite of the onion. "Happy birthday," she said, and then she bit where I bit and my mother bit where my amah bit and then the Japanese came in. They took the pot and poured the grass dish out the window.

"This is not a kitchen," they said. "This is where you sleep."

. . .

My father came to visit when he could. When he did, my mother sat still on her mat. Her eyes moved all over him. My amah checked his earlobes for thickness. His feet were brown, as if they were dug from dirt — potatoes from a field. I thought how we could boil them. How broken open they would steam.

"We are many up there," he said, and pointed to the mountains past the Sea of Trees.

"Marcelle," he said to my mother, "we will come down."

My father left. My amah said to us children, "Sound is what we hear at sunrise. Taste is a stop in the road. Seeing is the talking of ghosts. Animals teach us sleep — geese make us the pillow, the honey slowness of almost sleep is taught to us by bears." She pointed to our mats. "So everyone get to bed."

The Japanese played ball. Out our window we could see them running toward the jeeps they used as goals. We picked our favorite players. Bet on our teams. Our window was the closest to the field. Women balled rice in their fists, then placed these bets on the sill. I waved the flies away, kept count of who had wagered what. I thought, what if my man on my team jumped into the jeep and drove through the Sea of Trees? I would surprise him from the back, tell him where to go.

"The mountains," I would say. "I have to see my father."

My mother had Poulet one day while a game was going on. She spread her legs and her yells mixed with the yells of the players and the cheers of the Japanese standing on the sides of the field. That day the women bet their balls of rice on the baby. More thought boy than girl, and when she came out girl, the losers spit on their rice balls. Poulet came out yellow. My mother, wet from fever, held my arm with both her hands as if she were rowing and I was her oar.

When my amah asked for milk, they cut a hole in her leg.

"Look what the saber did," she said, and she took my fist and put it in the hole in her leg. Then I rolled my fist back and forth on her bone.

Later my amah stole the milk instead. My mother fed Poulet the milk, saying it would take away the yellow of her skin. My amah laughed. "For that you will need a river of milk," she said, "and I've only got two legs."

Not in French, like usual, but in Chinese, my mother told my amah to be quiet.

At night they told me stories. My amah told me how she lit a firecracker and put it into the ass of her father's best horse. My mother told me about the day I was born. My father's dogs stood over me like oxen in the manger. My father was down in the kitchen eating oranges the servants kept in china bowls around the house. It was the Year of the Dog. Our family, long known for selling medicines, lined the streets with their roots and their leaves, gave buyers a tiger's price. A girl had been born to Yeu, the dynasty lived on. And Yeu waited in the kitchen, eating one orange after the other, the servants taking the peels to keep under their pillows.

"Dreams of the groves," my amah said, "keep the family tight-knit."

IN THE DIRT, FATHER JEAN-CLAUDE DREW ME A MAP OF his homeland. He took off his cross and used it to draw mountains capped with snow and houses with roofs that were as pointed as steeples.

"Here's the bar," he said, and he drew me the inside, where the woman stood who served him drinks and where the liquor bottles lined the shelves.

Father Jean-Claude looked for a long time at his map and then he handed me the cross and told me to draw a map of whatever I wanted while he took a nap with his head under a bush, saying there he could sleep shielded from the power of the red-hot sun.

Later, when the last light was going down behind the mountains, Father Jean-Claude sat up and looked at what I had drawn.

"Where's this?" he said while leaves in his hair fell onto his shoulders.

"Here," I said.

"Here's the Sea of Trees," I said.

"I can see that, but what about the latrines, or the grave, didn't you draw those?"

I shook my head.

"This isn't right," he said, and he took the cross from me and drew in the fifteen makeshift bamboo prisoners' huts, where he said we laid our two hundred sweaty heads every night, and he drew the guardhouse towers and the general's place and the broken-down hall the nuns had called the Great Room when this place had been a convent. He drew people sleeping on the floorboards in the huts and some of us in piles on the side of the road.

Then Madame Lin walked by. She bent over my map and Father Jean-Claude looked down her dress. She took up the cross and drew the flowers by the marsh and the fishline out behind our place where our washed slips and underclothes were hung to dry.

· · ·

I woke up one night to the Japanese. They were sitting my mother back down on her mat.

"Where were you going?" they said.

"Nowhere," my mother said.

"Where were you going?" the Japanese said.

"To the toilet," my mother said.

"Where were you going?" the Japanese said.

"To the mountains," my mother said

In the moonlight they looked like brothers and my mother their sister gone off with a boy they didn't like, anything in particular they couldn't say, just their sister shouldn't be off with a boy, not with older brothers around.

It rained for days and the shovels slipped from our hands as we filled the field with sand so that the Japanese could play their games. Poulet on my back, I imagined I looked like a mother, with a husband, a house and some crop to be picked on her land. The slick shovel handle I meant to ask my husband about, see if on his next ride into town he could buy us a new one. The Japanese watching under umbrellas were trees on our land, when they moved it was the breeze in their branches.

"Keep the jeeps the jeeps, don't imagine them to be something else, that way we can drive out of this place," said my mother, who was shoveling next to me.

In the field, we stopped shoveling and held our hands above our eyes so we could see in the rain. I saw the Chief of the Montagnards. His testicles were swollen so big from the stream water that his wife pulled a wheelbarrow beneath him so he could walk without his testicles ripping off and falling to the ground. My mother took my hand and brought me closer to her while we stood and watched the chief and his wife and the wheelbarrow go by.

When the Chief of the Montagnards stopped in front of the Japanese, the Japanese bowed to him and the chief rested his hand on his swollen testicles in the wheelbarrow. No one could hear what the chief or the Japanese said. It sounded like the chief was

5

singing. Madame Lin said that he and the Japanese talked of peace and the end, and that the chief was going to disband his small mountain army, which had existed for centuries, even before the Japanese had come to this land. Madame Lin said that at least she wished that was what they were thinking, so that maybe more clothes and jewelry would be traded back and forth between the Montagnards and the camp and she could make herself a char- treuse dress, the same color as the robes the chief had worn one day when he came down the mountain months before.

The women watched how the wife cupped her hand to lift the water from the wheelbarrow and pour it on the Chief of the Mon- tagnard's testicles.

Before they went back through the Sea of Trees, the chief and his wife spoke to my mother.

"Marcelle," I heard the chief say, but that was all I could hear and then they left.

Later, the Japanese gave my mother fish eyes and asked her what the Chief of the Montagnards had said to her. My mother chewed on her fish eyes but she did not answer. The Japanese hit her face and the fish eyes flew out of her mouth, marked with her teeth. I picked them out of the dirt and chewed on them while I watched the Japanese play ball.

My father told us what had happened to him while he was living in the mountains with the Montagnards. He said he woke up in his grass hut and a woman was sitting in his chair and she took off her head and started brushing her hair.

"She was the most beautiful woman I've ever seen," he said. "And the sound of the brush going through her hair sounded like words whose meanings I did not know. When she left I found her long hair on the floor of my hut, mixed in with the dirt fallen from the cleft hooves of the wild pigs that would come in looking for rice, for the Chinese apples whose seeds shone like rubies, for anything they could eat. On my hard dirt floor, their small hooves sounded like women walking. Picture high-heeled shoes and transparent gowns. Foraging, grunting and then leaving, they wiggled their asses and their corkscrew tails shook as they trotted back up to the higher plateaus. It was the woman," my father said, "who took off her head and started brushing her hair who told me when it was safe to come down and visit you, when the Japanese would be shy of guards who bordered the Sea of Trees. Sometimes this woman would sing, her voice sounding like it was coming from all over. She was a kind of weather we've never known, a kind of rain or wind, a kind of night sky a color no one had ever seen before. There were the mountains and there was her singing," my father said.

"You fucked her then?" my mother said. She had once found receipts from hotels in my father's trouser pockets. She had found strands of hair on the front of his shirts, long and shaped like rivers drawn on maps.

"And where," my mother wanted to know, "did you put it inside her? The hole between her legs or the hole in her neck? Lucky girl," my mother said, "to be fucked in the head."

"Marcelle," my father said to my mother in French, "she was a ghost."

"Oui?" my mother said.

. . .

In the Great Room I stood on my mother's feet again and she danced me around the symboled borders of the oriental carpet. At the symbol for water she stopped and told me what it was the Chief of the Montagnards had said to her. My father was planning to set us free. With spears, with guns and sabers, he and the Montagnards would come one night or one day and they would spring from the Sea of Trees and beat back the Japanese.

When my mother told me this, white moths were flying through our legs and settling on the carpet.

"It's either the silk in our skirts or the wool in the carpet," my mother said.

She caught the moths and rubbed the powder from their wings

onto my eyes, so that when I looked in the Great Room's mirror I had half-moons above my eyes, so they seemed bigger like my mother's eyes, and I looked out the window, toward the mountains, and I thought I could see my father there, Yeu, walking with his face turned to the side, his nose large, banner-like, father straight and tall as a pole.

. . .

The day the Chief of the Montagnards came with his children, his boy pointed to his father's testicles in the wheelbarrow and said to me, "Someday all this will be mine."

The day of the Great Game, the Japanese came from all over. From roads that led to places we did not know of, from roads we knew led to Saigon, from roads where others had been taken and never seen again, the Japanese players came in jeeps. Their sabers and guns were collected and spread on tarps and then the Japanese changed their clothes. They put on their colors. The Japanese red sun was raised. Generals drank from small cups, and Japanese women came from the backs of the jeeps to cook and serve the food. From our place we watched the women. Wearing wooden shoes, they walked among the tables covered with cloths and ladled out noodles. Their long sleeves never got in the way but stayed close like folded wings at their sides.

"How beautiful," we all said, and we decided who was the prettiest, who wore the nicest dress, who walked the way we thought she should walk, who would be the first to be whipped, or made wife, or fucked in the kitchen, the man's saber hitting the stove, nicking the table's legs, her legs — drawing blood from the lily-white skin.

"Oh, yes, they are all beautiful," we agreed, and with arms on dusty window ledges we watched them move through the Japanese men.

The player man I bet on did not win.

"Year of the Pig," my amah screamed at me. "What did you expect? Pigs give you dreams of the mud, and in the morning your sheets look like you've slept with your shoes on. Besides, he couldn't run with legs as fat as tree trunks and knees that knock."

· · ·

Days later, when they pulled him from the marsh, we found out that the bloated man was one of our men. He was the husband of Leandri, a woman who made us dolls. The brown hair she used for the dolls was from her own head, and all of us girls owned one of her creations and we all called our dolls our Leandris. When Leandri found out it was her husband, we were sitting on him, braiding our Leandris' hair the way the Japanese women had worn their hair.

Wrapped in a sack, he was like a couch, and we sat on him and leaned our backs against a bamboo hut and worked on perfecting the Japanese braid. Leandri pulled us off the sack and tore it open and fell onto her husband. As she hugged him, bits of his rotting skin clung to her cheek. When she walked back to our hut, the Japanese called her names — spirit from the Chinese grave of whores and fishwives.

When Poulet was just a few months old and I sat feeding her milk dripping from the corner of a sheet, my amah came over to me and told me to put Poulet down and to stand up. She had me lift up my arms, and she wrapped the sheet around my small breasts, tying it tightly in a knot at the back. The milk was cool on me and for a day I smelled like Poulet. But at night, when I asked my amah to untie the sheet, she said, "No, from now on you are just a girl and not a woman. The Japanese will not want to touch you or take you to the Sea of Trees. I don't want to see you coming back to camp with dirt in your hair and blood running down your legs."

I wore the sheet all the time. Once in a while my mother would untie it and tie it tighter for me. My elbows sticking out, my mother asked, "Who is the chicken here? You or my little Poulet?"

· · ·

Once when I was playing the circle game, the Japanese pulled me off the dead man I was sitting on and took me to where they held prisoners and they sat me in a chair and they brought out a Frenchman and they said, "Tell us what he says."

His name was Michel Riquelme. One lens of his glasses was missing and the lens that remained magnified his eye and made it bulge so that he seemed to look at you with it more closely.

"Speaking of eyes," he once said to me, "I took out a man's eye in a bar with the end of my cane."

The Japanese said, "Tell him to stand up tall. Tell him, Keep your head down, your answers short, yes or no, your hands low, don't grab for rice or for water. Clean your ass after you shit, clean your teeth with your finger, clean your cell with the water given to you to drink, watch your mouth. Tell him, Your translator's a half-breed, and in the eyes of the gods she counts as two of the lowliest girls that ever slipped out of the belly of a French whore made with the seed of a Chinese clown."

With the eye stuck on the end of the cane like a cigar, Michel Riquelme said, he left the bar and dropped the eye in the Seine. Pupil up, it floated and bobbed, taking in Notre Dame, the starlit Paris sky.

"What did he say?" the Japanese said.

Michel Riquelme spoke French quickly. Often he would answer the questions and tell me about his life at the same time. "For fun we ran a stick through a hoop down the street — I don't know about the guerrillas — days it rained we made boats out of orange peels. Toothpicks were their masts, and we sailed them in the gutters — guerrillas never came to me or my men on December twenty-third."

I fell in love with Michel Riquelme.

"Year of the Rabbit," my amah said when she found out. "You'll have dreams of the garden," she said.

ON MY MOTHER'S BIRTHDAY WE WENT TO THE MARSH. There we put a table and chairs in the knee-deep water so that while we ate in the hot afternoon sun we cooled the bottoms of our legs. Come to curl around our ankles were the floating grass blades.

From the marsh my mother looked toward the mountains.

"One year Yeu gave me dancing lessons for my birthday. Out on our balcony he sang in perfect French, 'Parlez-moi d'amour.' I put my head on his chest and heard his heart going — it kept time with the song," my mother said, and then she started singing it and we joined in, my amah and me, and we splashed our feet in the marsh and the marsh water went up and hit our faces and our hair and then the Japanese came and they told us to take our table and our chairs back to where we found them, and "Do you think this is your house?" they asked us, and they laughed, saying to each other, "They think this is their house." They ran to one side of the marsh and said, "Here is the bedroom," and then they ran to the other side of the marsh, the legs of their trousers getting wet, their saber points dunking in the water, and they said, "Look here, the kitchen," and then they ran to another side of the marsh. "The toilet," they yelled, and they dropped their pants and peed in the water, making it look like circles in the marsh come up from fish feeding at the surface.

Later, from my window, I saw the Japanese lying down by the trees, they were watching the sun set and chewing on long blades of grass. I was drawing another map of our place in the dirt. I was just drawing where we lived, how our huts faced each other and how you could stand in your doorway and wave to someone across the way. I drew the general's hut, which was one hundred paces from ours. His had a porch and on the floor of the porch was a lion skin. The soldiers told the story of how the general shot the lion when he was just a boy. I could hear Father Jean-Claude's voice telling me it was all wrong, I should be drawing the guardhouse tower and how connected to it was the never-ending barbed wire that penned us in our camp. Then I thought that what Madame Lin would have drawn was something other than huts or guardhouses, probably the garden we grew behind our row of huts. In the garden the bean plants sprouted white flowers and Madame Lin plucked them and put them behind her ear. She would hold out her arms to one side and move them like ocean waves and say that the Japanese were mistaken, she was not really Chinese but rather a Fiji islander, and they should set her free and take her back to her father on his island, where he would give them necklaces made of shells and wine served in coconut bowls and steaks cut from monkey and whale.

THE DAY THE JAPANESE FIRST CAME I WAS STANDING ON my mother's feet and she was dancing me on our balcony. She was singing "Parlez-moi d'amour," and my father's dogs were jumping at us.

"Cutting in?" my mother asked them, and I could see their teeth, and their breath smelled like the bones brought home for them from the market. Then my mother said, "Ça va?" but she wasn't talking to the dogs and she wasn't talking to me. She was looking out over the field and she had her hand over her eyes like we were on a boat and she was trying to see land.

"He's coming," she said.

So soon? So early? I thought.

"He's not alone," she said. My mother ran downstairs. From the balcony I could see my father turn to the side. I could see his straight nose. Straight as the garden rows. Corn planted that way, at an angle to the morning sun, catches stronger rays at midday and grows sweeter and faster. This is what my father had told me.

"Jesus," my mother was screaming. "The Japanese! The Japanese! The Japanese!"

At first I thought it was part of the song she was singing.

They were holding my father by the arms.

Let him go, I wanted to scream out to the Japanese. He will not fall, I thought. But I did not scream out because everyone else was screaming and I did not think I would be heard.

My father was screaming, "Get back into the house!"

The Japanese were screaming words that, at the time, I could not understand.

It was not until the Japanese pulled out their guns and shot my father's dogs that I realized that the dogs were barking so loudly.

The dogs leaped into the air falling on their sides. Dust rose from where they lay even after their legs had stopped moving.

When the Japanese came to me I was singing my mother's song.

I was hearing my father yell, "Marcelle! Marcelle! Marcelle!" even though my father was standing right next to my mother.

I was watching a Japanese face come down so close to mine that I thought it was going to kiss me and I lifted up my face a little to let it.

Outside, stalks brushed my arms and legs and it felt like hands were touching me. I heard a noise like my father digging in the garden and hitting rock, but then I turned and saw it was the Japanese. They were hitting my father and mother with the butts of their guns.

Even with a hand over my mouth I was still singing "Parlez-moi d'amour."

MY MOTHER READ THE NOTE FROM THE CHIEF OF THE
Montagnards when the Japanese were playing ball. My amah was
rocking Poulet and telling her about the house where we once lived
— the porcelain bridge, the carp in the pond, the smell of lotus on
the paths, the one-thumbed crooked gardener who stole from the
rose garden and later sold the roses from a cart at the market.

After my mother read the note she folded it and put it into the
sheet knotted at my back. "Promise me you won't read it," she said.
"You're to give it to Michel Riquelme."

I had to carry the note in the knot of my sheet for days. At
night, when I moved on my mat, the paper's edges got caught in
the bamboo ticking. I thought how can I ever give it to Michel
Riquelme without the Japanese seeing me?

Those nights I did not sleep. Outside, the Japanese were walking by our place, their sabers scraping the walls. Inside, my amah
was screaming in Chinese. In her dreams she would put her fist in
the hole in her leg, holding her hand like the saber was in it and she
was trying to draw it out.

"Ayaaaah!" she would say, and pull out the saber in her dreams,
her fist rising above her head and my mother waking up to calm
my amah down.

. . .

Every Wednesday was Rat Day. We stomped our feet on the ground
and yelled, and the rats from the rafters and from under the floorboards would come running out, back and forth across our feet,
over our mats. With planks pulled down from the dividers in the
latrines, we aimed for their heads.

"Banzai!" we would scream, laughing and picking up the rats
by their tails and tossing them to the cook, who carried them out to
the kitchen in a covered pot.

"Banzai," the Japanese said when they saw us through the windows. Watching us they would smoke cigarettes and bet on how many rats we would catch.

The day the general was bitten by a horse it was Rat Day. No one saw the horse bite the general, but while we were yelling and crashing the boards on the rats' heads, we heard the horse whinny loudly and charge past our windows. We thought the general had been shot.

The Japanese stopped betting on our rats and ran to where the general lay on the ground, blood soaking through his fingers where he held them to the bite on his shoulder. The Japanese pried his hand from the bite and sent someone off to round up and destroy the runaway horse. At their dinner that night we could smell horse stew all over the camp and it smelled sweet and not like the meat of a horse who could take a bite out of his master's flesh. We wondered how they had cut it, in cubes or strips. We guessed at the spices and the greens they had added.

"Coriander," my mother said.

"Pepper," Leandri said.

"I smell the Chinese apple," I said. "Would they use that?"

"Perhaps it is the sweet smell we are smelling," my mother said.

Then the Japanese came in and they threw our mats into the air and they lifted up loose floorboards and they called out that they were looking for medicine for the general, and that if any of us had some we were to hand it over, because if the general's shoulder worsened overnight, there would be lashings in the morning, dunkings in the latrine and a dead body or two.

The Japanese found no medicine for the general in our hut. My mother, long past wearing cologne, offered up a bottle, opening it and letting it pass under the noses of the Japanese.

In French, to my mother, Leandri said, "Don't think that will get you out of here — it's going to take more than a bottle of cologne to do that." Then the Japanese made my mother put on her silk skirt and take the bottle to their horse-bitten general.

Later, back from the general's, smoking cigarettes he had given her, my mother sat on the end of her mat and told us what had happened.

"Walking over to his hut I kept trying to remember when I'd gotten the cologne. And then I remembered that Yeu had given it to me after he had told me that in place of brushing their teeth, the old Chinese ate water chestnuts after their meals. I had laughed at that, and he said, 'You French are no better, with baths of cologne instead of baths of soap and water.' I laughed again, thinking about it, while walking to the general, and the Japanese yelled at me. 'No laughing,' they yelled, so of course I laughed harder, and while I was laughing I was thinking how I couldn't let the bottle drop and spill in the dirt, and then the Japanese opened the door of the general's place and I saw the general lying on his cot, without his shirt, his belly as broad and smooth as a woman's, and I kept on laughing and the general said to his men, 'What's this, you've brought me a hyena?' but then I noticed the splendor in the general's room and I stopped laughing.

"On the walls there were tapestries woven with silk and with gold, depicting beautiful women bent at rivers, walking with flowers, men on horseback, the horses' manes spread out behind them like the wings of birds of prey. On the table was a pot of steaming tea. The floor was recently swept. 'I must be careful not to slip,' I told myself.

"'With all respect,' I said to the general and bowed, 'I am afraid that all I have to offer you is this one bottle of cologne.'

"'Lai, lai,' the Japanese said to me, knowing I knew Chinese. So I went up to the general and opened the stopper on the bottle and moved his bandages to the side and I poured all the cologne into the bite in his skin. You could see the tooth marks so clearly that if the horse were to bite him in the same spot again, its teeth would fit, like a bare foot in its footprint in the sand. When the general screamed the Japanese crossed their sabers in front of my neck, but when the general didn't roll over and die, they let me stand. The general took my hand. To kiss it, I thought to myself, but he was just holding on to me so I could help him to his feet. He went to his desk and sat in the chair and someone poured him some tea.

"'Please sit down,' he said, and I was given a chair. The tea smelled like a holiday — I couldn't remember which one. Easter or Christmas. I thought maybe it was brewed with clove.

"'The French make quality cologne,' he said to me, and he touched his hand to his shoulder and then wiped it off under his fatty breast.

"'There is a Frenchman my daughter translates for, as prisoner he receives no cigarettes, would it be possible?' I said.

"'Cigarettes too?' the general said. 'Of course that is what the French do, and they drink, don't they?' he said.

"'Yes,' I said, 'but it is the smoking he misses the most.' The general pushed his pack of cigarettes across to me on the table and I put them inside my blouse.

"'But what about you?' the general said.

"'A sheet, to sleep under, safe from mosquitoes,' I said. The general spoke to his men and they came back with a sheet.

"When I left the general I took a look at the tapestry hanging behind him. It was one I hadn't noticed before, it was so plain, showing only a man pulling a wagon up a snow-capped mountain. When the general saw me looking, he said, 'This is from my country,' and passed his flattened hand over the tapestry's threads."

IT WAS 1942 AND WE WERE IN KONTUM, INDOCHINA. Radios were scarce, but Michel Riquelme knew all the words to "Parlez-moi d'amour," and he sang them out his window while we sat in the road or shoveled the ground. Sometimes Leandri and my mother and I would join in, and we would dance on the dirt and Michel Riquelme would throw us kisses. Sometimes, when my mother and I were in the Great Room, we could hear Michel Riquelme singing far down the road and through the trees, and it sounded like the radio playing and my mother danced me on her feet around the room and we could have been at home, dancing through our rooms or dancing on the balcony. But then I would look down and see the moth-eaten carpet under our feet as we passed over the worn symbols for fire and water, metal, air and earth.

The Japanese stood outside the double doors and called for me.

"Half-breed," they yelled. "North Eye, South Eye — come on, it's time to talk to the French pig."

So I left my mother dancing alone in the Great Room, and when I turned to wave goodbye to her, I could see that her back was to me and she was dancing facing the window. The sun lit her brown hair and her blouse and her skirt and her bare feet and all of her in the pink light of dusk.

"What's she doing?" the Japanese asked me.

"Looking for my father in the mountains," I said. Then the Japanese made a chair for me out of their arms.

"Jump in, little dog," they said, and as I jumped into their arms my legs hit their sabers and the cool blades felt like the window on my face when I stood in the Great Room with my mother looking for my father in the mountains.

Out from under me the Japanese let go the chair made from their arms and they sat me on the desk in the prisoner's hut. Under my sheet I was sweating and in the pocket of my sunsuit I had the pack of cigarettes. Michel Riquelme was brought into the room and made to stand. When he saw me he smiled and winked.

"Like the one-eyed man," he said to me in French.

"The general said I could give him these cigarettes," I said to the Japanese.

I held out the cigarettes to Michel Riquelme and he reached for them, but then I held on to them and pulled back so he knew that they were not to be smoked, but to be opened up later, by the light of the moon that came through the thatch of the roof.

"Ask him why he doesn't smoke them," the Japanese said. "Waiting for the war to end?" they said, and they laughed.

Michel Riquelme laughed too and then he said, "Did I ever tell you gentlemen about the man in a bar whose eye I poked out with a cane?" and I translated for the Japanese.

"Tell him we've got more time on our hands than the Buddha from the Three Thousand Worlds," the Japanese said, and sat back to listen.

"Well, then," Michel Riquelme said, and this time instead of just listening to Michel Riquelme's story, I translated it for the Japanese while sitting on their desk, letting my bare feet bang against the file drawers, and I changed my speech from the rhythm of the French to the rhythm of the Japanese. Michel Riquelme and I had the Japanese laughing over his story and we looked at each other after the story was over and we smiled at each other like people who have won after playing on the same team, and it was not us, I thought, the Japanese were laughing at, but the story, and the man's eye, which Michel Riquelme said had found its way from the Seine to the Nile, to the China Sea, to the Inland Sea, and was now vacationing somewhere in the waters of the Philippines.

· · ·

Back in our place, my mother held me by the shoulders and she said, "Tell me again how you gave him the cigarettes." And using her hand like it was the pack of cigarettes, I held on to her fingers and pulled back on them, to show her how Michel Riquelme would know not to smoke them, but to read the note inside them sent from the Chief of the Montagnards.

"Are you sure he knows?" my mother said.

"Oui, Maman," I said.

"Show me again," she said, and again I held her hand while we sat on our mats and my amah watched us.

"Is there a way to win this game?" my amah said.

· · ·

That night, lying in bed, my mother told us about the night when my father first asked for her hand.

"We were on a boat from France to China," she said.

In the dark I could see the end of my mother's cigarette burning, moving as she brought it to her mouth and as her hands spoke with her words.

"I was off to buy silk for the hats I was selling and he was returning to China with secrets — at least that's what he told me. He said he would fetch a price for them and then he tried on my hat and brought the veil over his eyes.

"His French was not flawed by an accent, and I remember looking at his straight nose, so different from the Chinese I had seen before, and I wondered if physical features were any indication of how well you would speak other tongues.

"The hat did not fit him, and it blew off over the rail, but he caught it with one hand, almost going overboard, and I remember saying something, oh, I can't remember exactly, but something like, 'I hope that's not how you handle your secrets,' and then he asked for my hand and he touched each knuckle as if he were wiping something off it or rubbing it on, and he said, 'Don't worry, I can keep a secret.'"

We shared our hut with four other families. Light came in from the spaces between the boards of the walls. When my mother spoke, everyone listened. I could see the listeners propped on their elbows. Some were stroking the faces of their children who slept curled beside them. Others were staring up at the ceiling, where the rats lived and ran overhead while my mother told her story.

"Later, when we dined, I saw how his fingers were long, and then we put down our forks and put our hands up facing each other, and his fingers reached far above mine, as if instead of three digits, this man had four.

"I thought is this the way it is with all Chinese? And I sat watching him cut his food, spearing it with his fork.

"He said I wasn't eating so he fed me his food with his fork. I looked at his nose and thought that it must have been a nose his father had before him, and his father's father and his father's father — so far back it must have gone because it was such a beautiful nose, a thing passed on. I wanted my children to have that nose. He who wore that nose, I thought to myself, could slice through the air, go top speed, leave a wake."

My mother stopped her story and said to me, "Tian, stand up, show them the nose," and she held her cigarette in her mouth and with both hands she lifted me up under the arms and had me stand where the shafts of light coming through the boards were the widest.

"See, there it is," my mother said, and all the others lying down stood up to look at me.

Then she ran her finger down the bridge to the point of my nose and said, "This is a story. A story better than I could tell about how first I met Yeu on a boat to China. A story better because it has no ending, because my daughter's children will have this nose, and their children, and their children. I don't know why," my mother said, sitting back on her mat, pulling me down with her. "I don't know why I didn't just have Tian stand up first, before I told you the story, because she is the story of me and Yeu. I could have saved myself all those words," my mother said, and she lay down on her mat and soon fell asleep.

I took the burning cigarette out of her mouth and I finished it for her, blowing the smoke through my nose.

"Oh, like the dragon now," my amah said from her mat, frightening me because I did not know that I was still being watched.

. . .

That night my father came in through the window. On his head he wore the skull of a wild pig. Some of the meat of the pig still dangled from the bone and hung in the sockets where the pig's eyes had once been. My father moved aside the meat that hung there as if it were hair and he was trying to see out from behind it.

"Papa!" I yelled, and jumped up from my mat and waved. He leaped over the others who were asleep to get to me with his arm held out. I thought he was going to embrace me, but instead he put his hand over my mouth. On his hand I smelled pine and dirt, and I felt his calluses rub against my lips. For a long time he did not say anything, he just held his hand over my mouth and looked around the room. I watched him and the only thing that was moving was the meat hanging down in the sockets of the wild pig's eyes.

"Sit and be quiet," he said to me, and pushed me down onto my mat. Then he went to my mother and stood over her and put his hand on her leg. I could see that his hand was darker than her skin. His fingers looked like the fingers of a darker man, and I could not see them as the fingers that my mother had admired on the boat from France to China, but I could see them as fingers eating from the gourds fashioned into bowls that Madame Lin had once told me the Montagnards used in their huts, and I pictured my father eating wild pig out of a bowl with his hands.

"Swine," my mother said, waking up, and she pushed his hand away.

"Marcelle," he said, and fell on her chest where her robe opened and I could see how her breast looked flat as a plate from the weight of him. And then my mother beat with her fists on his back and the thud-thud of my mother's fists was like the sound of the Japanese hitting us with their guns.

All the children woke and held their Leandri dolls close to themselves and when Leandri woke she held herself and we watched my father on top of my mother.

Leandri stood and picked up the sheet the general had given my mother and threw it on top of them, and then she told us to come away from my mother and father, that she had a story to tell us and that she could only tell it under the space in the roof where the moonlight fell strongest. And Leandri, with her hair cut all different lengths to make the hair for our dolls, sat in the light from the moon and told us children, even the older ones, and those as old as my amah, the story of the young Leandri.

"I dreamed of being a model," she said. "At home, in front of the mirror, for my mother's friends, or for the girls at school, I posed.

"Everywhere I went I tried to look at myself. At lakes my brother would be pointing out the fish and I would be staring at the way my hair curved with the curve of my chin. Ribs as sharp as elbows were what I dreamed of, and I felt for them on my chest. I thought about tall things only, and I never looked down unless there was a body of water to catch sight of myself in. To learn about grace I watched birds and how they flocked. Geese veed and my neck craned to keep them in sight as long as possible before they flew out of my range.

"The day I was allowed to wear lipstick I walked the streets of Paris kissing all the café windows. Men at tables, heads bent and reading their papers, looked up at me. To buy clothes I stole from my brother's rare coin collection. From Spain I had ancient reales, and on the coins the rulers' heads were so worn down they were unrecognizable. I shopped in a boutique where the owner knew the value and had his own collection.

"Silk was my fabric of choice. Under silk the bones at my hips and my ribs seemed to protrude more sharply when the clothes fell over them and I realized that the most beautiful thing about me was those bones, and I talked to my bones and told them I would do everything I could to let them show and almost break through my skin.

"When I was older, and I really became a model, instead of eating I would swallow balls of cotton soaked in olive oil. The other models asked me how I stayed so thin, and when I told them they started eating cotton balls too. Our mouths were circled in oil that shone under the lights of our dressing rooms. After the shows we would feed, using our combs to fish out the balls of cotton soaking in jars of olive oil.

"It was in the hospital, after I collapsed, that I met my husband. He was the one who turned me. Three times a day, from my left side where I looked out the window, to my right where I could see myself in the mirror above the sink.

"'You're so light I could turn you with just my pinkie fingers,' he would say to me. And then he brought me extra pillows to put between my legs so that while lying on my side I would not bruise the flesh around my kneecaps. In the pockets of his uniform he kept chocolates, which he popped into my mouth while he sat and talked to me.

"It was in the hospital that he proposed to me. I had one of his chocolates in my mouth and he said, 'I can never understand you with your mouth full of chocolate, so whatever you say, I'll take it as a yes.'

"Years later, teasing him, I would say that what I said to him in response was no, that I would not marry him. And it was years later, when I was in my husband's office in Saigon and he was popping one of his chocolates into my mouth, that the door banged open and in came the Japanese. With the chocolate still in my mouth they tied my hands behind my back and I remember trying to scream out 'No!' But I couldn't say it the way I wanted to, the chocolate was in my mouth and the words came out muffled and soft.

"Then I thought I heard my husband laughing and I thought he was laughing because I still couldn't say no, but then I realized that he wasn't laughing and that the Japanese were breaking my husband's hands by putting them into the desk drawer and slamming the drawer closed. Afterward my husband's hands — the hands that had turned me so easily — hung from his wrists like they had been sewn on and could be ripped off with a slight tug.

"And then the Japanese took us away and my husband left on one train and I left on another, and the next time I saw him it was here in Kontum, in a burlap sack in the marsh, the rotting flesh peeling off his face."

When Leandri was finished with her story, I could hear my father singing. We all turned around to see my mother and father dancing, and my father was singing my mother's song, "Parlez-moi d'amour." And they danced over our mats and our sheets and our piles of clothes and our sticks for our stick games and our rocks for our rock games. My father still wore the skull of the wild pig on his head and my mother's robe fell low on her shoulders, revealing her collarbone, which looked more like a necklace than what one would think a thin woman's bones should look like.

· · ·

When the Japanese came in my father ran for the window, but there were Japanese waiting for him on the other side, and I could see their saber points raised, ready to strike.

From their belts hung oil lamps that cast light in a circle around them. One of them caught my father and threw him to the ground, where he lay in their circle of light. The pig skull fell off his head and rolled into the darkness. I could hear someone pick it up, and I thought that if it were one of the children who had gotten it, I would make him give it to me later.

The Japanese took my father away. My mother was screaming and the Japanese slapped her, but she did not stop. She ran to the window and watched as they pushed him and hit him. Leandri went to my mother and pulled her back in. My mother still screamed and Leandri slapped her and then my mother stopped screaming and started to cry. She cried all the rest of the night while I held her from behind, my arm across her chest. She held my arm with both her hands and I remembered the time she gave birth to Poulet and held my arm like she was rowing and I was her oar.

In the morning she pushed my arm away like a blanket, jumped out of bed, and still in her robe ran down the road to the Great Room. I followed after her, and along the way I could see in the dirt where the Japanese had dragged something. Opening the double doors to the Great Room, my mother lost the belt from her robe and I picked it up and followed her inside. She walked to the Great Mirror and there she let the robe fall. She looked at herself in the mirror and she said, "I have two sisters, Claudine and Germaine, a brother named Robert. I grew up in Biarritz and ate sardines for my lunch. My mother grew chives and basil in our window boxes. My father had a bicycle and rode me to school on the handlebars. After a party we would go to the sea late at night and take off our clothes and swim. Back home we would hang our gowns on the balcony. Salt stained the hems forming up-and-down lines that looked like mountains."

"Maman," I said, "your belt," and I held it up so she could see it while she looked in the Great Mirror. She took it from me and then she turned and wrapped the belt around my neck.

"This is the way to tie a tie," she said, and she made the loop around the neck big enough so I could look down and see how she was tying the knot.

"I used to stand behind my father on a chair and tie his tie for him in the mirror," she said.

"Where is he now?" I said.

"He walked into the sea one day and he kept on going. The sea is strange that way," my mother said. "You can swim in the sea and swim back, but once you walk in, it is hard to turn around. Maybe it has something to do with your shoes getting stuck in all that sand," she said, and then she made me look in the Great Mirror with the loose tie tied around my neck.

"You look like a man who has come home late to his wife from a bar," my mother said.

I slung my arm around my mother's neck and went weak at the knees, slurring words and saying, "Baby, please, oh honey, forgive me," and stumbling over the Great Room's carpet, falling on my back onto the symbol for air and then closing my eyes and snoring a loud, open-mouthed snore. When I opened my eyes I was laughing, but my mother was not near me, she had gone to the window and she was looking at the mountains. I picked up her robe and put it on her shoulders.

"I can see the Montagnards lined up," she said. "They are getting ready to come down and free Yeu, and free us."

"Where?" I said. "Show me."

She pointed to the mountains.

"Where?" I said again. "I still can't see."

. . .

"These are the days of the snake," my amah said when it was so hot that the ground cracked and you stood and walked a few feet only every now and then because of the flies or because of the smell of something rotting coming your way.

It was on one of these days that the general was carried out on a stretcher. It was known that the heat made him faint and that he liked the stretcher, that he drummed his hands on the bamboo poles at either side when he was carried along. On this day they took him to the prison cell where they were keeping my father and Michel Riquelme. As he passed by me and my mother, he had the men carrying him stop and he said to my mother, "You shouldn't have put that note in the cigarettes. The Frenchman was planning to escape with the help of your husband. But I suppose you already knew that, and that you already read the note. What's the need for treachery? Don't we treat you well enough, under the circumstances? Remember the sheet I gave you to keep you safe from mosquitoes at night? You'll think of me years later, when you are not down with malaria. When you are not feverish in your bed and cursing the gods. In Japan malaria victims are put with the insane. You are lucky we are not in Japan," the general said.

My mother raised her head from the ground where she lay and looked at the general and said, "Luckier than we know."

"Put your eyes down!" the general said, and hit the bamboo pole at the side of his stretcher so that the men carried him on.

After that my mother and I lay down again on the hot ground in front of the huts and she showed me how to make angels in the dirt. My amah came by and asked us if we were snakes under the house. Then me and my mother stood up and we looked at the angels we had made.

"They will rise at night and fly over the moon," my amah said.

"Snakes don't fly," my mother said.

"Being married to a Chinaman has not made you wise to the creatures," my amah said. "Snakes are fairies, rats are quail in the spring, and a hare lives in the moon. Also, I've tasted your roast duck before, you need to turn it while it cooks in the oven."

"I'm covered in dirt," my mother said. "Let's go to the marsh and wash ourselves."

In the marsh my amah taught Poulet how to swim.

"Chickens can't fly," she said to Poulet, "so they better learn how to swim," and Poulet kicked her small legs and beat the water with her hands.

IT WAS THE END OF OUR FIRST YEAR IN KONTUM, AND Poulet was learning how to swim before she learned how to walk.

"Let walking be the last thing she learns," my mother said. "If she walked around here I would worry about her feet getting dirty, her hands getting splinters from the walls, her face eye-level with the knees of the Japanese guards."

We hardly ever sang "Parlez-moi d'amour," anything but that, and when we found ourselves singing it, we stopped and made the tune slide into something else.

At the marsh we sang my mother's country's song, and Leandri and all the other Frenchwomen joined in. While Leandri sang, she unknotted the sheet from my chest and washed it in the marsh and then tied it back on, wet, so that I was kept cool during the day. While singing we heard screams from the prison cells, and so my mother and Leandri sang louder, like true patriots, but I listened for my father's voice and I could hear it and I thought to myself that it wasn't the way I had ever heard his voice before and that screaming that way must be a way to kill yourself — the body, I thought, would break from within. Michel Riquelme's voice I imagined to be somebody else's, even though I knew he was the only other one in there. I imagined it to be the voice of a man I didn't know, better yet the voice of a Japanese being tortured for telling secrets he shouldn't have told.

At the marsh I overheard my mother and my amah talking.

"She's still in love with him," my amah said. "Didn't you know your daughter was in love?"

"Love?" my mother said. "What does she know about love?"

"She is the oldest girl here, so who do you think she learns love from except from the youngest woman? Leandri is teaching her without even knowing it. Soon your Tian will be throwing down that doll Leandri made her and she will be walking up and down the road trying to walk the way Leandri walks."

And it was true, a few days later I was trying to walk down the road the way that Leandri walked. Leandri's hips were thin, like a boy's, but she did not walk like a boy, she did not walk like she could even throw a rock or jump over a stream. She looked like if she threw a rock or jumped a stream her legs would crack in half, her hips fall off and clatter onto the flat rocks by the side of a stream. When I tried to walk like Leandri, I walked thinking I was in Paris, that the streets were crowded, that men were looking at me, that I saw myself in storefront windows wearing lipstick, the Seine and Notre Dame were in my field of vision and not the latrines and the red-sun Japanese flag flying over the guardhouse tower.

This is the way I walked when they told me to go into the prison cell and translate for Michel Riquelme and my father. When I walked in they were on the wooden floor, their arms and legs tied with rags. I recognized strips of the clothes I had once worn. My father wore a daisy pattern at his wrists. Around Michel Riquelme's wrists was the belt from my mother's robe.

I walked back and forth in the cell, still walking like I thought Leandri walked, until a Japanese guard stopped me and made me stand in front of my father.

"Translate," the guard said. And I did. I do not remember what it was that I translated. I did not listen to the words that came out of my mouth. I remember trying to stand the way Leandri might stand. I tried pursing my lips while I talked. Michel Riquelme did not look up. I thought maybe they had hit his head so hard that he could not lift it. They stood me in front of Michel Riquelme and they said, "Translate."

When Michel Riquelme lifted his head to me, I saw that they had gouged out one of his eyes. With his one eye still there, he winked at me. I ran to my father and put my arms around him, but because his hands were tied he could not hold me. The guards put a saber between us and moved us apart. I looked at my father and he looked at me, and it was only by keeping my eyes on my father that I was able to translate whatever Michel Riquelme said.

Days later we woke to find Michel Riquelme in the middle of the playing field. A Japanese flag was stuck in his belly and it billowed in the morning breeze. His one eye stared straight up and in it we could see the passing clouds overhead.

"Catch a cicada," my amah said to me, so I went to the tall grass and I caught one. My amah pulled off its wings and put it into Michel Riquelme's mouth.

"Now he will always have music," she said, and the insect, as if it still had wings, tried to fly off Michel Riquelme's bloated tongue.

Other women brought rice balls and set them by his side. "For his hunger," they said.

Leandri brought one of her dolls and put it in the crook of his arm. I wondered where his other eye was. I wondered if the Japanese had thrown it into the marsh and it was floating, looking up, on its way to the Mekong, reflecting clouds and birds and more northern skies.

. . .

I looked everywhere for the pig skull my father had worn that night he came to our hut. I asked all the young ones if they had taken it, but none of them had. I thought then that the Japanese must have taken it — that it hung on a nail in some guards' hut and sometimes they would take it down and act like my father, dancing around the room. I thought my father was the kind of man the Japanese probably told stories about, and wove his likeness into tapestries to decorate their walls.

I dreamt my mother was dancing me on her feet in the Great Room and we were passing over the symbols on the oriental carpet. Instead of there just being the symbols for fire and water, metal, air and earth, there was also the symbol for Yeu, my father. My mother stopped dancing when we came to it and then slowly the symbol rose from the woolen carpet and floated above our heads and then Yeu, the symbol for my father, fell apart and it was raining woolen threads, which stuck to our faces like hair just cut with scissors.

When I woke from the dream, Leandri was cutting my hair.

"I've run out of my own and the children need more dolls," she said. From then on I wore my hair short, and everywhere I walked I could hear the children's voices saying, "Tian, Tian," not talking to me but to their new dolls.

. . .

"Do it for me," my mother said. "For him," she said before I had to go off to my father's prison cell. The note she handed to me asked if he loved her, would he please write back, did he remember their first night on the boat — what she would give to have his hand in hers.

"Maman, I can't give this to him in there," I said.

She fell to the floor, her hair sweeping up dust. My amah stood and tightened the sheet at my breasts and sang the fish song she always sang before I went to translate what my father said to the guards.

Leandri tried to pick my mother up, but my mother stayed down, curling her fingers into the floor as if it were a wall and she was going to climb it.

Then the Japanese came and took me to my father.

When I returned my mother was still on the floor, but she was sitting up and Leandri was cutting her hair. The sun's rays coming in through the holes in the walls hit the fallen hair and made it look pink in the light.

My mother was picking up her hair and looking at it. In French Leandri was telling my mother about the time her father took her to the zoo and introduced her to a gorilla. Her father told Leandri that the gorilla's name was Monsieur Kakabozo, and that Monsieur Kakabozo was Leandri's husband, that he had been betrothed to her at birth and wasn't he such a nice husband to have. "Look,

Leandri," the father had said, "how he cries at the corners of his big black eyes, waiting for you to grow to be a woman so you can slip through the bars and be joined as man and wife.

"Try that on your tongue, Madame Kakabozo," her father said. Leandri did not look at the cage, and her father said again, "Sweetheart, look at your husband, think of the hairy children you'll have, the neighbor tiger and panda for friends."

"Oh, the tiger," my amah said, listening to Leandri's story. "Think how lucky you could have been."

When my mother saw that I had come into the room, she stood up and said, "Well, what did he say?"

"He did not say anything," I said.

"Didn't he speak?" my mother said.

"He answered questions," I said.

"About the ship? About me?" My mother took me by the shoulders and held me against the wall. Behind me I could feel the knot in my sheet pressing into my backbone.

Off in the corner my amah was taking small bits of soap and kneading them into one bar. When we laughed at her, she said we would be sorry when we were older if we did not learn the value of saving. "You'll have no husbands if you don't learn," she said. We told her we didn't care about husbands, and she said she didn't blame us, she had never bothered to have one herself. "But look how pretty," she said, and held up the final bar of soap, mottled with yellows, pinks and greens.

Leandri was shaking out hair from the skirt of her dress.

I looked into my mother's eyes and I could see that her eyes were cloudy. I had never seen her eyes looking that way, as if she had poured milk into them, or as if her eyes were film projected too many times and the sharp lines of the image were softening, glowing white.

"No, about the Chinese," I answered her.

My mother slapped me, and then a guard who was walking by

the open window stuck his bayonet through and held it under my mother's chin.

"That's the general's translator you're slapping, be careful," he said, and then he walked on.

In a whisper my mother said to me, "You're still my daughter, and I can slap you whenever I goddamn please."

"BANZAI!" WE ALL SCREAMED AND HIT THE RATS WITH our boards. When I bent over, the sheet around my breasts ripped and the youngest ones came up around me to see where my sunsuit had torn. The sheet unwrapped from my chest and fell under my sunsuit around my waist, where it sat on my hipbone.

My amah sewed the sheet back together and said, "Now your sheet is scarred but stronger than ever, and like iron tracks you can now bear the weight of trains on your back, and when there are no trains," she said, "you can bear the heavy mountain snow, and where there is no snow, you can bear the weight of a man as he stands on the ties and looks to see if he can see the town below him. At the least, the sheet won't rip again for a day."

The general called for my mother.

"Bitten by a horse again?" Leandri said to the Japanese who had come to escort my mother.

"What happened to her hair?" one Japanese asked.

"My hair?" Leandri said. "My hair was blown off by wind that touched the gargoyles of Notre Dame. My hair was burnt off by the bombs in the north. My hair was pulled, strand by strand, off my head by my husband, he wanted string to clean between his teeth. My hair was stared off my head by monkeys at the zoo. My hair was —" Leandri never finished, because one of the Japanese came at her and stuck a stick between her teeth and told her to keep it there until he came back with my mother.

Leandri stood with the stick in her teeth and I watched as her saliva stained the wood dark.

· · ·

Three days later, my mother came back from the general's hut. It was morning and my amah was sweeping with a broom she had made out of reeds from the marsh. When she swept, our hut smelled like the marsh — we were the animals who lived along its shores or built nests on the rocks that reached above the water line.

Outside, the Japanese were getting ready for a game. Every once in a while we could see through our window the ball they used arcing in the sky, and we could hear them yelling to each other and we could hear the sound of them running into each other, a sound like tails of gigantic fish flapping on a dock.

My mother's skin was bruised. My first thought when I saw her was that the bruises would change color, that for the next few weeks we would watch the color change and we would have something to do.

"For three days I smelled Bastille Day," my mother said. "And just like Bastille Day, where you cannot see your hand in front of your face for the smoke, I could not see my hand in front of me because they wrapped a cloth around my eyes. But there was the burning smell and the flashes of light through the cloth. Often there was the smell of food or of blood. He drank cow's blood. I could smell the shit and the hay on the soldier's coat when he brought the blood into the room.

"'Madame,' the general would say, 'blood is like wine — it makes the room spin.' So with him drunk, and me blindfolded, the general made me dance with him. Around his room we turned while I smelled the blood on his breath, and his naked ball of a belly rubbed against mine."

"Where did you get this?" Leandri said, and touched my mother's bruised arm.

"My arm?"

"The bruise," Leandri said.

"Get it?" my mother said. "It sounds like you thought I wanted it, that I went out of my way just to have it."

"Who gave it to you? Who hit you?" Leandri said.

"Did I tell you," my mother said, "about the tapestry of the mountain in that man's room?"

In the field the Japanese had stopped in the middle of a game. Through the window I could see them wetting cloths in a water-filled bowl and then wiping each other's sweaty necks. Two Japanese were standing face to face, and one Japanese was holding the other's head and wiping blood from a cut on his brow.

"What about Yeu?" Leandri said. "Did you ask?"

"You can ask about his home country. You can ask about the women. The rice. The liquor and wine. But you ask about this camp and he hits. With sticks, with the chair, with the back of his hand, he attacks and you are driven down to smell the dirt under your nose. I did ask about Yeu. I asked to have him let go, and then I was blindfolded. So in darkness I pictured Yeu's face. I went backwards. I tried to picture all over again the first time I met him. For three days in the general's place I imagined I was on the ship where Yeu and I first met. Dolphins followed and breached from white-capped waves. Yeu took my hand and we watched them from the deck."

"Dolphins," my amah said. "Like the Year of the Tiger or Dragon should be a year one can be born in."

Outside the Japanese played ball. The women came over to our place and bet their rice balls and touched my mother's arm and told her what a brute the general was, what a fuck from the bowels of our earth, what a cad from hell and then they asked about the things he had in his place, what the food was like, were there bean cakes? Was there milk? Sheets? A clock that told the right time?

That night my mother and I went to the Great Room so that she could turn to the side and see in the mirror the places on her back where the general had hit her. When she could not see all of it, she asked me.

"Tell me what it looks like," she said.

"Here is one in the shape of a bird," I said.

"Good," she said. "Then the bastard will get up and fly away."

. . .

Someone broke free. It was not anyone we knew, but someone who arrived after we did. He tried to run through the Sea of Trees on a day so hot and still we all knew it was not the wind making the leaves rustle, but a person running, and the Japanese knew it too.

"Bravo," my mother said when he was caught. "Now the next one must succeed."

One day the Japanese left me alone with my father.

"I've been thinking about the woman who took off her head and brushed her hair," he said to me

"Maman wants to know if you remember how she could not eat when she first met you on the ship, and how the sight of your hands stopped her hunger."

"Find out who that woman was," my father said.

When I went back to my mother she asked me what my father said.

"He loves you," I told her.

"I knew it," my mother said, and she put some sugar in my hand.

That night we saw a rat come running out from the hole in the floorboards with a rosary around its neck.

"This is where nuns once lived," Leandri said.

We looked beneath all of the floorboards, searching for whatever the nuns may have left behind.

"What are you looking for?" my amah said. "God is not here."

We found a few more rosaries, a few more rats and a diary.

"Property of Sister Matilde," the first page read. Leandri was the one who sat us in a circle and read the diary out loud.

Trees here are like a necklace with a hidden clasp closing us in. I've walked the perimeter looking for a good way out, but there is none. The roads are all straight lines and anyone walking down them would be seen as far as the horizon. Anyone who wants to leave here should look toward the mountains, where no roads go and the only path to follow is made by the tracks of the wheelbarrow pushed along by the wife of the Chief of the Montagnards.

Up there, in the mountains, one can almost see Saigon, but down here vision is not interrupted, and this strains the eye more to look for miles at nothing.

A shut-down factory that made wooden rulers has given us leftover rulers to burn for our fires. At the oven, the sisters and I watch the centimeters going up in flames. We have figured that if we lined up all the rulers we've burned, then we'd have enough distance from here to Cho Lon — at least that is what the sisters have figured.

"This woman shouldn't have been a nun," Leandri said.

"No one really wants to be a nun," my mother said.

We kept the rat and named it Sister Matilde. We knew her because she still wore the rosary, and at night we could hear her going across the floor, the rosary beads clicking against each other, the cross sometimes dragging on the boards.

I didn't know where to begin to look for the woman who took off her head and started brushing her hair. I thought maybe it had been Sister Matilde. The next time I saw my father, I told him.

"A nun, really?" he said. "Why would they chop off the head of a nun?"

"She wanted to leave. They must have found out," I said.

"Who? There were no Japanese then," my father said.

"Maman wants to know if you remember the cologne you once gave her," I said.

"Try again," my father said. "That nun is not the one who took off her head and started brushing her hair."

...

In the morning we heard doves. My amah, lying on her mat on the floor, turned toward us and said, "In my village we would put wooden whistles on their tails and send them into flight. Circling flocks made a melody — the fast flyers whistling high notes, the slower ones low notes."

· · ·

Smallpox came to our camp. There was a hunt for doves' eggs to prevent Poulet from getting it. Early in the morning we would go down to the marsh and follow the doves. We found some eggs with broken shells, but we never found the whole ones with yolks. My amah collected the broken ones and with mortar and pestle she ground them into powder, then with water made a white paste that she spread on Poulet's face.

It was then that Poulet became a kwei-tsze and the other women would not hold her or look at her for fear the ghost-like kwei-tsze would rob them of their spirits.

When the Japanese saw Poulet, they brought her milk and melon and rattles made from leather strips with glass beads tied at the ends. When they brought the objects to the doorstep they would leave them on a cloth and walk backwards, always facing Poulet and always watching her eyes.

It was when Poulet was a kwei-tsze that I was allowed to bring her with me while I translated for my father. The Japanese would move aside when I brought her in. My father would kiss Poulet on her mouth — he could not hold her with his hands tied behind his back.

"Maman wants to know if you remember when you danced with her on the balcony," I said to him.

"She wore a transparent gown," my father said, looking at the wall. "Through the cloth I could see her belly. While she sat there with her head in her hands, brushing her hair, I thought to myself, if only I could touch her, she would still be there and not disappear. I was ready to give away anything I owned for that. Take my sight, I should have said to her, my child, steal my home, cut off my legs — I wanted to trade them to stay at her side."

· · ·

I was in the Great Room when we heard the bombs.

"Allied," my mother said, and with me still on her feet we went to the window, which shook in its frame. The siren sounded and the Japanese player whom I had bet my rice balls on came to the Great Room and told us to hurry, it was time to go down to the shelter.

"Let's keep dancing," my mother said, and for the first time in a long time she sang "Parlez-moi d'amour," and she danced me around the symboled borders of the oriental carpet while the bombs fell.

Soon afterward, though, the bombs came too close and we had to leave the Great Room.

There were five shelters, which were holes in the ground lined with concrete. Thirty-seven of us stayed in one of them. Father Jean-Claude preached to us in the dark and my amah sang the frog song, the stone song and the Buddha's Laugh.

"Father Jean-Claude is the skunk," my amah would say, because Father Jean-Claude's stomach, he said, was not made for bombings, and while he was preaching, telling us about the loving arms of God and how He could see through the concrete and shine down into our shelter, Father Jean-Claude was, as my mother said, "farting for all of France."

"For all of China, Indochina and Japan," my amah said. "This man is the goat let go in the compost heap, a beast feeding on the old bolted lettuce and squash of a poor farmer's field gone to rot."

"Stop farting!" Leandri yelled out one day when Father Jean-Claude was preaching. "Let me out of here — I'd rather face bombs than the smell coming out of this man," and she ran to the hatch of the shelter and started to pull on it.

It opened suddenly. The sound of bombing was so loud we put our hands over our ears. So much dirt was flying, we tried to put our hands over our eyes as well. We thought it was raining because we could feel things falling on our heads — they were small rocks sent up by the bombs hitting the ground near the shelter.

"Oh, God," Father Jean-Claude said.

"Christ," my mother said.

"Fresh air!" Leandri said, and she tried to run off. My mother stopped her, jumping onto her back and pulling her down into the shelter.

When the bombing was over, it was the Montagnards who opened the hatch for us.

Later everyone said that when they first saw the chief there with his wheelbarrow and his wife, they thought they were dreaming. The chief was wearing orange and red robes, the wife was wearing a necklace made of coins, and the chief's testicles lying in the wheelbarrow were painted with black dots, so that my amah said they looked like urchins from the sea.

It was the chief's birthday and he had invited the Japanese to his party where the Sea of Trees began and where the grass ended.

Dirty, pale and smelling like Father Jean-Claude's farts, everyone climbed out of the shelters and walked over to the party.

The Japanese were already there, drinking the chief's wine and playing a game with a ball.

My mother went to my father. "Yeu, are you all right?" she yelled, and walked in circles around the prisoner's hut.

The Japanese shouted at my mother to go away. "French whore, your husband doesn't care about you. He's inside there with other women, fucking them in the sockets of their eyes, putting it in holes you never even knew existed, sucking out of them bouquets of lotus, honeyed ducks, the spirit of the dragon and luck of the tiger's paw. Whore," they yelled, "get back to the Seine where your kind sell themselves to the river rats and dogs along the banks."

My mother fell on the ground in front of me and asked, "Is it true what the Japanese said?"

I was eating melon they had given me at the party, the juice was dripping down me and I was licking my arms. I looked at my mother. In the daylight I could see dust and dirt collected in her hair. I could see a pattern of what looked like a woman's face. I thought it might be the face of the woman my father saw who took off her head and started brushing her hair. Only the woman wasn't beautiful the way my father had described. She looked old, with few teeth, tangled hair and sunken eyes.

"No, it is not true," I said to my mother. "There is only Yeu in that prison cell. There are no women. Only a room, the guards and his bowl."

Leandri came over and picked my mother up off the ground. "Qu'est-ce que tu fais?" she said, and began to comb my mother's hair with her fingers.

Leandri was wearing a skirt and under its thin cloth I could see her bones showing through and I thought they were beautiful, and then I saw the Japanese and they were also looking at Leandri in her skirt.

I wanted to take off the sheet around my breasts. I thought the Japanese should see them. I started to untie it but my amah came over and she threw me down and she sat on my back and said to me, "Imagine I am a Japanese," and she took my nipples in her hands and she squeezed them so hard that when she let me stand up there was blood coming through the sheet and blood coming through the front of my sunsuit.

I went back to our hut to change my clothes. No one was there. I sat on Leandri's mat, under the sheet hung to keep out mosquitoes, and I imagined I was Leandri. I put my hands down at my hips and felt for my bones. I spread the blood coming from my breasts on my lips like lipstick. I twisted my hair around my fingers, trying to hold the hair in a curl.

It was then a Japanese walked in. He held a deck of cards and he sat on the mat next to me and he said, "Let's play."

We played poker all the ways it can be played. When it came to strip, we still played. He pulled off his boots, his shirt and his pants. I pulled off my clothes and I sat there with the playing cards fanned in my hand, thinking they could act as a shield.

"I am Hideho," he said as he played.

"Tian," I said.

"Tian, is that all?" he said.

"No, really it is Christiane, but Tian is easier," I said.

"Tian is for children. I'm calling you Christiane. Turn around, Christiane," he said, and then I felt his hand at the knot in the sheet at my back. "Lift up your arms," he said, and I did and he unwrapped the sheet around my breasts and I felt his hands kneading them as if there were something inside my breasts he was trying to find. I wondered if the blood had dried and if he could feel it caked on my nipples.

"Christiane," he said, but it did not sound like a question, so I did not answer him.

Then he stopped, and he tied my sheet back and put on his clothes and he said we would play some other time and he left our place.

That night, when I took off my clothes to go to sleep, my amah came over to me and touched the knot in my sheet.

"Tied like the Japanese butterfly," she said. "Too bad he left you no wings to fly with. Like a larva, you can only roll around where he has set you down. In other words," she said, "don't fall in love."

I tried to fall asleep, but I could not. I heard my mother talking to Leandri and telling her how the Chief of the Montagnards had asked the Japanese to set my father free, that the chief had told them that my father had been in long enough and had no more answers left to give, and the chief said if my father wasn't set free then he would stop the cloth, the eggs, the tobacco and rice from moving over his mountains from up north.

I wondered what Michel Riquelme's eye was seeing. I wondered if it went north or south — Saigon or Hanoi. I pictured it floating in the salty waters of the south, making its way around jagged rocks sticking out of the mouths of the Mekong. Then I pictured it up north, floating in the Red River, watching fireworks rain down on it from a town's holiday display.

When I woke up I heard screaming. I thought that my amah was having her dream where she tries to pull the saber out of the hole in her leg. But it was not that. It was Leandri screaming outside.

She was near the Sea of Trees. When I got closer, I saw that someone was on top of her. She was trying to scream again, but now there was a cloth tied around her mouth.

On top of her I could see a man. I saw his boots and I could hear his saber scraping on the ground as he pushed into Leandri. On his head he wore my father's wild-pig skull and I almost called out my father's name, thinking for a moment that it was Yeu.

I got closer by running from one tree to the next. When I was very close, I saw it was Hideho on top of Leandri. I wished it was my father on top of her instead, and I wished that Leandri hadn't looked up to see that I was standing there.

The pig skull on Hideho's head was pushed far back, and it looked as if the pig were on top of Hideho, doing to Hideho what Hideho was doing to Leandri. After Hideho was finished, he put the pig skull on top of Leandri's head and walked away while fastening his pants and buckling his belt.

When I got to Leandri I wanted to leave her that way, her mouth bound and her hands tied. She did not look up at me and I figured that is how she wanted to be left.

The pig skull toppled off her head and onto the ground. I picked it up and I could feel on its underside the sweat from Hideho's brow.

I put the skull up under my arm and I untied Leandri's hands and mouth. Free, she grabbed the skull out from under my arm and threw it far into the Sea of Trees. I was amazed that her bony arm did not detach from her socket with the force of the throw and follow flying after the skull.

I tried to help her stand.

"No, nothing has happened," she said, and she walked off ahead of me.

· · ·

The day the Japanese let my father return to our place, my mother set up cigarettes in a circle at the head of his mat.

"What's this, a shrine?" my amah said.

The day my father came back it was Wednesday and it was Rat Day. The first rat he killed was Sister Matilde. The ceramic beads she wore lay smashed on the ground.

My mother told the children to be quiet. It was just a rat, after all.

"Come with me to the Great Room," my mother said to my father.

"Not now, Marcelle," he said.

· · ·

When Poulet was not a kwei-tsze anymore, and my amah washed her face of the dove-egg paste because the threat of smallpox had passed, the guards were not afraid of her, and instead they took Poulet in their arms and passed her from one to the next.

"Bored of your games in the field?" my mother said to them.

"She is not a bird," my amah said.

"What would a beak-nosed sea turtle know?" a guard said to my amah.

My amah spit on his jacket. The guard boxed her ears with a board. For months afterward, my amah could not hear. She would wake up in the middle of the night with blood coming out of her ears and staining her mat.

"I hear the flesh," my amah would say when she woke up. "I

hear the doors of the heart, the walls of the veins, the slides and ramps of the brain. What I'm trying to say is I can't really hear at all."

My father asked me one day where his pig skull was. I told him that I did not know. He got up and said he was going out. "I'll come back to get you out of here." he said.

"I heard that, Yeu," my amah said, wiggling her finger in her ear.

. . .

My mother cried in the Great Room. We went to see her.

My amah cried out for an elephant.

"What kind?" we asked.

"One that understands human speech, eats grass, eats sugar cane, drinks wine, dreads smoke, fire, lions and serpents, is strong and can get us the hell out of here," my amah said.

"Leave me alone," my mother said. "Leave the elephants out too. I need a cigarette. A drink. Some solitude."

. . .

That night we had grasshopper soup. My mother did not eat.

"Hey, I'm the only skinny one here, eat!" Leandri said to my mother and made my mother take a rice ball.

Madame Lin came by that night and brought my mother a drink. She said she had traded it for stockings and a garter.

"This is the sexiest whiskey in all of Indochina," she said.

Madame Lin wore dresses that were too small for her, so her breasts showed like they were the heads of babies popping up from the cloth. And that is what she called them, her babies. That night we played hand and knuckle and hoof. Madame Lin showed us hoof, and we rolled on our mats playing it, our skirts and dresses sliding up above our bellies as we played, and Madame Lin's babies sliding up too, out of her tight dress.

Our laughter brought the Japanese. They asked us if we were children, if we really wanted the general to be wakened by our noise, he would have our heads fixed between boards, have our hands put in his boiling tea water, have our fingers bent backwards, our shins kicked and our ears boxed.

All this only made Madame Lin laugh harder and so we all laughed and the Japanese sat down with us on our mats and laughed too, taking turns playing foot with Madame Lin while their sabers, still at their sides, scraped on our wooden floorboards.

That night before we slept, my amah sang the fox song. Pointing up she said there he is, the fox with a man's ears, crawling on the beams.

"Leave your rice balls for him and he will let you live a long life and bring you wealth," my amah told us.

In the morning we left our rice balls on the beams for the fox with a man's ears and later that day the rice balls were gone.

• • •

"Yeu will come for us soon," my mother said while we bathed in the marsh.

• • •

The day there were no rats on Rat Day we became scared. There had been no continuous rain, no fire or heat wave or cat we knew of to keep them away.

"Pests," my amah said. "Be thankful they're gone."

But others thought that the rats had all been killed by something that could kill the rest of us as well.

"Who knows," said Leandri, "what potions and fumes the Japanese have learned to concoct from the Germans and that they are anxious to try on us."

"Look how my babies have grown brown spots, that's not normal," said Madame Lin, showing Leandri her breasts.

"It's like your breasts are the backs of your hands," my mother said. "They are getting old."

"My babies? Old?" Madame Lin said.

"Shh," my amah said. "Can't you hear the clicking of the dragon's scales? He is moving over the earth and forming new lands."

"Yeah, like turning China into Japan," Leandri said.

"No, I'm wrong, it's not a dragon, it's the Japanese fixing a jeep," my amah said.

"Where's Poulet?" my mother asked. Everyone looked under the porch to see if she was playing in the cool dirt, but she was not there. She was not inside, sleeping on a mat in the afternoon sunlight, and she was not with the older girls.

"The marsh!" my mother screamed, and we all ran.

The marsh was quiet. The tall grass did not move in the wind. The grasshoppers were not hopping and a striped snake lay on a rock in the sun.

Thrashing through the water, my mother was waist-deep, calling out for Poulet.

When we found her, Poulet was sitting on a dead man's body.

"Not my husband again," Leandri said when she heard.

The dead man was bloated and Poulet sat on his belly while she chewed on a cattail. With one hand she played with her toes. When she looked up she saw us and smiled, and her mouth was brown from the end of the cattail. The dead man was not wearing any clothes and we could not tell what he was.

"Japanese," Madame Lin said.

"Vietnamese," Leandri said.

"French," said someone else.

"How are his nails trimmed?" said my amah, who was too far away to see.

"Like daggers," said Madame Lin.

"Like claws," said Leandri.

"This could be my husband," my mother said, picking up Poulet and handing her to me so she could get a better look at the man.

My mother began to faint, clutching a handful of cattails that tore at their roots as she fell over backwards into the water.

The Japanese pulled my mother from the marsh and stuck her face into the dead man's genitals and asked her, "Do you know them? Are they the balls of your Yeu? Don't you know?"

IT WAS NEW YEAR'S EVE OF 1944 AND WE HAD FOUND a Buddha's hand.

"These are its fingers," my amah said, and then she held up the fruit to the mountains, saying the mountains were as good as any shrine and her hands would have to serve as the porcelain bowl the fruit should be offered in.

My mother wanted us to make resolutions, but my amah said it was best to wish for typhoons, droughts and more wars — that way the gods would think our minds gone and deny us our requests.

While I was wishing for a tidal wave at the marsh, Hideho came up behind me.

He asked me what I was doing, and I told him I was wishing for a tidal wave. He laughed so hard he fell back on the grass and then yelled in pain because he had lain back on the handle of his saber.

Then he leaned over and kissed my ear.

"Is that lemons I smell?" he said.

"It's the Buddha's hand," I said.

He ran his fingers through my hair.

I felt the marsh water lap at my legs, and something else, a reed come sailing by and shoring up against my ankle bones.

Hideho picked up the reed and drew with it like a pen under my skirt, on the insides of my legs.

Then it was not the reed up against my legs, but Hideho, lifting up my skirt.

He did not go slowly. I could hear his feet pushing into the mud. From his pushing inside me I thought I would split in two like the wishbone off a cooked chicken. A wish on me I could bring luck, money and lovers.

I tried to bring my head up, but Hideho kept it down. I could not breathe.

When I woke up Hideho was gone and my amah was looking inside my mouth.

"Brown, like the water from the marsh," she said, and then she made me stand up, button my shirt and pull down my skirt.

"No, I want to stay here," I told her.

"You can't," she said.

"Why, is there a snake flying down from the moon? Is the earth cracking underfoot? Are the wild pigs stampeding down the mountain? Is it the Year of the Dragon and I've forgotten the candied ginger?" I said.

"No, dinner's ready," she said.

· · ·

No one knew why, but dinners were getting better. I remember once there was rabbit cooked with thyme.

"Who caught this rabbit? Who has a garden with thyme?" we all asked.

"It's Yeu, he's sending food down our way from the mountain," my mother said.

"Bullshit," Leandri said as she used her fingernail to pick thyme from between her two front teeth. "Someone's been stealing, and whoever it is better tell us so that we don't all get roped down on boards in the sun or beaten with belts or pissed on or burned."

"Thank God, a dry wine," Father Jean-Claude said, and dipped his fingers into the sauce.

· · ·

We put a willow twig into the right hand of the dead man at the marsh.

"This is so he can sweep away demons," my amah said.

"Oh, here we go again," my mother said. "For the love of Christ, just burn him in the bushes, or better yet, send him down the marsh. If his legs get stuck on the bank, the hog deer will come and set him free with their noses when they smell him to see what he is."

"And put a stone in his mouth, we haven't got a coin," my amah said.

"No stones, no willow twigs, no crickets, cicadas or grasshoppers, just let him be. Does he look Chinese to you?" my mother said. She lifted up the dead man by the neck, and water dripped off his shirt and into the marsh as if he had just gotten up himself and was waist-high in water, ready to walk.

"Check his teeth. Chinamen don't clean them and lotus tea stains the ivory after time," Leandri said.

"Check the hair on his chest," Madame Lin said.

"Check the whites of his eyes," someone else said.

"No," my mother said, "just let him go. He's not one of us. He's not your husband, your uncle, your cousin, your brother, your boy. Send him on." So we did, and I watched him float past the place by the marsh where Hideho had pulled up my skirt.

When the Japanese came they took the dead man out of the water. One Japanese had a pistol. He put it up the dead man's nostril.

After he shot him, my mother said, "Good, now he belongs to the Japanese."

At night my belly itched me.

"Snake skin," my amah said, and made me lie on the rocks by the path warmed by the sun.

"She's right, a rash called snake skin, caused from eating poor food," my mother said, and she found me some oil made from the rough skin of shark.

"Turn over," she said, and I did. I lay on the rocks while she poured the oil onto the scabs on my belly.

The oil made us think of a shark soup we hadn't eaten for so long. When I woke, a boy was licking my belly. One of my scabs was hanging from the corner of his mouth.

• • •

The second time my father was caught by the Japanese they put a cloth belt around his eyes. I yelled for him on the path. He turned his head toward me, and like a schoolgirl's ribbon on the back of her straw hat, the ends of the cloth belt crossed and lifted with the wind.

"Papa!" I yelled, and the Japanese yelled for me to be quiet.

I was happy to see him. I wanted to run and tell my mother. She would ask me to pick mint and grind it with oil to spread on her wrists and her breasts and her legs and the places where perfume would go. Leandri would brush my mother's hair and my amah would roll pills made of dust, saying they were really ground gold and we would live long.

"Papa!" I yelled again, and this time it was my father who shouted for me to be quiet. He was taken to a cell dug into the ground. The roof was made of bamboo poles tied together with rope.

"We'll never be freed," my mother said when she learned my father had been captured again.

"You sound happy about that," my amah said while she and my mother made a swallow-ashes charm.

"With Yeu down in the ground, I can walk by and see him whenever I want to. But up in the mountains, who knows where he is and who he is sleeping with." My mother mixed the swallow-ashes charm with water and fed it to Poulet.

"What about me? Won't the demons get me too?" I said, so she gave me some ashes to eat and I showed her my black tongue.

"You've been lying," my mother said to me.

"That's not Chinese, that's French," my amah said, meaning the part about your tongue turning black when you lie.

At night I wondered which demon might catch me. Would it be the one who steals your soul or would it be the one who takes your money, your eyes or your heart? I asked my amah what would happen to me if I was robbed of my soul, and she told me not to talk. She tied reeds together and slid them over my neck, saying they were a dog collar. A spirit robber who came for my soul wouldn't bother with the soul of a dog.

For months I was a dog. I let the children climb on my back and I walked on all fours. At a full moon I howled until the Japanese threw rocks at me.

Whenever she could, my mother would lie down on the ground by the hole where my father was kept. I could not hear what she said to him, but I could see her lips moving. I thought maybe she was talking to him about memories of the sea or of our home in Shanghai, or the German shepherds we'd had, or the games he'd played with the men from the club. I could picture my father sitting on the dirt and sweating in the dark as my mother talked on and on.

When the Japanese made my mother leave my father, I could see her pink skirt was covered in dirt, staining the silk in shapes like continents drawn on a map of the world. I tried to wipe the dirt away, but I couldn't get the skirt clean. At dinner, rice balls she held in her hand turned brown from the dirt on her fingertips.

· · ·

At night we heard a sound. Some thought it was a new kind of bird traveling south because too many trees up north had been burned by bombs and exploding planes.

Madame Lin thought it was babies floating down from Shanghai's children's hospital on barges made of rubber tires and bamboo poles. "We can mother them," she said.

"What will we feed them?" Leandri asked.

"I've got these buttons," said a small boy named Kwok, and he rattled a tin cigarette box.

I had a wooden box that once held Cuban cigars. There was no food in it, only a dead butterfly I had kept that had dots on its wings like a second set of eyes. I had taken the box from the hand of a girl who had fallen with fever on the path. Later, when they covered her body with dirt, her arm stuck out and her hand was still held in the air and her fingers looked as if they were still holding the box, or as if she were going to catch something that was falling from the sky.

"Maybe the sound is the Montagnards coming down from the mountains," my mother said. "Oh, no, I hope that doesn't mean we'll be set free," she said.

Father Jean-Claude shook his head. "Up there the Montagnards are starving. There is no more food above where the trees grow and the wild pigs have all been killed. The Montagnards are too weak to come down here. No," he said, "it is only the wind changing course, getting ready for winter."

"It's a radio," said a girl named May-ling. She went out back and pushed aside leaves and branches, showing us a radio she hid there. She said she liked the way the dials spun between her fingers.

We couldn't reach any stations.

"Who has the most fillings?" my mother asked, and walked around the room making all of us open up our mouths to see how much metal we had.

Kwok and two other boys had the most. They went outside, standing cheek to cheek, biting down on the antenna while my mother slowly turned the dial.

"Get some music," Leandri said. "Try for Saigon."

"It's too late, everything's off the air. Don't waste the batteries," Father Jean-Claude said.

We went to bed. Before I fell asleep I saw May-ling move her fingers in her sleep as if she were still turning the dials on the radio.

In the morning we tried the radio again.

"Shh, I think it's music," my mother said.

"That's static, bad lines," Leandri said, but my mother insisted it was music and she made Kwok and the two children walk with her around the room while she held the radio and searched for a direction that would pick up the strongest waves.

My amah laughed at my mother, saying there was already music. She went outside and put her ear to the trunk of a tree, saying its rings were like the tuning fork and rang out notes in the key of C and D. Really, she said, she was listening for birds, to trap one for our meal.

"Goddamn it, why can't I get music?" my mother said.

Then we heard words in Japanese.

"It sounds like the general's voice," I said. "It's about the Vichy camp. They're going there for dinner."

"How fucking grand," Leandri said.

"Oh, what I would do for some wine," Father Jean-Claude said.

"Shh, it's a raid," I said. "They're sneaking up with thirty men hiding in the trucks transporting the general and his officers — no one is to be left alive. No bother digging graves, just use gasoline and set them on fire. Take everything they've got — the tents, the poles, their clothes and boots, their books, their maps, their mirrors and their food."

"Dance to that," Leandri said to my mother.

"Oh, the Vichy, maybe they have a phonograph," my mother said, and she danced around the room with me and she looked above my head as if instead of dancing with me she was dancing with my father and the space above my head was my father's eyes.

I was glad about the raid. If the Japanese stole a phonograph from the French I would sit outside beneath the general's window and listen to the music.

My mother stopped dancing and put her hands to her head. "A raid? We have to tell the French. I know people at that camp. My brother's friend René is there," she said.

"How can we tell them?" Leandri said.

"How? Simple. The Japanese and the Vichy are still amicable — I've seen a few Vichy drive through here on their way to Hanoi. Hell, the general even gives them tea. Maybe we can get them a message when they're here," my mother said.

"They won't believe you," Madame Lin said. "They'll turn you in and the general will beat you to death and rip out your teeth for that gold crown you have."

"What will they serve at the dinner?" I said.

"Pheasant, they are close to where they flock," Father Jean-Claude said.

"Will they have dessert?"

"Yellow cake made from powdered milk," he answered. "I'll be there in spirit." Father Jean-Claude had picked up the habit of sucking on the metal cross around his neck, since the time when rice didn't get through for three days and we ate grasshoppers cooked in boiling water with blades of grass thrown in.

"Even for the killing?" I asked.

"No, I'll leave just before that and after finishing my wine," he said.

"Have a cigarette for me," my mother said.

"Bless you, child, of course," Father Jean-Claude said.

"I've got an idea," she said. "Find me a pen and some paper."

We all groaned.

"Hah, pen and paper. What would you like to trade for that? What have you got? Have you got French diamond tiaras tucked away under your mat alongside your fancy-smelling cologne?" Madame Lin said.

"Blood," my amah said, and we all looked at her and thought that her ears were bleeding again. "Write in blood. We all have it, and it won't wash off in the rain."

"And for paper?" Leandri said.

"A board from the latrine will do," my amah said, and she handed us the one she always used for killing rats on Rat Day.

That night we sat around a bowl and we cut the tips of our fingers with a shard of glass. Our blood dripped and mixed together in the bowl. Leandri fashioned a thin brush out of hair. My mother kneeled over the bowl and dipped the brush into our blood. On the board she wrote the French a message about the raid our Japanese general had planned.

I hoped there would be enough blood left over so that I could write more words on the walls. But for strength my amah had us lick the bowl clean.

· · ·

The Vichy drove through in jeeps on a day when there was no sun, just low gray fog.

"With the sun as a symbol for their flag, this is not a day for the Japanese," my mother said. She took the board with our message written in blood from under her mat and went outside. Soon she came back running.

"Did it work?" we all asked.

"I don't know," she said. She was out of breath. Standing, she bent over and put her head down. "Oh, God, I hope so," she said.

The day the Japanese were to dine at the French camp we watched them sitting outside and cleaning their guns and sharpening their bayonets.

When they were ready to leave, the general was carried to his jeep in his bamboo stretcher. I ran with the children alongside him.

"Au revoir!" he called to us, waving.

When we could no longer hear the sound of their jeeps driving down the road, we ran to the general's windows and tried to look inside and see the tapestries on his wall. But the guards who stayed behind came at us and banged on our hands with the butts of their guns to keep us from hanging off the general's window ledge.

With swollen hands and fingers we left the general's place and played blind tiger in the road that led to Saigon.

My mother and my amah and Leandri and Father Jean-Claude and Madame Lin all sat on the porch and watched us play. If they had had cigarettes they would have smoked them, but without them they just sat, leaning against the wall and waiting for the Japanese to come home.

There was no moon. It was difficult to see in the dark.

"Get to bed," my mother said to us, and we ran to her laughing, with sweat at our hairlines.

"So early?" we said. Some of us continued playing blind tiger inside, chasing each other around our mats on the floor.

Before sleep, on our mats, we played ox. We used our fingers as horns to poke each other in the back.

"Play the bear now, sleep," my amah said.

In the middle of the night we heard the general's scream.

We thought a horse had bitten him again.

We jumped to our windows. The sky was clearing and clouds went quickly past the moon. We asked each other who could see if the general was bleeding, if his arms had been torn from their sockets, if his eyes had rolled back up into his head. But before anyone could answer, the general jumped off his stretcher and ran into our hut screaming words in Japanese I did not understand.

The guards tried to keep him back, but he was strong and broke free of their grip.

He went first for a six-year-old boy named Shueh-jen. He took out his bayonet and cut off Shueh-jen's earlobe. Shueh-jen cupped his hand around his ear, and then he bent over and picked up the piece of his earlobe and put it into his pocket.

The general, still screaming, hit at the walls with his bayonet. A rat came running out from a rafter. Exhausted finally, the general sat down on Leandri's mat and put his head in his hands. Then he fell asleep.

That night Leandri slept with me on my mat and we watched the general's belly as it rose and fell with his breaths.

"What happened at the Vichy camp?" Father Jean-Claude whispered to my mother in the dark.

"Nothing, that's why he's so upset," my mother whispered back.

"They got your message, then?" Father Jean-Claude asked.

"I think so, yes, but we'll never know for sure and we must never ask," and then my mother closed her eyes and we all fell asleep to the sound of the general's breathing.

In the morning the general woke and walked to the window and pulled his pants down and peed out onto the road. The guards brought his bamboo stretcher and the general lay down on it and they headed off to his quarters. In the stretcher he fell back to sleep, and his arm hung down, his fingers dragging in the dirt as they went.

FOR FEAR THE HEAVENLY DOG WOULD COME DOWN AND take Poulet's spirit, we caught a dog and cut a piece of its fur and put it in a pouch we sewed to the lining of Poulet's dress. No one knew what kind of dog it was or where it had come from. The children wanted to keep it, like the rat Sister Matilde, so they could ride on its back.

"We can make a saddle out of this," they said, and lifted up a bicycle seat they had found.

"He's got legs, not wheels," my amah said, and she took the leather seat from them and said leather had flavor and she would use it in a soup made from willow and reeds.

That night my amah could not sleep. She dreamed the Heavenly Dog came down through the slats in our roof and took up Poulet between its teeth. In the morning, she said the pouch of dog's hair sewn to Poulet's dress was not enough, that something else must be done so that the Heavenly Dog would not be tempted by the baby's flesh.

On an evening when the Japanese were at the back of the camp playing ball, my amah took Poulet to the road that led to Saigon to teach her to walk so that she wouldn't resemble a baby and so the Heavenly Dog would not eat her. Down on all fours, my amah crawled next to Poulet while Poulet stood on two legs and held on to my amah's head for balance.

From the field we could hear the players shout at goals scored, at the gain of team ground. Poulet laughed and shouted too.

"That's right," my amah said to her, "those are cheers for your walking."

"What have you done?" my mother said when she saw Poulet walking, holding on to the slatted walls for balance.

"She wanted to learn. You must let her do what children do even though we're in this place," my amah said.

"Who said you could teach my child how to walk?" my mother said.

My amah lay on her mat and turned her back to my mother while she screamed down at her.

"Oh, please, can't anyone get any sleep around here?" Leandri said, and she threw a wooden board at my mother, who caught it midflight. A splinter pierced the skin of my mother's hand. She dropped the board and held her wrist, looking at her palm, the splinter sticking out at an angle. My amah stood up to look.

"If it moves in the sun, we will be able to tell the right time," my amah said.

My mother laughed. Her hair shook loose and hung in ringlets around her eyes. Leandri, who had had her eyes shut, opened them, and she helped my mother pull the splinter out.

I saw my mother and Leandri talking on the steps. Leandri was poking the splinter through the spaces between her teeth, pulling out white bits of rice. My mother had been laughing with Leandri, and all of her hair now swung about her face and covered her eyes and all I could see of her was her open mouth and her teeth. That night, they did not sleep on their mats, but stayed outside on the steps, talking and laughing and watching the sun rise. When our guard woke and saw my mother and Leandri, arms around each other, sleeping on the steps, he unbuckled his belt, pulled it through the loops of his pants and hit at their bare ankles. Later, like cheeks, their ankle bones shone red as if they had been out in the cold. We applied cool rocks taken from the marsh and wrapped in the hems of their skirts. My mother cried out, but not from the pain. Down on her mat she could see through a slit to the outside, where Poulet was walking straight for the field where the Japanese were playing a game.

"Not me," my mother yelled, "Poulet!" and she pointed to the space between the boards.

I ran toward the field but the Japanese got to Poulet first. In the way of a pass, she was picked up and thrown to the sidelines. She landed on her face and did not move. I could hear my mother screaming.

Mud covered Poulet's face. I scraped it away. When she opened her eyes she smiled. Bits of mud from above her lip dropped into her mouth.

"Tian," she said.

"Are you all right?" I said, and she nodded and more mud fell off her. Then I lifted her onto my shoulders and told her that from now on I would be her legs and take her wherever she wanted to go.

In our hut, when I let her slide down me and into my mother's arms, I saw that the mud from Poulet's legs had dried like a black scarf running down the sides of my neck.

"Leave it," my amah said when I tried to peel off the dried mud. "You'll need it for warmth come the Year of the Horse."

. . .

The Chief of the Montagnards came down. His wife ran beside him, trying to keep the wheelbarrow from rolling too quickly down the mountain. They stopped in front of the general's quarters. The general came out with two other men and bowls of tea and food we all guessed was fish, or chicken, or anything we hadn't eaten in a long time. When I saw it was rice, my mother said, "Don't tell the others, they won't believe you."

My mother pushed the others aside so she could get up close and hear what the chief said to the general. I could not hear because my amah was at my ear, telling me the names of the jewels our family once owned:

"A Marie Antoinette ring, golden earrings that weighed so much they dragged the wearer's lobes down to the ground, pocket watches whose gears were diamond-studded, gold bathroom spigots so high of carat that when turned, the soft gold bent so much that the water would not run, and the bathroom was closed off and wasn't even called the bathroom anymore, but the room of melting gold. That's what we had before all this," my amah said.

"Shh," Leandri said, "I'm trying to hear what he's saying."

"Nothing, he's come just for food, it's not politics, it's starvation," my amah said.

My mother came running back to us.

"What?" I said.

But my mother would not say. She pushed us back and told us to run.

We all laughed.

"Where?" Leandri said.

"The marsh?" I said.

"The mountains?" my amah said.

My mother ran without us.

"That way's Saigon," Leandri called out, and we watched my mother running, her skirt tight around her legs where the silk would not give with her stride.

Then we looked back at the Chief of the Montagnards, and everyone saw it was rice he was eating because when the Japanese shot him in the head, bits of rice flew out of his mouth as if he had heard a good joke.

"Those fucking Japanese," I heard my amah say.

Hearing the shot, my mother suddenly stopped running as if she too had been shot.

Then they shot the Chief of the Montagnard's wife. She fell over into the wheelbarrow, and water sloshed out of it. I wondered where the chief's son was, the one who had told me that someday his father's testicles would be his. He had not come down from the mountain with his father, and I thought the Japanese weren't going to give those testicles up. I could hear my amah saying something, giving me a recipe for a medicine made with testicles.

"Sliced with the grain of the flesh," I heard her say, "can cure like the tiger's eyes, but against the grain can kill a man dead."

Later I picked up some of the grains of rice and I kept them under my mat. At night I heard a rat by my ear, pawing at the woven straw for the loose grains.

. . .

"Christ," my father told us he had said when he heard the shots go off.

He said he had known it was the chief and his wife they had shot because he dreamt the woman who took off her head and started brushing her hair had come to him, only it wasn't her hair she was brushing, but the chief's.

After they shot the chief and his wife, the Japanese let my father out of the hole and they put a shovel in his hand and made him dig by the Sea of Trees.

When the rain came I watched my father shovel up the dirt and throw it over his shoulder. When he stopped, it was just for a second, to wipe the rain from his eyes.

"The rain will keep him cool," my amah said as I watched out the window. From where I stood I could see my mother lying in the dirt near my father. A guard stood with one boot on the middle of her back. She tried to move like a snake through the mud toward my father, but the foot pinned her down so she could only inch forward. The spray of dirt from my father's shovel landed closer to her each time.

"Let's catch the rain," my amah said, so she and Poulet and Leandri and I went out and caught the rain in our hands and we drank it.

"I taste Shanghai," my amah said, and then she made us drink from her hand. "Taste the filament from the Street of Ironworkers?" she said.

The rain did taste like metal.

"No, this is from Notre Dame," Leandri said. "This has slid over the gargoyles' wings and down into the Seine."

The guards brought my mother and father to the door of our hut and threw them on the ground. Mud weighed down their hair and covered their eyes. My father was too tired to move. Knees up, he wedged his hands in between them. I brought him a smooth flat stone and put it under his head.

"Yeu," my mother said, and crawled over to him and spooned herself around him.

"This is not a bed," the guards said, and they started kicking my mother and my father. "Get up," they said and they poked their sabers at their bellies and backs.

"Leave them alone, they are only sleeping," my amah said.

The Japanese left.

That night I heard voices between the falling drops of rain. I thought it was my mother and my father talking about the place where we used to live. I heard the word "balcony" and I heard the word "dance." I thought they were remembering birthdays and dinners and walks they had walked and rides they had ridden and parties they had given.

The rain gone, the late morning sun dried the mud hard. My father took off all his clothes and beat them with a stick, making the dried mud fly around us on the road.

Even after he had gotten all the mud off his pants and his shirt, he still beat them. My mother ran up behind him and tried to take the stick from him, but it hit her in the face.

The mark on her cheek was black. My amah said it was from the dirt and mud on the stick, but my mother said it was from the poisons in my father's blackened soul. She went back to our hut and smoked a cigarette. "Come here, sit down next to me," she said, so I did, liking the smell of her cigarette and the way the smoke blew out of her mouth when she sighed.

"He's not going to get us free," my mother said.

"Yeu?" I said.

"Yes, your father. Without the help of the chief he can't do a thing."

"Look at these." I showed my mother the rice grains I had picked off the ground after the chief had been shot.

She did not look at the rice, but at the wall.

"It's almost Rat Day," I said.

"No, it *is* Rat Day," my mother said and then she threw her cigarette down, picked up a board and hit at all the walls, sending dust and dirt down on my head and all over our floor. It sounded more like ten of my mother hitting the walls, not just one woman with a bony neck.

All the children ran in, and my amah and Leandri and my father. A few rats ran across our mats, but my mother didn't go for them. She just kept hitting the walls.

"Stop her," my amah said to my father. But he bent over and picked up the burning cigarette she had thrown on the floor and he started smoking it.

"Aren't you going to stop her?" my amah said again, her hands over her ears to keep them from bleeding from the noise.

When the Japanese came in they laughed at my mother hitting the walls. My father laughed too, and they slapped him on the back with their hands and told him wasn't it nicer where they had him locked up before and not in this room with a woman half out of her mind?

"Shall we cut off her head?" one of the Japanese said to my father.

My father smiled. The guard laughed and then held a bayonet up to my mother's neck. She still swung with her board at the walls.

"Marcelle!" Leandri cried, and she went to my mother.

I ran to my father.

"Stop them," I said. I dug my nails into his leg. He puffed on the last of the cigarette and threw it back down on the ground.

"That's all right, I've already got a woman with no head," he said, and he put a hand on the guard's shoulder. The guard put away his bayonet.

. . .

In the Great Room I stood on my mother's feet and I said, "Dance." But she did not dance. She looked at herself in the mirror.

"We'll never be set free," she said.

"Come on," I said, and then I started singing "Parlez-moi d'amour" until she started to move. We danced over water, the symbol worn down so much you couldn't see it was water and we only knew it was because we were the ones who had worn it down with our dancing. Outside I could see the Sea of Trees, but there was nothing to look for there — not my father, not the chief and his wife. The trees looked thin, as if they had lost their leaves and winter had come to the tropics of Kontum.

· · ·

The Japanese started entertaining my father. The general would come by on his stretcher, banging on the bamboo poles, and call for him.

Walking alongside the stretcher, my father would tour the compound with the general. Behind the stretcher marched a line of guards in case my father decided to injure the general.

· · ·

"It's the Year of the Horse," my amah said. With the sharp stone that she used to scratch off the days, she put a mark on the wooden slat of the wall.

We celebrated by going to the marsh. I floated on my back and my mother pushed me at my feet, saying, "And who is this dead man I have come across in the marsh? Does anyone know him? Is he a Chinaman? A Frog? A Jap?" and the others tickled my feet because my amah said that if you tickle a dead Chinaman's feet you can hear his laughter coming from behind you as he passes through the gates of the dead. And then they poked at my belly, saying you can tell a Frog because of the way the belly bounces back like a spring from all the butter he's eaten. A Jap, they said, has a crease in the ear. This is the mark of a devil, they said, so they pulled at my earlobes and folded them over, closing the marsh water in. Later, when I stood and leaned to one side, the water fluttered there.

"It's the butterfly's wings," my amah said, and made me stand tall to let the butterfly have a clear path of escape. Really, she told me this so I would keep a straight back and not grow a hump when I aged.

· · ·

The general and my father played chess. Pawns were pebbles, knights were buttons, queens were beetles. Kings, also pebbles, were wrapped in colored tin foil from chocolates eaten long ago. While the general gauged his next move, my father would unpeel the wrapper from his king and tell me to smell the faint smell of chocolate that still clung to it. I would lick my lips and my father would smile and then wrap his pebble back up. The wrapper was so old that after a while it was hard to smell the chocolate and instead I smelled the marsh, where the pebble had been found.

My mother came running. "Yeu, the Japanese!" she screamed.

"What's she screaming?" the general said as he moved a pebble on the board.

My father shook his head. "I don't know," he said, and he played his move.

Two days later, my mother was still screaming, "The Japanese!" They put her in one of the covered bomb shelters so we could all sleep at night and so the animals off by the Sea of Trees would stop howling.

But putting Marcelle beneath the ground made things worse. We couldn't understand her words, but my amah said my mother's screaming was the rolling of the earth, the ground flexing muscles, throwing the weight of itself up and over, down and under.

"Shit," Leandri said to me, "I wish she'd just shut up. I can't even hear my heart pounding or the blood traveling in my ears. Your mother is keeping me from hearing myself alive."

My father slept, though, and as he did I watched how his chest rose and fell with every breath and I wondered what he dreamed so I lay my head down on his chest. I tried to see what he dreamed, but all that I could see was the Sea of Trees moving up and down as he breathed in and out.

70

Three days later, when my mother stopped screaming, they let her out of the bomb shelter. But as I wiped the dirt off her skirt, I could hear her throat making a clicking noise, and when I looked up at her, I could see she was still mouthing the words "The Japanese, the Japanese, the Japanese."

· · ·

My amah caught a fever and lay on her mat and pretended she was eating rice.

"Let me finish eating," she said when I took a cloth and wiped her brow.

My father played chess with the general all night long. To see their moves the general lit small fires from bundled newspapers containing news of the war which he never read.

I went to the Great Room and took my mother with me. Holding her by the hand, I stood her over earth. She sat on the symbol cross-legged and looked out the window, pointing. "I can see Yeu in the mountains."

"Papa's playing chess with the general," I said.

"Bastard, he hasn't come to see me yet," she said.

I sat on fire.

"Watch out, you'll burn," she said.

I moved to water.

"That's better," she said.

We lay on our backs and looked at the ceiling.

"Do you think he'll come down from the mountains?" she said.

"Maman, he's already down."

"He's got to come save us," she said.

Just then, my amah walked in the door. Striding across air, she said, "It's over. It's time to go home."

"Who won?" I asked, thinking of the chess game.

"We did," my amah said. "Now get up, let's pack. Soon there'll be trucks and troops. I don't want them throwing out what's ours."

"The Japanese?" my mother said.

"No, us, the Allies, we won," my amah said.

"What's she saying? I can't understand her." My mother said and turned to me.

"The war, for Chrissakes," my amah said.

"Talk about the hare in the moon, the Buddha's hand, the snakes on the path, the fox in the rafters, the ghost in our souls," my mother said. "I just can't understand a word you're saying."

My amah left the Great Room, letting the door slam behind her. My mother stood up and put her hands against the window that faced the mountains.

I thought about the skull of the pig my father once wore over his head. I thought I'd better get back to our hut and see if it showed its face there so I could claim it as mine. I pictured wearing it on my head as we filed down the road to Saigon.

My mother flapped her arms in the air.

"What are you doing?" I said.

"Signaling your father, letting him know I'm here," she said.

"Then go outside, stand in front of the general's place," I said.

"But he's up there, he's got to come down first," she said.

I left my mother standing on the symboled borders of the oriental carpet, flapping her arms in front of the window.

Running back to our hut, I could see my father and the general still playing chess. My father lifted up his arm, it must have been his move. Then I heard a shot, and I saw he wasn't holding the chess piece any longer and that now both his arms were raised and he was flapping them just like my mother in the Great Room. I thought the two of them would take off and meet above our heads, floating over the camp, the guardhouse tower, the Japanese.

Having seen my father play chess with the general, the Chinese must have thought my father was Japanese. One soldier held him up by his neck and threw him against the wall and put a gun to his head.

"He's not Japanese!" I yelled. The soldier did not hear and he hit my father with the butt of his gun.

Then I heard Leandri and my amah and Father Jean-Claude

and all the others screaming, "The Chinese!" and they pointed. Down the mountain ran the Chinese troops, who set us free.

My father lay on the ground, holding his head in his hands.

I ran to him, but the Chinese soldier knocked me aside and went through my father's pockets, pulling out broken cigarettes. Tobacco scattered in the air as he turned the pockets inside out.

Hideho was shot. His head snapped back. Blood ran down his neck as if it had been slit. I thought for a moment that maybe the Chinese didn't use guns but scythes. More were shot all around me. "Japs bleed as much as pigs," I once heard someone say. I thought I could hear the dry ground soaking up the blood, making popping sounds.

"The war is over," said my amah, carrying Poulet on her back and a bundle in her hand.

"Where are you going?" Leandri asked.

"Saigon first," my amah said. "Come on."

Father Jean-Claude laughed and sat down. "No need for walking, old woman. There will be trucks lined with mattresses, covers of goose down, and fish and noodles and possibly wine."

That night I went to our hut and looked for the skull of the pig my father had worn on his head. Our hut didn't look like our hut anymore. The Chinese were all over our room, sleeping on our mats. There was some kind of smell. It was boots and sweat and thyme.

"Thyme?" Leandri said when I told her of the strange Chinese men sleeping on our mats.

"Yes, and they're talking in their sleep, screaming out words in Chinese. It's like they're all having the same nightmare, and they're all trying to wake up from it."

"That's our place, they have no right," Leandri said. "Let's get them out."

So Leandri and I went for help. We tried to wake up my father, who still lay on the ground, but when we shook him he said, "She took off her leg and started painting her toenails."

Father Jean-Claude's shirt was full of blood. He was giving last rites.

"What is it you want to take out of there?" he said to us, shutting the eyelids of a man just shot.

"We've got things," Leandri said.

"Sheets," I said.

"Right," Leandri said. "Sheets. And what about the children's dolls, and Marcelle has some cologne."

"Didn't she use that on the general?" Father Jean-Claude asked.

"All right, I've got a journal then," Leandri said.

"You do?" I said. "What did you write on?"

"It's from the first week," Leandri said. "After that I ran out of paper."

"Let them sleep, leave them alone," Father Jean-Claude said, and from the pocket of a dead Japanese guard he pulled out a cigarette and smoked it.

We went to my mother. In the Great Room she lay on the carpet, her arms and legs stretched out as if she were trying to touch all the symbols at the same time.

Leandri used her foot to try to push my mother's legs together.

"Get up," she said. "We've got to kick out the Chinese."

"Do you remember when the Japanese first came?" my mother said.

"Oh, Jesus," Leandri said. She went to the mirror and looked at herself in it and she licked the tips of her fingers and ran them across her eyebrows.

"Are you all right?" she said, and looked at me standing behind her in the mirror.

"Me?" I said.

"Yes, you. With Marcelle like this and Yeu like that," she said. "Mon Dieu, I've got lines here so deep I look old. I'm still a beauty, though, aren't I?" she said, and with both hands she held up her hair on top of her head.

The pink light of dusk came into the Great Room. I walked to the window that faced the mountains.

"This is my favorite time of day," I said.

A few more Chinese came down. Knapsacks on their backs, they looked like boys walking home from school.

My amah came into the room with Yeu on her back. As she passed through the doorway, his bare feet bumped against the frame. She let him drop next to my mother on the carpet.

"The Chinese are here!" my mother said.

"Come on, let's dance," Leandri said.

I stood on her feet and she danced me around the symboled border of the oriental carpet.

My amah sat on water and sang opera through her nose.

Poulet came in the door walking on her hands.

Passing by the mirror, I saw us all lit up pink by the light of dusk. "Where are we?" I almost said out loud, and I thought how the Great Room would have spoken, the symbols rising off the carpet around us — fire, water, metal, air and earth — whispering, circling our ears, the fine woolen threads floating back down to the ground after they'd told us their answers.

. . .

For days it was worse than with the Japanese. We did not know the Chinese. The bottoms of their pants were stained and smelled like the mountain river waters they had waded through. They had chewing gum from England. Cigarettes from France. Yankee guns. Cracked heels, bottled water, baby talc, a Spanish wine.

The chewing gum was stale. It broke apart in our mouths in bits that sometimes slipped down by mistake and we swallowed them while trying to chew and make them whole.

"Achh, fuck!" Leandri said, and spit her gum out and instead put in her mouth a dried fish eye.

"Hau bu hau?" my amah said to her.

"Très hau," Leandri said, nodding her head and chewing.

"Très hau. Hah," my amah said. "Now you're speaking like the snake with a split tongue, one side French, the other Chinese."

"But my head is the wild boar," Leandri said, and out from under her pile of things she took out the pig skull my father had worn.

When Leandri saw I wanted it, she held it above me. "Let's see, Cinderella," she said. The wild-pig skull went over my eyes and stopped at the bridge of my nose. Under the bones, it was cool. I smelled the smell of Leandri's clothes. There was a knock on the skull. It was my mother.

"Take it off, we've got to pack," she said, and threw all that we had into the sheet the general had given her to keep her safe from mosquitoes. In the middle of the sheet my mother threw her moth-eaten skirts and the near-empty bottle of cologne.

"What have you got?" my mother said, and I threw in the broken rosary from Sister Matilde and the ripped sheets I had worn over my breasts. The wild-pig skull I still wore.

. . .

When my mother asked my amah what she wanted to pack, my amah left the hut and came back later with a broken piece of the Great Room's mirror.

"What's this for?" my mother asked. "To chase off evil spirits?"

"No, to look at ourselves," my amah said.

The Chinese came in and did a check — we had packed too much. "Bring half of that," they said, pointing to our things in the middle of my mother's sheet. My mother tore the sheet in half and then she bundled up the right side and knotted the corners. She left behind everything on the left side of the ripped sheet — her skirts and her near-empty bottle of cologne. What she took was my old ripped sheet, which she wrapped around the broken piece of mirror.

When it was time to go, we could not find my father.

"I'll look in the bomb shelter," said Father Jean-Claude.

"I'll check the Great Room," said Leandri.

My mother went to the latrines.

I went to the marsh. I walked in the water up to my ankles. I pulled the tall grass to one side.

I called my father's name. "Yeu," I called, because I thought if I called for "Papa" he would not answer me and he would think I was someone else's daughter looking for her father in the marsh.

When I found him he was floating. Face up, eyes closed, he said, "I am taking in the sun." He floated into the shade, and then he asked me to move him back to a spot where the sun hit strongest. I pulled him by his pant cuffs, the marsh water parting as we went.

"Maman wants to know what you'll pack," I said to him.

"Was the chessboard saved?" he asked.

"I think so," I said.

"That's all that I want then," he said, and he brought his arm up out of the water and held on to me.

"I don't want to leave," he said.

"You don't want to go home?"

"No, I want to go back up to the mountains. I just dreamed she took off her arm and started to cover it with bracelets and slide rings onto her fingers."

"Papa, we're going to go back to Saigon, then Shanghai. Maman says we'll eat pork and thousand-year-old eggs. Leandri's going to take me to Paris. I'll see the Seine. The starlit sky."

Later, when I saw my mother, she asked me what he had said.

"He talked about the woman who took off her head," I said.

My mother slapped my face. "What did he really say?" she said.

"He said pack the chessboard, it's the only thing he wants," I said.

"Go get it," my mother said, and she sent me out of our place.

Along the way I passed Japanese. Tied at their ankles, they sat on the path and called to me as I walked by.

"Hey, half-breed," they yelled, "got any food?"

"No," I said, "just a cigarette," and I put it in my mouth as I walked by them.

I went to the Chinese. A game of chess was going on.

"How about a trade," I said, and when the two players looked at me I took the cigarette from my mouth and held it their way. One man took it.

"I want the board," I said.

"Do you have a match?" he said.

I gave him one and he lit the cigarette. Then I reached over and slid the board out from between the two Chinese.

"No, that we're keeping," one said, and he gave me back the lit cigarette.

Walking past the Japanese I flicked the cigarette. "Catch," I said, and the burning cigarette landed on the back of a Japanese who was sleeping.

...

The rain came again. It came down in sheets that flooded the paths and flooded our hut and flooded the latrines, and the Chinese said it was as good a time as any to leave this godforsaken place, so we set out on the road that led to Saigon.

It was Rat Day when we left. The last thing I did before we started walking down the road was look back at our place and I thought how, months from now, without us being there to kill the rats they would overpopulate, running out of space, scrambling over one another, three and four rats thick, standing on each other's backs, rising high against our walls, almost able to reach the marks in the wood where my amah had scratched with a sharp stone, numbering our days.

"Where are those trucks?" Father Jean-Claude asked the Chinese.

"What trucks?" they said.

"For us, to go to Saigon," Father Jean-Claude said.

"Oh, those," the Chinese said. "We sent the Japanese back to the city on them."

"What about us?" Father Jean-Claude said.

"We walk the whole way, except for the places where we cross rivers, then we swim," the Chinese said.

"Good God, with all that, I'll need a new brassiere," Madame Lin said, and put her hands under her bosoms and pushed them so they came up from the low neckline of her faded dress.

MY FATHER WALKED BEHIND. MY MOTHER TRIED TO walk with him, but every time she went to his side, he would get behind her.

"What's happened to him?" my mother asked me.

"He doesn't want to leave," I said.

"Yeu, darling, think about going back home. The rooms, the land, the balconies," my mother said. My father did not look at her.

"Look at the trees," my amah said.

"Why? They look like the same trees we passed hours ago," Leandri said.

"That's right, and when you go to Saigon, you'll see the same trees," my amah said.

"What's she talking about now?" Father Jean-Claude said while lying on a long flat rock and sucking on his cross. The rest of us stopped too. I watched the Chinese walk in front of us.

"Let them keep going, we can stay here," my father said when he caught up to us and sat down on the rock by the feet of Father Jean-Claude. My mother ran to my father and knelt on the ground and put her head in his lap. My father looked down at the top of my mother's head. Around us the leaves of the trees were wide and flat. Banana, I heard someone call them. But I could not see any fruit. The dirt was rich and black. I wanted to take some back to the camp and see how fast our garden would grow. I found a leech between my toes. I watched it swell with my blood to the size of a grape before I burned it off. The leaves were so close together it made it difficult to see if the sky was cloudy or blue. Because there was no clearing, the air was heavy and our faces shone. I wiped my face on my sleeve. Father Jean-Claude began to snore.

"Yeu?" my mother said, and then looked up at my father. He was looking back to where we had just come from.

"He's not here," my amah said.

"What do you mean?" my mother said.

"He's up in the mountains, with the woman who took off her head and brushed her hair."

"Yeu, it's me, your Marcelle," my mother said.

Leandri went up to Father Jean-Claude and pinched his nose. He snorted in between snores and woke up.

"What? What?" he said. His cross had slipped to his side, and he picked it up and put it back in his mouth. Then he went back to sleep.

"Is this where we stay for the night?" I asked. All around us there were trees, so many it seemed that if we tried to reach out for each other in the middle of the night we wouldn't be able to. We would jam our hands against a tree trunk, find bark beneath our nails.

"We wait until they tell us where to sleep," Leandri said, and she pointed up ahead to where the Chinese walked on.

"Let's not lose them," my amah said. She took my hand and she took Poulet's hand and we went toward the Chinese. I turned around and saw Leandri pulling Father Jean-Claude up to his feet from his nap, and I saw my father standing, and my mother trying to take his hand, but he put his hand behind his back. Then my mother tried to reach behind his back to take his hand anyway, but he turned away from her so she couldn't, and to me it looked like dancing, so I started to sing "Parlez-moi d'amour."

Up ahead, the Chinese heard me. That night they had me sing all the words to the song for them so they could learn it.

Some Chinese had fish. It came in a cloth bag, and it was salted and yellow and wrapped in leaves. When the bag was empty, the Chinese passed it around, and we wet our fingertips with saliva and stuck our hands into the bottom of the bag and brought up big grains of salt and sucked on our fingers. While the Chinese sang "Parlez-moi d'amour," the big grains of salt that clung to their lips fell off, landing on their uniforms.

"Shut them up," my mother said while she lay alone by a tree, trying to sleep.

Poulet sat on my amah's lap. My amah had found a clearing in the trees and together they looked at the moon and they pointed to the stars. I couldn't hear what my amah was saying, but I could see her talking, her head moving up and down and her hand moving the hair from in front of Poulet's eyes so that she could get a good look at the sky.

A Chinese talked to my father. He was the lieutenant. On his hat he wore medals that swung from side to side as he spoke. My father listened. The lieutenant pulled out maps and twirled a compass over lines showing rivers and gray shapes designating mountains and land.

I fell asleep to the Chinese singing. In the middle of the night I woke up. My father was folding maps and putting them into his shirt. He looked at me. I waved to him. I wanted him to lie next to me and tell me stories, especially the story about the woman he loved who took off her head and brushed her hair. But he leaned against a tree and closed his eyes.

"He's back now, but he'll leave again," my amah said, scaring me because I thought she was asleep.

"Where?" I said.

"Nanking," my amah said. "You know, to fight the war."

"The war is over," I said. "Go back to sleep, there's blood in your ears tonight," I said.

"Not in my ears, in the streets of Nanking. With the war over, the Nationalists and the Communists are fighting like cocks. Yeu will join the Nationalists as general. Put your head against his chest and his medals will dig into your cheeks."

My mother woke up. "Old woman, be quiet, you're scaring the girl. Yeu isn't going anywhere. We're going back home. I'm planning a party. The grass will need cutting, but after that, we'll set up tables out back. I want American music. Candles everywhere. A suckling pig, roasted potatoes, a fat crispy duck. The band will play and Yeu and I will dance. Our old friends will watch and lift their glasses of wine to us."

"Am I invited?" I heard Father Jean-Claude say.

"Oh, all sorts of wine, German, French, Spanish, white, red, yellow, green, oh Portuguese and Pelopponese. Malay and Thai. I want wine coming out of our ears and I want it pouring from our shoes," my mother said.

The next morning we crossed a river.

"What's this called?" I asked. I waded through with Poulet sitting up on my shoulders and the pig skull on my head.

"The River We Cross," my amah said.

"That's not its name."

"The River Around Us," she said.

"All I want to know is, how far to Saigon?" I said. My breath made my face hot as I spoke with the skull on my head.

"Days," Leandri said. "Rat Day will come twice before we get to the gates of the city."

I looked down at the water swirling brown around my legs and I thought I felt something bumping up against me — a twig, a small fish, Michel Riquelme's eye. When I reached down to pick it up, it escaped through my fingers.

I thought about our hut. I wondered who would live there now besides the breeding rats. Maybe the woman who took off her head would haunt the Great Room. I pictured her taking off her head and brushing her hair while standing in front of the Great Room's mirror. I wondered if she'd stand on water or if she'd stand on fire instead.

In the next river we crossed I lost the skull of the pig. It was on my head and when I slipped in the mud the fast-moving water swept the skull downriver. Without it I was cold, even under a hot milky-yellow sun that made our scalps sweat and made our temples drip and the sweat slide down our cheeks and down our necks.

"Oh, God, look at him," my mother said, and she pointed to my father, who was now walking at the front with the rest of the Chinese.

"It's what I said, he'll go to Nanking next," my amah said.

My mother started running to catch up with my father. She ran so fast it looked as if she were running away from something and not straight for it. Leandri even turned around to see if she'd better start running herself for the cover of safety.

Before my mother got to him she fell face forward, tripping, not over vines, rocks or roots, but over her own two feet. We ran, laughing, to help her stand up. I went on one side and Leandri on the other. But she did not want to stand up, and every time we tried to lift her, she let her knees go limp and fell into a heap. After trying a long time, Leandri and I were laughing so hard we had to hold on to ourselves and then sit down with my mother in the dirt, not wanting to go farther, just wanting to sit and to laugh.

There were so many stars that night we were scared.

"Who knows if the sky can hold them all," my amah said.

Leandri said the stars made it hard for her to breathe.

"Wish them away," my mother said.

So I did, and I fell asleep wishing.

The Americans came. Flying in circles, dropping packs of cigarettes to the ground, they waved to us. I thought I could see the men at the controls of the planes through the windows. I thought how I could marry one of them. We'd say our vows in the air, standing on the wings, the wind so loud that we'd say our vows with our hands and our heads, waving and nodding, "I do."

WE STOOD ON A CORNER IN SAIGON.

"Buy! Buy!" said little girls crowding around us, holding up cups of melon and meat skewered on thin bamboo sticks. Black specks of soot had fallen onto the glistening fruit. I was wearing new rope-soled shoes the Chinese had given us after we had arrived. My feet hurt, and I was thinking that if I were back at our place I could go to the marsh and give them a dunk.

So many people moved around us I could not see whole bodies, only parts of legs and arms, a broken button split in half on a shirt, a package, an earring hanging from an earlobe, a set of teeth. I held Poulet. She grabbed at a saffron-colored scarf a woman was wearing over her shoulder. It was a color Poulet must never have seen before. The woman was French, and when I said "Pardonnez moi" to her, she stepped back and looked at me.

"You speak French?" she said.

"Oui, I am part," I said, and then she took off the scarf and wrapped it around Poulet's neck.

"Where are we?" my amah said, squatting on the sidewalk and staring down at the gutter, where paper trash floated and orange rinds were swept along in sewage. And then she said, "What year is this?"

"Are your ears bleeding again?" my mother asked.

"Year of the Cock, 1945," I said.

"Christ, the city, I'd forgotten," my mother said, looking around her. She sat down next to my amah and stared at the trash and the orange rinds.

In Saigon they danced all night. Radios were put out on window ledges facing courtyards where people danced. The music was American and everyone seemed to know the words. I was lost. I could only think of the words from "Parlez-moi d'amour."

. . .

We waited for my father in a building filled with cots set up for those of us who had no place to sleep. My father was coming to say goodbye. When he came down the street I thought he was a general. There were other soldiers with him who walked a few steps behind. He wore black boots. They were so shiny in the sunlight I thought he had mirrors wrapped around his legs. Up close I saw the medals on his jacket. He did not say anything to me. He kissed me on the forehead, climbed into a jeep, and someone drove him off. Over the American music from the radio I could hear my mother. I thought she knew the words and that she was singing along. When I went inside to where she lay on her cot, I could see that she was crying and not singing at all. My amah sat down with her on the cot and stroked her back.

"These are the dove's feathers," I heard my amah say as she let her fingers walk up and down my mother's skin.

We had lost Leandri. The next day I walked past the rows of cots, calling out her name. Morning sun coming in the windows lit up everyone sleeping and I saw sweat on their cheeks.

"She's gone forever," my amah said, but I didn't listen. I ran outside and Poulet followed me and we ran down small streets and into doorways where people leaned against walls, sleeping, smelling of wine or the urine that we could see had run out from between their legs and stained the sidewalk. When we got to the edge of the city, I picked up Poulet and pointed to the hills in front of us.

"You can see Leandri from here," I said to Poulet. But Poulet could not see, so I pointed to what I thought was a house on the hill.

"Wave, she's looking out the window," I said, and Poulet and I waved goodbye.

"She's gone back to France, then," my amah said when we saw her.

"Or to Kontum. She left a brown skirt there. I saw it under the steps before we left, hiding like a dog too hot for anything but the shade under a house," my mother said.

Every day there were new people on the cots. In the mornings I would walk around to see what things people had brought with them. I traded a piece of the Great Room's mirror for a turtle. The turtle was drying and its skin was turning white as if it had been dipped in flour. I thought if I fed the turtle leaves, its white-flour color would disappear and it would grow to the size of a sea turtle and Poulet and I could sit on its back, use scarves or belts as reins through its mouth, and it would take us to places we wanted to go — Nanking to see our father, over the hills, through water, to Leandri.

When my amah saw the turtle she said, "This is exactly what we need," and then she cut off the arms and legs of the turtle and seared the meat, giving a shave to a man on the street in trade for the use of his fire he kept burning for his tea and his meals.

"Open your mouths," she said to us, and we took the meat and chewed.

I imagined mine tasted like bread. My mother said she imagined hers tasted like Peking duck. Father Jean-Claude said rabbit in brandy. I thought Leandri would have said that it tasted like turtle.

After ten days in Saigon my mother looked around us and said, "This is freedom?" and then she put her head back down on her pillow with her eyes open and looked at the ceiling.

"What are you doing?" I asked her.

"Thinking of ways to get out of here," she said.

There were ships and trucks and junkets and bicycles and donkeys and carts that could take us away, but we stayed.

I learned new games. There was the one where I caught flies by snatching them up in my fist. I put the flies into a paper bag, which I held up to the light of a lamp, and watched them fly in circles and then fall, collecting on top of each other in the bottom of the bag.

My mother woke because I was catching flies that sat on her

sweating hairline. Her eyes opened and my balled fists moving fast must have looked to her like I was throwing punches.

"Who are you fighting?" she asked.

"Maman, you've drooled onto your bed sheet. What does that mean?" I said.

"It means she slept with her mouth open," my amah said.

. . .

Poulet learned the crocodile song and the frog song. All day she would sing while we sat on the street and watched the people and carts and cars go by. After hours of slapping the street like the frog jumps from lily pad to lily pad, her palms were black and stuck with gravel. "She looks like a street urchin," my mother said, and she threw a coin into Poulet's outstretched palm when Poulet was picking out the bits of gravel.

We heard no word from Yeu. At night my amah pulled out strands of my hair and studied the roots for a sign of his return. My mother, not able to sleep because of her long sweaty naps at midday, sat on the window ledge staring up at the sky.

"I'm wishing on stars," she would say.

"No old wives' tales," my amah said. "They never come true."

Looking at Poulet as she slept, I could see she was still singing the crocodile song, her head moving from side to side like a crocodile marching off to war.

"Look how fast she's growing," my amah said.

. . .

We left for Shanghai on a train. My mother had said how nice it would be to see the countryside from our window, but when we saw our train the windows were boarded up. There was not even a crack where sunlight could enter. Stepping into our car was like stepping into the night. It was so dark. Gas lamps were lit, but it was still difficult to see. The people who did not sleep smoked cigarettes and looked straight ahead. We found seats and waited. My mother thought that once we got out of Saigon, men would come around with crowbars and pull the nails from the boards, allowing us a view of the land. But men never came. My amah kept her eyes closed for days. She said what she could dream of seeing was better than what she could see in our dark train. My mother stared at the boards covering the windows. When we stopped at a station she turned to the boards and held her hands up against them, to see if they'd move and to see if sunlight, moonlight or any kind of light would show through.

Poulet and I played the train game.

"Where are we now?" she would ask, and I would tell her we were passing through Africa — watch out for your rice and your fish, the tiger's mouth is pressed against our windows, his fur hot from the sun hitting down on the plains and his teeth as big as the fins of sharks swimming deep waters.

Father Jean-Claude made friends in the dark, in the part of the train where the gas lamps weren't burning and where everyone was always on the floor, drinking or snoring or calling out names in their sleep. My mother wanted a drink.

"Father Jean-Claude!" my mother yelled, and she got up from her seat and stumbled through the aisle, holding on to the tops of the seats as she went to the back of the darkened train. "Father Jean-Claude!" We heard her turn over sleeping men to look at their faces.

She never found him. When the sleeping men woke they said the last time they had seen him was back at the border.

"He left with our wine," they said.

My mother went to the windows and tried to pull off the boards, hitting with her shoe at the nails hammered in sideways into the wood, trying to bend the nails so she could pull them straight out.

My amah opened her eyes.

"I see your husband," she said. My mother stopped pulling at the boards.

"Where?"

"Have you looked at Poulet?" my amah said. "Have you seen

how her fingers will be just like his, thin like tapered candles, the thumbs as long as the first finger, the veins strong enough for cording bundles weighing pounds and as fat around as trunks of trees? This is Yeu right here," my amah said and she sat Poulet on her lap and showed her how to dance her knuckles on the boarded-up windows to make a sound like horses trotting over paved roads.

My mother sat down. "Where are we?" she said.

"We must be close," I said.

"How long has it been?"

I looked at her hair in the lamplight. It was flat in the back where she had been sleeping with her head against the seat. In the front, there was a bit of rice hanging from a strand. When she talked it moved up and down. She had been wearing stockings, no shoes. The stockings were black at the edges of her feet from walking up and down the dirty car. We had been on the train a long time.

"We'll be there soon," I said.

"Get me out of here," she said, and then she sat holding her right hand with her left hand. When we asked her why, she said, "This is so I don't reach out and grab hold of my throat."

"You'd kill yourself, then?" my amah asked.

"No, there's a scream caught inside me and I'm afraid of pulling it out."

"You'll have that scream caught inside you longer than this train ride. Come the Year of the Monkey it will shrink with the cold winter air. But it will come back. Think about the rats we killed at Kontum," my amah said.

"Will that stop the scream?" my mother said.

"No, but the rats were really amazing the way they kept coming back. We must have killed hundreds, and probably there were still hundreds more."

. . .

When the train got to Shanghai, soldiers came through the cars and told everyone to cover their eyes with thin cloth so that the sunlight wouldn't hurt them. On the platform we noticed smells.

"Smell the pork buns?" my amah said while we waited with covered eyes.

"I smell my husband," my mother said.

"You can't smell as far as Nanking from here," my amah said.

We took off the cloths covering our eyes and hailed a taxi to drive us to our house.

"Look, old Liang's is closed," my amah said, pointing to a shop near our house that used to sell linen and thread.

"I left the silverware drawer open, I remember I did that," my mother said.

The taxi stopped.

"YOU MUST HAVE MADE A MISTAKE, MY MOTHER SAID to the driver.

But there was no mistake. It was our house. But it was not our house as we had left it. Someone had torn down the wooden shutters and let the grass get overgrown and the water from the birdbaths drain and the tiles on the paths crack and the doors fall off their hinges.

"The Communists," my mother said.

"Light lotus blossom candles," my amah said. "Check for the jewels and the gold, get a dog to stand in the doorway, hang a broom upside down, crush a lizard's tail, collect rainwater. Watch your step, there are scales on the paths left from the tail of a dragon. Oh, and someone's broken all the windows, so be careful not to step on glass."

"The fucking Communists," my mother said, and she sat down on our overgrown lawn and pulled up the grass at her sides, throwing it into the air, where it scattered and blew in the strong wind off the Yangtze River.

Inside the house we chased rats with boards we found on the floor. One rat stared up at my mother from her empty but still open silverware drawer. My mother brought down her board so hard on the rat's head that the drawer came crashing down and trapped the rat inside it. Later, when we rested, sitting in the middle of the floor, our hair stuck to our sweating faces, and we studied the blisters on our hands from hitting with the rough boards. We heard the trapped rat squeaking and throwing itself against the sides of the overturned silverware drawer, trying to get free. My mother, panting, said, "Let this one go," but when she saw it taking off she ran after it and clobbered it on the head again with her board.

"I changed my mind. It doesn't deserve to go free."

I went up to my old room. The only thing left was a mattress on the floor.

I lay down on it. The smell of cologne came up to me from whoever had slept on it last. I rolled over onto the floor and slept there instead. When I woke up it was evening. The sun was going down and bats flew in circles outside my broken window. I went to the balcony in my mother's room and looked out over the grounds. I saw where the Japanese had first come to get us through our field. I thought I could see them again. I squinted my eyes. I imagined I could see Michel Riquelme with them, Leandri and Father Jean-Claude. I waved out over the grass, burnt and dry from the summer sun, and the bats called out their calls. From downstairs I heard pans on the stove. Someone was cooking.

· · ·

"Crickets give you dreams of the wind," my amah said.

"Not the grass?" I said.

"They hop through air," she said, and ladled out the soup she had made with crickets she had caught in the garden while I slept.

· · ·

My mother went to see if there was a letter from my father. When she came back her hands were swollen and red. "From banging on the post office door where they've held up our mail," she said, and put her sore hands into the pond.

"Didn't we used to have goldfish in here?" she asked.

· · ·

Poulet rode on my back through the garden, where nothing grew. I was her horse and she was our great-grandmother Li, who would go out into the Chinese forest to shoot down glass plates thrown up into the sky by her servants.

"Ka-pow! Ka-pow!" I said when Poulet aimed her finger up, and then I would rear, acting like a horse startled by gunshot.

"Don't go too far, birds will soon sleep and bats will fly," my amah said.

· · ·

With Poulet on my back, I trotted out of the garden and onto the street in front of our house. I went on all fours, keeping close to the turning wheels of carts and close to cats sleeping in doorways. Poulet called out, "Ka-pow, ka-pow," and I just kept going.

I was looking for Leandri. I thought she might be in Shanghai. I thought if I could find her I would tell her to come live with us, that there was enough room and that she could sleep where I slept and that there was a pond she could see herself in and that we were already starting to put back into the house what had once been in it. My mother had found a silver fork in the dirt and she cleaned it off and put it back in the silverware drawer. My amah had found a wooden spoon and she started to dig up the grounds, looking for the gold and the ruby rings she said she had hid before the Japanese came to take us away.

I looked for Leandri below bridges and inside tunnels and alongside railroad tracks. I found a dog without a leg by a river. He hopped after me and we named him Short, because that was how much time we gave him to live.

"Have you seen Leandri?" we asked Short. He smelled the hems of our skirts and licked our legs for salt.

We slept that night by the river and I dreamed of the marsh back in Kontum. I dreamed a bloated dead man carried by the marsh went by me, and when he came close he was my father holding the head of a woman whose long hair fanned the water and whose eyes were the color of saffron.

In the morning we woke and heard Short hopping over the ground and over sticks and leaves. With his nose he was lifting up rocks, licking grubs, chewing green moss, eating a meal.

The way he ate, we thought to change his name to Long. Poulet wanted to take him home or give him as a present to Leandri. But when he tried to lift his only back leg to piss against a tree and he fell, I said he wouldn't be a dog much longer, but a dead dog, and those are two different things.

On the way home we found a piece of Chinese apple, the skin still embedded with ruby-red seeds. Before we ate them we pressed them to our lips and rubbed hard — we were Leandri wearing lipstick, walking through the streets of Paris, our bones showing through our skirts and men turning their heads to see our rear ends and our legs and our broad backs as we walked, hips forward, leading, as if the street were a runway and we were modeling clothes.

Walking home we looked for Leandri behind a warehouse with a sign out front that said "Lumber," but there was no lumber in it, only Nationalists doing it to whores. We could tell they were Nationalists by their uniforms, which lay on the ground. The uniforms didn't have patches of red five-pointed stars sewn on their sleeves the way the Communist uniforms did.

The whores were telling the Nationalists to hurry up, and they threatened to stop midway, saying Nationalist money was only good enough for as long as it took to steam up a chaodze. The men said it was so long ago since anyone had had a chaodze, and they stopped and pulled aside the sewn-together clothing that served as curtains separating them from the other Nationalists doing it with other whores and they tried to figure out which of them it was who had last eaten a steamed chaodze.

"Oh, get off me, you're making me hungry," said the whores. They made the Nationalists leave and then one whore pulled a flour bun out from under her vest, which was covered with small round mirrors. Sunlight hit the mirrors and the makeshift curtains caught the dotted reflections. I watched, thinking wasn't it beautiful and where could I find myself a vest like hers.

I walked up to her and I asked, "Where did you get it?" and I put a finger on one of the mirrors on her vest.

"India," she said, and she finished her flour bun and then ran her tongue up and down her palm, licking the last traces of flavor. Her fingers were long, as long as my father's. I thought this whore looked more like my father's daughter than I looked like my father's daughter.

"What's your name?" I said.

I did not hear her answer. Just then, a Communist walked in

and said "Get out of here" to me and Poulet. We left but stood around the doorway of the building. We could hear the whore scream and then we heard what sounded like him hitting her across the back or the face or the legs. He shouted at her to stay the fuck still or he would break her neck. We heard the whore call him a name and then we heard what we thought must have been her neck getting broken. It sounded like someone walking on a gravel path. When he came around the corner, buttoning his pants, we ran back to the whore.

She looked like she had been stepped on. There was a boot print on the side of her neck.

Getting her out of the vest was not so easy, and we pulled too hard in one place and tore the vest at the seam under the arm. A few of the mirrors fell to the floor and Poulet picked them up while I put the vest on. We went back out to the street and I thought everyone would see how beautiful I was wearing the whore's Indian vest.

On the street there were no Nationalists, only Communists. When they saw me and Poulet, they yelled at us to get in the back of a truck and they pointed guns at us. I got Poulet to jump up on my back and we ran, and Poulet used her finger to pretend to shoot down the Communists who were chasing us.

"Ka-pow! Ka-pow!" she said.

I ran down to the docks. The Communists stopped chasing us. Now they went after a group of Nationalists who had jumped into a boat and set out fast, rowing clear of the harbor. The Communists stood at the end of the dock and tossed grenades, which exploded, sending up so much water we couldn't see. Wave upon wave churned the water white where it had been an army green, as if tanks and jeeps had once sunk to the bottom and reflected their colors back up to the surface.

Poulet and I headed for home. I wore the vest, and the whole way back Poulet asked if she could wear it and why couldn't she wear it and when would she get to wear it and I did not say anything but kept looking around to see if anyone noticed me wearing the vest from India. We only passed people curled on the street, asleep in the sun, their hands between their knees as if the weather were cold and not the kind of hot that it was, the kind that made you too tired to wave a fly from your face or shout a warning, even if a child were walking in front of a car or a tile were falling from a roof, and instead you just watched all the danger happen around you without speaking a word, your eyes heavy at the lids where oil from your skin sat and weighed them down, closing off your vision.

When we walked into our house I took off the vest, heavy with my sweat, and I hung it on a doorknob to dry. I called out for my amah and I called out for my mother, but no one answered. I walked up the stairs and into my mother's bedroom, where I stood on the balcony and looked out over the overgrown weeds. I remembered that when the Japanese had first come I could not see over the railing of our balcony but had to look between the bars. Now that I was taller I could rest my hands on the railing the way I had seen my father do so many times before. I remembered looking out through the bars at our dogs we once had as they ran through the trees, their tails up and curled, my father following behind them, saying their names, telling them to heel, and the dogs would run back to his side, heads lowered, walking the pace he had commanded.

When I heard Poulet fall down the stairs I thought our dogs had come back to life and they were bounding up the steps to jump on me. When they did not come into the room, and I realized the sound on the stairs was not something coming up but something going down, I went to look.

Poulet had fallen so that her leg was bent out to the side, akimbo, her arms spread out and her head face-down. Maybe if it weren't for the heat I would have run down the stairs, but instead I put my hand on the rail and walked slowly down. I stopped in the middle to scratch my arm, there was some kind of bug bite there.

At the bottom step I said her name.

"Poulet." It was not a question, it was just her name. I sat down next to her and kept scratching my arm. I looked down at it. I could not remember being bitten. After a long time I went and got the whore's mirrored Indian vest and then I put it across her shoulders and lay down next to her and put my arm around her and looked at my eyes in the small round mirrors.

When I woke up Poulet was calling out my name and I had just been dreaming that I had run into the woman who had taken off her head and was brushing her hair and she was wearing the whore's Indian vest while she told me that she had been with my father and that he was going to be all right.

"Fang shing," don't worry, the woman said, so when I woke up and heard Poulet call out my name, I said it to her, "Fang shing," even though I was worried and I did not know what to do about Poulet's leg, which was bent in a way I had never seen a leg bent before and I looked at it for a long time thinking I might never see a leg bent backwards in that way again. It looked more like Poulet had learned to do some trick and throw her leg out like it had been taken off and turned around and twisted and then put back on. So at any time I expected Poulet to sit up laughing and turn her leg back around.

Then I heard the crowing of a hen outside the window. "That means the ruin of the family," I once heard my amah say about the unlikely crowing of hens. I got up and went to the window just to be sure I wasn't wrong. I wished it was still daylight so I could look up and see if maybe it wasn't a hen but the Chinese red crow that stood on its three feet and lived in the sun.

Again Poulet called out my name. I took the whore's mirrored vest and put it in front of her so she could look at it while she lay on the floor and I tried to think of what to do next.

I decided to wait the night, to see if maybe by morning my mother and my amah would arrive and tell me what to do. Maybe my amah would have us read the veins in jade or have us drink tea from a rhino's horn. Maybe my mother could carry Poulet piggyback and take her to the infirmary in a taxi. I thought if my father were here he'd take hold of Poulet's leg and twist it right back the way it should go. He would tell Poulet to look at the moon and ask if she knew that if you opened your mouth and let in the beams from the moon, you would live forever.

"Fuck," I said out loud, thinking that's what Leandri would have said, because in the morning when I woke up next to Poulet, she was sweating against my back. I said, "Shit." I took the whore's Indian vest and wiped Poulet down.

"Come on," I said to her. I threw her onto my back and she screamed. Her leg wouldn't hook under my arm, and reaching for it was like reaching for a sleeve I couldn't find while putting on a coat.

On the street I wore the mirrored vest over my head to keep from burning in the sun. I heard Poulet whimper so I started to sing "Parlez-moi d'amour." I sang it loudly and people in the houses I passed yelled for me to be quiet, but I kept singing until I arrived at the door of Doctor Chen.

"Ayyahh," he said when he put Poulet down on his wooden table and looked at her leg.

"Where's your mother?" he said.

"I don't know," I said.

"The Communists?" he said while he took Poulet's leg and broke it again.

"What?" I said. I could not hear him over Poulet's screaming. He said it again and I shook my head.

"It's bad," he said, taking a piece of wood and sawing it to match the size of Poulet's leg.

"It happened last night," I said.

"No, the Communists. They're all over. I tried to go to the

municipal station, they wouldn't let me in. 'I've just come for documents,' I said. Then one of them put his gun to me like this."

Doctor Chen took the point of the saw and held it up under my chin. I could smell the wood shavings.

"'How do you like that?' the goddamn Communist said. I didn't answer him, as if that deserved an answer, but he said it again, 'How do you like that?'"

Doctor Chen pressed the point of the saw harder up under my chin. Poulet was screaming louder.

"'How do you like that?'" Doctor Chen was also screaming. "And what did I say?"

"I don't know," I said, my voice sounding strange because of the point of the saw.

"Guess."

"Go to hell?" I said.

"No. I did not say 'Go to hell.' I said, 'Good day.'"

"'Good day'?" I said.

"That's right. No, no, that's wrong. 'Good day, sir.' That's what I really said."

"'Good day, sir'?"

"I'm a gentleman. He should act like one too. And so then what do you think he did?"

"Hit you?" I said.

"No," Doctor Chen said, and then he put down the saw and started to attach the piece of wood to Poulet's leg with strips of cloth he had ripped with his teeth. "Nothing, he let me pass. There's a lesson for you," he said.

"Now how do I carry her?" I said, pointing to Poulet.

"What's this?" Doctor Chen said, lifting up the whore's Indian vest and looking at the mirrors sewn onto it.

"I'll need a cart or a horse," I said.

Doctor Chen tried the vest on. "It fits," he said.

"It's Poulet's," I said.

"Take this wheelbarrow, then," he said. He cleared out a wheelbarrow he had filled with bottles of rubbing alcohol and then he lowered Poulet into it. I pushed Poulet out the door, the wheel of the wheelbarrow squeaking. The fumes from the rubbing alcohol that had leaked into the wood made our eyes sting and our nostrils burn.

I went to the Street of Promise and looked in the window at the Store of a Million Items. I thought maybe my mother and my amah had gone in there, looking for forks and plates and knives, paper liner for the kitchen shelf or hooks for our ladles and our pots. I wanted to wheel Poulet inside the store, but a man came out and locked the door behind him.

"Closed?" I asked. The man did not answer me. He walked down the street staring at the pavement. I tried to pull open the doors, even though I could see they were locked.

On long tables in the store I could see tall vases with symbols for the five poisons on them. The viper, the scorpion, the centipede, the toad and the spider. I stepped away from the window and read the sign above the shop again — it was not the Store of a Million Items, it was a store without a name — only a symbol of a lizard was painted on the signboard. I pushed Poulet to the street corner. I was lost. We weren't on the Street of Promise, we were on a street called the Street of the Four Heavenly Kings.

Poulet sang the crocodile song while I wheeled her down the street. Someone threw garbage down from a window. It landed on top of Poulet in the wheelbarrow. She stopped her singing and took a piece of paper that had been used to wrap some kind of meat and she licked the wrapper clean.

"Beef?" I said.

"No, pig," she said, and let the wrapper go. It lifted with a breeze up above our heads.

I headed for the water. Rounding the corner for the Shanghai docks I could hear the motors of boats and the horn of a large steamer. Then I saw Father Jean-Claude.

He was flat on his back on the dock by a boat with a sail being sewn by a woman sitting on the shoulders of a man. The woman was holding a large curved needle in her mouth and calling down.

"Father Jean-Claude, Father Jean-Claude," the woman said, "wake up, you drunk old fart, and help us with this sail."

I walked over to him and Poulet and I looked down at his stubbled face. He was sucking on his cross. He opened bloodshot eyes and belched.

"Huh?" he said.

"Thank you, wake him up for me," the woman said.

"You've got to get up, Father," I said.

"You girls?" he said. He propped himself on his elbows as if he were going to sit up, but then he lay down again and closed his eyes. When he spoke to us a second time his eyes were still closed.

"I thought I'd never see you again," he said.

"I'm looking for my mother," I said.

The woman sewing the sail came down off the man's shoulders.

"Open your eyes or I'll sew them shut," the woman said, and she leaned over and dragged the needle down the side of Father Jean-Claude's face. He opened his eyes. He grabbed hold of the woman's thin wrist and she stopped.

Then she looked at us. "He owes me money," she said. "He drank three cases of my wine in two days. I'd kill him if he weren't a goddamned priest."

"The Lord thanks you," Father Jean-Claude said.

"Have you seen her?" I asked.

Father Jean-Claude took his hand from the woman's wrist and held on to mine.

"Lift me up," he said.

. . .

As we made our way down Diplomat Row, Poulet sat on Father Jean-Claude's lap in the wheelbarrow while I wheeled them past sellers selling fish, nuts and seeds by the pound, glass jars capped with cloth held by twine, filled with pickled ginger and root from the angelica tree. Father Jean-Claude talked to everyone he saw — the sellers, the street sweepers, the children playing statue — arms out, standing still in a courtyard.

Father Jean-Claude described my mother and my amah to everyone, asking if they had seen the two.

"French, medium height, hair almost red, and an amah, eyes look like they're almost closed, but she sees everything," he said. No one had seen them. It was getting dark. We went back along the dock. The masts sticking up from all the boats looked as if they were piercing through the setting sun. I thought I saw my father, but when the man turned around he was a Communist, with a red five-pointed star sewn onto his shirt, carrying a gun and wearing a bandage over his eye. I thought I saw Michel Riquelme, but when he turned around it was an old man with a white goatee. I had to sit down.

"Park here," Father Jean-Claude said, and we stopped by a shipment of wine barrels. Father Jean-Claude said the rosary and cupped his hand under a leak in one of the barrels.

My rope-soled shoes had broken. I took them off and threw them into the water, where they floated for a while and then sank. I pictured them walking by themselves on the harbor floor, side-stepping rusted cans and broken bottles, heading for the current, out to open sea.

We went back to the boat owned by the woman who was sewing the sail.

"They need to sleep here tonight," Father Jean-Claude said to the woman. The woman showed us below, where we could sleep on folded cloth she used to repair the sails.

Father Jean-Claude thanked the woman and kissed her on the mouth.

"From God," he said after he kissed her, and the woman called his ancestors turtle eggs and said they were related to loaves of bread and descended from a long line of mothers who were French whores and fathers who were opium addicts and uncles who were thieves and brothers who were dogs of the mongrel kind.

At night, while I lay on the folded cloth and Poulet held me in her sleep, Father Jean-Claude told me that he had jumped off the train from Saigon because he was afraid that at the Shanghai station he'd be followed by Communists, accused as an aide to the Nationalists and sent straight back to a camp, for the Lord only knew how long, until this war was over too.

"Can they do that?" I asked.

"They can do that, and they can kill you," he said.

. . .

On the boat the next morning I woke up to my mother looking down at me and my amah, saying if she had a tiger's claw charm she would put it around my neck, because that's what we'd need considering where we were going, and she'd throw in an amulet of peachwood too, and she'd have me wear a nail that had been used to board up a coffin, and braid some of my hair with the hair of a dog.

My mother looked at Poulet and said, "My God, what's happened to her leg?"

"Probably the wild boar," my amah said.

"The stairs," I said.

"Have you seen your father?" my mother said.

"I thought I did, once, but it wasn't him," I said.

Father Jean-Claude walked in.

"You've found them then?" he said to my mother.

"Yes, thank you, but they haven't heard from their father either. Are you sure no one knows how he is?"

Father Jean-Claude took a drink from the flask he was holding, then he wiped his face and he sat down on a torn sail.

"I have no idea where he is. From Nanking there's been no word."

"Let's look at the sky," my amah said, and she took me and

Poulet up to the deck. In the clouds we found bears playing flutes and belly dancers dancing.

On the docks we sang "Parlez-moi d'amour" in whispers. Louder would have gotten us into trouble, my mother said. Singing in whispers, I danced on my mother's feet and we went in circles on the wharf, with the splintered wooden boards beneath us and the fish smell of the green harbor water.

"We're getting out of here," my mother said, and she stopped dancing and went to ask how much passage was on board a ship to Saigon.

A gray-haired man with food stuck in his beard held tickets he fanned at passersby.

"Saigon, Saigon, Saigon," he said, and moved in a slow circle. We watched him turning and then, from a few feet away, my mother called out, "How much?" I could not hear his answer.

My mother turned us away from him, and we walked on down the wharf. She stopped to sit on a bench and count her money.

"Not enough," she said.

"Bargain," my amah said.

"With what?" my mother said.

While my amah talked she took a strand of her hair and flossed her teeth with it.

"You've only got one thing left," my amah said. "Use it." She looked at me and said, "Take off her ring."

My mother wore a diamond engagement ring. The band was white gold and the diamond as old as the first fathers of the Yeu dynasty.

"We haven't eaten in days," my mother said. "What in God's name are you cleaning out from between your teeth?"

"Bits of Kontum," my amah said, and then she reached over and tried to take my mother's diamond ring off her finger. My mother balled her hand into a fist.

"We could stay in Shanghai and in a few weeks when there

really is no rice and there are even more Communists and they have taken your children, then they can cut your finger off and they can just take the ring."

"But this is my marriage," my mother said, holding the diamond up and looking at it against the sunlight.

My amah pointed to me and Poulet. "And these are your children," she said.

...

On the quay there was a man singing "O sole mio." I did not know if he was going to board the boat or if he was saying goodbye to someone who was already on it. He stood with a suitcase next to his leg. My mother held our tickets in her hand. Where her ring used to be I could see her skin was white.

I wanted to go up to the man and ask him if he knew "Parlez-moi d'amour." His voice sounded like Michel Riquelme's voice. I thought if I heard Michel Riquelme's voice, I could see his face again more clearly. Over time, I had forgotten which eye it was that had been gouged from his head.

My mother thought she saw my father in the crowd.

"Not him," my amah said without even looking.

"How do you know? Some cloud shape told you? Some tea leaf you read? Or the dead fish floating belly-up in the water?" my mother said.

"I know because Yeu isn't stupid enough to set foot in Shanghai and get himself killed by the Communists."

The man stopped singing. He sat down on his suitcase and put his head in his hands. He stayed that way only a moment before the leather strap around the suitcase broke and he lost his balance and fell on the quay along with his clothes, which scattered around him.

He was Italian and his name was Mr. Spain. When my mother told him her name, he said "Marcelle" sounded like water being poured from a pitcher. We helped him pick up his white shirts and his trousers from off the quay. When all the clothes were back inside the suitcase my mother told him that "Mr. Spain" sounded like he should be from Spain, and how did he ever get another country's name than his own? Mr. Spain said it could have been worse, he could have been named his father's name, which was Mr. of the Green River from Up North.

"That's bad," my amah said. "If a river's green, its fish are green, and green fish from any country taste like they've been living on grass trampled by ghosts and spirits gone for swims at night when moons were full and tigers dreaming of catching their kill."

"We don't have tigers in Italy," Mr. Spain said. My amah didn't hear him, though. She was now giving Poulet a ride on her shoulders and asking her if she could see people's thoughts more clearly now that she was at the level of their heads.

Mr. Spain was also going to Saigon. He had paid for the ticket with his last lire. In Saigon, he said, he hoped to see his wife and children. The littlest had learned to whistle, the oldest could do math. "My wife," he said, and then he stopped the story.

"Time to board," my mother said, but she did not walk toward the boat. Instead she told us to wait and she walked to a dirt lot close to shore and she got on her knees and bent her head and she kissed the ground. When she returned there was dirt on her mouth, filling in the lines on her lips.

OUR TICKETS DID NOT BUY US CABINS. WE WERE USHERED far below where we could not hear each other speak over the noise of the ship, its engines blowing steam and its gears and chains turning. Passing the last porthole we would get a chance to look through, my amah told me to watch the sun setting over the water, that it might be the last of the sun we'd see for days, and that even though it was setting, I should think of it as rising — my life lasting longer that way.

Down below, we played sky. Shadows cast on the walls by our lit candles took the place of clouds. I saw a turtle. Poulet saw a goat. My amah saw the feathered phoenix. Mr. Spain saw Africa. My mother saw my father's nose.

When the candles went out, I could see the burning ends of my mother's and Mr. Spain's cigarettes while I tried to sleep. They talked about Italy. They talked about its cypress trees and its sea and its mountains. Mr. Spain said that in his town there was a pig who slept under the tables in the bar. Often there would be sawdust on his snout where he had rooted for peanuts and olives fallen from plates. Mr. Spain said the men in the bar elected the pig mayor and they put a hat on his head and people came to the pig to ask him what they should and should not do with their lives. And Mr. Spain said the pig answered the people. He told a farmer to burn his crops, and a housewife to stay with her husband, and a lover to forget about love and move to the city.

"What did you ever ask the pig?" I heard my mother say to Mr. Spain. At first Mr. Spain did not answer, and I thought he had fallen asleep, but then I saw the end of his cigarette glow.

"I asked him about Shanghai," Mr. Spain finally said, quietly.

"What about Shanghai?" my mother said.

"I asked him if I should come here," Mr. Spain said.

My mother did not say anything, but then I heard my amah.

"What did the pig say?"

"The pig said no, but I came anyway. I should have listened to that pig," Mr. Spain said. My mother laughed and then my amah laughed and Mr. Spain laughed too, and I could not help but laugh myself and then all the others sleeping around us woke up and told us to be quiet and we laughed harder until I fell asleep, my cheeks wet with tears.

When I woke up, it seemed as if everyone else had fallen asleep except for my mother. She was sitting next to me and she was whispering, saying my father's name over and over again. I lit a candle. Her face looked orange. She was sweating and the sweat beaded on her upper lip and beaded on her forehead and ran down the length of her nose, where it dripped off the tip. In the heat of the belly of the ship I thought she was melting, and she was saying my father's name over and over again because saying it before had once made her feel better and saying it now would keep her from melting, leaving her just a skeleton, elbows resting on kneecaps, skull in her hands, collarbone sticking out so far and looking so strong that if you took it away all the other bones would fall to the floor.

"Ayaah," I heard my amah say, and she sat up and pointed to a shadow the candle flame was making on the wall of the ship.

"The dragon," she said, and then she lay down and went back to sleep.

· · ·

We ate rice we had in cloth bags that we laid over the steaming pipes to cook.

Mr. Spain had eggs. He stuck a needle through the shell and sucked out the raw white and yolk. Later he gave me and Poulet the empty shells and we drew patterns on the outside and then we held the eggs up to the light and looked at the patterns through the hole made by the needle.

My amah held the candle under her chin and told us the ghost story about the boy who became water and seeped under doorways and appeared to you as a vision made of steam, rising up from the floor, swaying in front of you and calling out your name — a lure to come join him as a spirit of water.

My mother went around to other passengers and introduced herself. Sometimes even waking them from sleep, she would shake their shoulders, asking them to please talk to her, she was looking for her husband and had they heard of him? He is tall, I heard her say, his nose long and straight. "Tian, come here and show them your nose," she would say. I would try and hide behind other people, under clothes, under stairs, so that I would not have to stand up and show everyone my nose.

Mr. Spain helped me hide. He said he once had an aunt who always tried to show other people a triangle he had in the green of his eye. He held a candle and let me look. It was a black triangle like a slice of pie.

"It's a splinter of cedrela," my amah said, peering into Mr. Spain's eye. "Where are the leaves?" she asked. "We could use them in our soup or spread them on your head to grow back your hair."

Mr. Spain touched his bald head. I thought if he could, he would take off his head like the ghost who brushed her hair.

"The dolphins are breaching," my amah said.

"How do you know?" we asked.

"The tips of my fingers are wrinkled," she said.

"If you know so much, then where is my husband?" my mother asked. She took a hairpin from her hair and used it to clean out the wax from her ears.

My amah took the hairpin from my mother and said, "Don't, you'll clog your ears with hair."

"I hear hair being brushed," my mother said. "Is it the sound of my husband's mistress?"

"No, it's the sound of your husband making love to his mistress," my amah said.

My mother threw one of Mr. Spain's eggs at my amah. Her shirt was covered with it, and she wiped it off with her fingers and fed it to Poulet.

"Are we there yet?" Mr. Spain asked, with his head leaning back against the wall.

No one answered. Maybe no one knew. Maybe there was a very long way to go and no one wanted to tell Mr. Spain how much longer we'd have to be together.

He was in the habit of unpacking his suitcase and then packing it again. He would pull out a white shirt, slowly unbutton the buttons, then button them again. He would pull out the collar stays and then put them in again. He would turn the shirt on its face and then unfold the arms and then cross them and fold them again. He would pull out his socks, which were folded up into themselves like balls, and then he would unfold them, laying them over the closed suitcase and pressing them flat with his hand. Then he would fold them into balls again, open the suitcase up and tuck the socks in the edges between the suitcase walls and his folded white shirts. He reminded me of a man I once saw who filled his pipe with opium, emptied it, filled it again, over and over until I finally saw him smoke it.

"Let me help you," my mother once said to Mr. Spain as he was opening up his suitcase. He shut it quickly.

"No thank you," he said, and he did not open the suitcase again until much later, when we were sleeping and all the candles were out. I could not see him open it up, but I heard him, and I heard the soft unfolding of the shirts and the folding of them again and Mr. Spain's breathing, starting off fast as he was opening the suitcase and then slowing down, calming as he touched his shirts and socks again.

"Light a candle, someone has died," my amah said.

"In Shanghai?" my mother said.

"No," my amah said.

"Here?" Mr. Spain asked.

"In that corner," my amah said, and she pointed to where we could not see in the darkness.

Mr. Spain walked to the corner of the ship with a lit candle.

"Who is it?" my mother called out to him. We did not hear an answer.

Again my mother called out, "Who is it? Are they dead?"

Mr. Spain came back. "I don't know who it is, I've never seen her before," he said.

"Dead?" my mother said.

"Yes," he said. "Who knows, a heart attack, something in her sleep."

"A nightmare," my amah said.

"We can't leave her here," my mother said.

"She'll stink. Tell the crew to take her out of here," my amah said.

"Go tell them," my mother said to me.

I climbed the stairs up to the deck. Behind me I could hear my mother calling, "Don't tell just anyone, tell a captain, someone with more than just epaulets."

I opened a door, enough so that I could see a guard smoking a cigarette, sitting on some steps that led to a higher deck.

It was nighttime. The ocean was so dark that the only way I knew it was there was by the sound of the ship moving through it. The guard flicked his cigarette, then leaned his head against the wall.

I walked past him. As I went up to the next deck, I heard an orchestra playing music. I looked in the windows. Everyone was dancing. I looked for my father. I thought I saw him dancing with a woman in a white dress with a low-cut back. I could see her shoulder blades. They looked sharp. I thought if she lay down on her back in that dress on a frozen lake she could cut the ice, skate across to the other side. The man dancing with her held his hand at the small of her back. The hand was dark, with long fingers.

"Papa," I said in a whisper, only because I hadn't said it in so long and because the man dancing with the woman could have been him and I would have liked that — I would have cut in on the woman and stood on my father's feet and had him dance me around instead.

I saw the food on the tables. There was a fish as big as a dolphin. Around it were lettuce and lemons and tomatoes split in half. White radishes cut like lotus flowers were at its head and tail. A table had ordered dessert. The waiter spooned out melted chocolate from a pan and twirled it on top of a pastry.

I opened the door. The room was warm from the people dancing and the plates of food and the orchestra playing. A woman passed by me, leading her partner by the hand to the dance floor. She smelled like butter and garlic, the meal she must have just eaten. She smelled so good I followed her and her partner to where the dance floor began. I turned around and thought a waiter was my father. I went back and sat at the empty table where the woman and her partner had sat before they went to dance. Their plates were still there and off them I ate what remained. Sautéed peeled new potatoes, a rack of lamb covered with mustard and thyme, a garlic mousse on the side. I had a sip of their wine. I thought if Father Jean-Claude were here he could tell me what kind of wine it was and where the grapes grew that it was made from.

The orchestra stopped playing. I heard people clapping. I got up from the chair and went to stand by the wall. The dancing couple whose table I sat at went back to their seats. I watched the doors to see if maybe my father would come in, a bow tie around his neck and the woman who took off her head at his arm.

Maybe it was the wine, or maybe it was the food, but when the orchestra started playing again, I started dancing. I danced where I stood and imagined I was in the Great Room dancing around the symboled borders of the oriental carpet. I closed my eyes. I breathed in and thought I could smell the Great Room's worn roof and water-damaged walls. I thought I could hear Leandri dancing next to me. I heard the sound of trees moving in the wind, like the Sea of Trees at Kontum. I thought if I opened my eyes I could look out the window and my mother would point to where she saw my father walking up the mountain and I would believe her.

When I stopped dancing, I looked out the porthole and could see that the sun was beginning to rise. Waiters were putting the dishes and the tablecloths on carts and pushing them back to the kitchen. My feet hurt from dancing. I grabbed a bread roll off a table. It had already turned stale and hard, but I held on to it. I went up to a higher deck. I walked down halls, past doors with brass handles. I could hear a man snoring behind one door. Someone was running a faucet. I stood in front of a door with a big red cross on it. I was thinking about knocking on the door when it opened. A man wearing a white coat and bedroom slippers asked me if I was all right. I told him I was fine. He asked what happened to my feet. He wanted to know where I had put my shoes. I told him someone down on the lowest deck had died.

"Lord Jesus," he said. He turned back into his cabin and I followed. He was a doctor. There was a skeleton hanging from a metal post. I touched its pelvic bone and I thought of Leandri.

"Is it a man or a woman?" I asked the doctor, pointing to the skeleton.

"A woman," he said. He was putting on his shoes. He wanted to know how the woman belowdecks had died. I told him I didn't know. I asked how this woman died, and I pointed at the skeleton. He did not answer me right away, and then, finally, he said influenza.

We walked down the stairs to the next deck, where there were people on chairs and people smoking cigarettes and looking out over the water. The air was full of mist, and when I touched my hair to put it behind my ears, it felt wet.

"She did not really die of influenza, did she?" I said to the doctor. The doctor, again, did not answer me right away and then he said she had been in a camp outside Shanghai and she had died of starvation. The doctor put his hand on my shoulder. I looked for my father on this deck. I turned around to see if he was behind me. The doctor's hand slid off my shoulder.

"Who are you looking for?" he asked.

"My father," I said.

"He's up here?"

"I don't know where he is," I said. "The last we heard, he was in Nanking." The doctor did not say anything. I watched as he pulled out a white mask from his pocket and tied it around his nose and mouth. He said something behind the mask, but it was difficult to hear him. He could have said that he heard my father was dead, or he could have said it was going to rain. I looked at the overcast morning sky. I could not see any animals or shapes in it because there were no clouds, just the gray that was thick around us, and soon we would not be able to see each other and we would have to reach out to know that the other was there.

"Which way?" he said loudly, and I led him through a door and took him down.

"Tell him the story of the pig!" my mother said to Mr. Spain the moment the doctor walked in the door. The doctor stopped walking.

"I can't see," he said.

"We have candles, your eyes just need time," Mr. Spain said.

"What color are his teeth?" my amah asked me.

"Who is dead?" the doctor asked.

"I am," my mother said, and then she laughed. She lit a candle and I could see that the silk skirt she wore was losing its hem and threads were dangling by her legs.

"Green?" my amah said to me.

The doctor took the candle from my mother and looked around the place.

"Do you know my husband?" my mother asked the doctor.

"I beg your pardon?"

"Tall, a straight nose, talks about a woman who took off her head and started brushing her hair. He's in love with her," my mother said.

Mr. Spain sat down and opened up his suitcase.

The doctor noticed Poulet's leg. He bent down and felt it. He stayed squatting, feeling Poulet's leg and looking around at us. He looked at me and I saw how his eyes were so round they looked like one of the mirrors sewn onto the whore's Indian vest.

"Yellow teeth mean he was born by the river, white teeth that he was born to the rich and has teeth made of porcelain kept high in locked cupboards away from the Kwei-tsze. Green, he has farmed, brown, he has tunneled," my amah said. "Get his mask before he leaves. We can steam it with rice, and when we wear it, we'll hear everything he has said. Also, it'll keep the smell from getting up our noses."

"She's over here," I said, and pointed to the corner where the dead woman was lying in the dark.

The doctor raised the woman's hand and held her wrist. Then he asked me to go back up with him. My mother stopped me before I left.

"He's got a radio, he's got news, find out about your father," she said. "Listen for anything about Nanking. See if he has a ship-to-shore phone."

"Don't forget the mask," my amah said. I gave her the hard roll I held in my hand.

Mr. Spain had all his shirts face-down in a circle around him. Poulet said he looked like the button in a daisy, and the shirts around him the petals. As I headed up the stairs behind the doctor I could see Mr. Spain slowly making the sleeves cross.

"I may need your help," the doctor said as we headed toward his cabin.

I couldn't think of what kind of help he could have wanted. He opened his cabin door and there was a tray of eggs and biscuits and coffee and jam.

"I never can finish all of what they bring me," he said, and then he had me wash my hands in a basin and he sat me down at his desk and told me to eat. I heard him call medics on his telephone. He told them to go below with a stretcher to try and find out who the dead woman was. I looked at the skeleton. I wanted to know how old she had been when she died.

The doctor didn't know. "Not more than twenty" was his answer. I looked at the bones in her foot and wondered where she had walked and what those bones had stepped on.

His mask lay on top of the garbage. I picked it up and put it inside my dress. After someone came to take the tray away, the doctor told me to lift up my feet and then he took out some cream and some cotton balls and he bent down in front of me and started applying the cream and rubbing my feet.

"You should have shoes," he said. He spent a long time rubbing the cream into my feet, even after the cream had soaked into my skin he kept rubbing them. He dried my feet with the cotton balls, wiping them along my insteps and my arches.

The medics phoned back. They couldn't find out the name of the dead woman, and they weren't going to do anything with her until someone could identify her.

"Move that woman, then worry about identifying her. There are other people boarded down there, and a dead body's going to make them all sick," the doctor said, and hung up the phone.

He sat in his chair and looked at the wall.

"Are they going to move her?" I asked.

"I don't know. They would rather wait until we got to Saigon. That way, they don't have as many questions to answer or papers to fill out." The doctor stood up, and as he did, the chair hit the skeleton. It started to fall over backwards, but he caught it with both hands. They looked like a couple of children playing at spinning each other around at top speed until one let go to send the other flying.

"Oh, come back here, Iris," the doctor said, and put the skeleton upright.

"Was Iris her real name?"

"I don't know. They didn't deliver her to me with a name, so I call her Iris." The doctor opened the door to leave. "I'll be back soon, why don't you sleep," he said.

When the doctor left I went back down to the lowest deck. At first, when I opened the door, I couldn't see inside and I thought my mother and my amah and Poulet had left. But then I saw the light from a candle flame. My amah came up to me and I gave her the doctor's mask, which she put around Poulet's nose.

"Did you try to find your father?" my mother asked. She was wearing a scarf over her nose and mouth and it was difficult to hear her at first.

"What?"

"Your father, did you call?" she said.

"It's not a real phone, it's just for the ship," I told her. She pulled the scarf up from her chin so she could smoke her cigarette.

"Go to other rooms, try the captain," she said. She pulled the scarf back down before she let the smoke out of her mouth. The smoke rose up into her eyes.

"Where's Mr. Spain?" I said.

"Over there, hiding his clothes from the smell," my mother said, and she pointed to a far corner of the ship where I could see Mr. Spain holding his suitcase to his chest.

"Get her out of here! Get her out of here!" he yelled.

"Not you, he means the dead woman," my mother said to me from under her scarf.

I went to the door to listen, to see if maybe the men the doctor had called were coming down the stairs with a stretcher. There was no sound, only Mr. Spain in the corner, still yelling to take the dead woman away.

"Go back up there and find your father," my mother said.

I spent the rest of the day going from deck to deck, trying to open doors that would not open. I tried picking a lock with a wire

I had found in the doctor's desk drawer. It worked, but the only things in the cabin were some sacks and a man's shoe. It could have been the size my father wore. I picked it up. The sole had bits of rock stuck in it. Marks from where the laces had been scarred the tongue black. I took the shoe back with me to the doctor's cabin. He was on the phone again, they still hadn't come to take the body away. When he got off the phone I asked if I could use it to make a call to Nanking. The doctor took the shoe out of my hand.

"What's this?" he said.

I almost answered, "It's a shoe," but I didn't. I asked again if I could call Nanking.

"It could take days to get through to Nanking on this," he said. "As many days as it would take for us to get to Saigon. You'll have a better chance trying to call from there," he said. I took the shoe back from the doctor.

That night I slept on the floor on a mat by the doctor's bed. The moonlight coming in from the porthole went through Iris and shadows of her ribs and skull and legs appeared against the wall. She looked as if she were walking tall above the doctor's head as he slept.

In the morning I took the shoe down to my mother. I opened the door and the smell of the dead woman was so strong I put my arm up to cover my nose.

"The heat from these pipes is making her smell ten days old instead of just two," my amah said when she saw me.

Mr. Spain was in the corner, lying with his face against the wall.

"Where's his suitcase?"

"He's holding it," my amah said.

I went up to Mr. Spain and touched him on the shoulder. "Are you all right?"

He turned around and looked at me. He wore a kerchief over his mouth that tied behind his head. His eyes were red. His knuckles looked white, maybe from holding on to the suitcase so tightly.

"He hasn't talked for hours. We tried to tell him you could take the suitcase to the doctor's cabin, but he wouldn't let go of it. He tried to go up a deck, but they wouldn't let him. They said no one's to come out or go in except you. Doctor's orders, they say," my mother said.

Others in the belly of the ship also wore scarves or shirts tied around their heads, covering their faces. Some had bottles of perfume that they held under their noses.

I heard a voice. It was so faint, I thought it was Poulet speaking, but then I heard it again. It was Mr. Spain. He was saying, "When?"

"When?" I said to him. He nodded and then pointed to the corner where the dead woman lay.

"I don't know, it takes time," I said. Mr. Spain closed his eyes and turned again with his suitcase to face the wall.

"Let's see the shoe," my mother said. "This is not his shoe. His foot was not shaped like some orangutan's paw. He never wore his heel down on the side like he was walking on a tilted road. He did not scuff the sides, he did not wear down the sole. Get rid of this," my mother said, and she threw the shoe far, over pipes. I heard it hit someone, who got mad and threw it back our way. It hit Mr. Spain, but he held his suitcase in front of him so the shoe did not hurt him.

"The Japanese," my mother started to whisper, and then she sat down and held Poulet in her arms and kept whispering it and Poulet whispered it with her, thinking it was some sort of game and Poulet smiled, saying, "The Japanese, the Japanese, the Japanese."

No one saw Mr. Spain walk over to the dead woman with the candle, but when we saw she was on fire, we realized what he had done. The flames were so bright that the first thing I thought was how well I could see everything. We were all so dirty. My mother had so much dirt on her legs it looked like she had been running through dry fallow fields kicking up dust, turning her legs a gray-brown. The woman burned and I heard screaming. She's dead, I thought, why is she screaming? But it was not the dead woman screaming, it was Mr. Spain. His suitcase had caught fire too. The old leather straps must have been dangling near the candle flame and the wicker suitcase caught quickly. He still held on to it while he screamed. The smoke spread everywhere. Now everyone was screaming, running for the door that led to the deck, but it was Mr. Spain, holding his suitcase, who made it out the door first. His clothes had caught fire and everyone made way for him to pass.

Everyone was running up the stairs behind Mr. Spain. Some still had their bottles of perfume in their hands as they ran, some still wore the scarves around their faces. I followed behind them, holding Poulet in my arms as my mother and my amah pushed at me from the back to hurry up faster out the door. The guard on deck tried to keep us back but he couldn't, and we ran onto the deck smelling of smoke and gasping, our hands at our necks.

Mr. Spain was running to the upper deck, where people were seated in lounge chairs, reading books or looking out over the water. He was a fireball holding on to a fireball which was his wicker suitcase.

The people on the deck screamed as he ran past.

"My God, he's on fire," we heard. We stayed on the lower deck.

"Mr. Spain! Mr. Spain! Stop!" we yelled from down below, or we tried to yell, but our throats were so filled with smoke that we really couldn't yell, and the noises that came out of us sounded more like hisses, so that Mr. Spain, if he was listening at all, must have thought that what he was hearing below him was not people but a bunch of snakes, piled on top of each other, moving and hissing and raising up their heads.

The last we saw of Mr. Spain was his body jumping over the side of the ship, still holding on to the suitcase of flames. I could see the soles of his shoes as he jumped over us, and I thought how they were the only parts of him that were not on fire.

When they found him he was still holding on to his suitcase, not with his arms all the way around it, but holding just on the edges, as if at any moment he was ready to open the hasps and show you his neatly folded shirts and his socks.

"Look, dolphins," my amah said, and we watched them playing and riding the waves.

We did not return to the lowest deck. Instead we slept shivering under staircases and covered ourselves with our smoke-damaged clothes to keep the ocean spray from making us colder. Because of the wind it was impossible to light candles, so Poulet and I played with the wax from the candles, molding it into cats, dogs and deer.

"Make Mr. Spain's pig," my amah said. "That way we will have someone to ask what we are to do next."

The pig I made looked more like a bear.

"That's all right. Remember, the bear teaches us sleep," my amah said.

"Old woman, please, can't you teach these children something useful, like how to sew or to cook or to clean?" my mother said.

I changed the bear into a dolphin, but it melted.

"Looks like lichee. God, I'm hungry," my mother said.

I went to the doctor. He gave me his breakfast again. I took it down to my mother. She did not eat the roll. She said she would save it for Yeu when she saw him.

. . .

When I was in the doctor's cabin I put my hand up against the bones of Iris's hand. Our hands were almost the same size. I figured if she were now a Kwei-tsze, then she probably lived in the forest where she could glide through trees, and she was probably not a Kwei-tsze here on a boat where there was nothing to do but read during the day and dance at night.

I picked up Poulet and put her on my shoulders and took her to watch the people dance. Poulet held on to the window and I told her not to push so hard, she might break it and the dancers would cut their feet on the glass.

"I see my father," she kept saying every time a man danced close to us.

"No, our father is taller than that," I would say, or, "No, our father doesn't have a mustache," or, "No, our father doesn't dance like a wooden fence post," or, "No, our father would be dancing with us if he were here dancing at all."

Poulet fell asleep on top of my shoulders while watching, but I stayed, the dancers coming close to the window and then twirling, moving farther away.

The last night of our voyage, the doctor asked me to dance with him. I was standing, looking in at the window by myself when the doctor came up from behind me and said, "Do you know how to dance?" and I told him that yes, I did, that I had learned by standing on my mother's feet in the Great Room at Kontum and that the symbols of fire, water, metal, air and earth on the carpet were well worn down from our dancing.

"Then let's go in," he said, and started to lead me into the room where everyone was dancing.

"But my clothes," I said. I looked down at my jumper. I had grown so much that I had to let out the hem, but it was still too short.

"All right, then let's dance here," he said, and he held me in his arms and we danced on the deck and then it started to rain, but we still danced, and the doctor told me I was a beautiful dancer and that he didn't think he had ever danced with someone who danced as well as I did.

Up close, the doctor smelled like cedar. I was going to ask him if it was a cologne, but then he stopped dancing with me and said he had to go back to his cabin and he thanked me for the dance and gave me his address in Saigon and he told me that if I ever needed anything, he would try and help me.

That night I tried to remember what Michel Riquelme smelled like, but I could not. I wondered if I had ever been close enough to him to know how he smelled. I remembered the smell of Hideho, though — he smelled like the marsh.

· · ·

"You can walk now," my amah said, and she pulled the boards away from Poulet's leg and Poulet walked around the deck, falling every once in a while but still walking, and my mother cried, watching her baby walk, saying out loud how she wished she could go back in time and that none of this had ever happened.

WHEN WE DOCKED IN SAIGON, THE FIRST THING MY mother did was take us to the consulate to try and find our father. We waited outside while she went in, and Poulet jumped on our amah's back and our amah took her up and down the steps of the consulate while Poulet pointed her finger up into the air, pretending to shoot down glass plates from the sky.

I stood on the steps and pulled down at my jumper, thinking if I stretched the material I could make it longer and get it to reach closer to my knees.

It was dark, and we were still waiting for my mother to come out of the consulate. When she finally came out she said they had closed and that she had been waiting on line the entire time and wasn't even able to talk to an official. She said she would try again tomorrow.

We were to stay with a relative of Madame Lin's. When Madame Han opened the door we knew she was related to Madame Lin because her breasts were just as big as Madame Lin's breasts. I wondered if she called them her babies the way Madame Lin had done. We slept in the kitchen. My place was by the stove, and when I lay on the floor I could see underneath the stove and see the droppings of mice and hear the mice squeaking at night. Madame Han said she would give me a pork bun for every mouse I caught. So I asked for a long strand of Madame Han's hair and I wrapped the hair around a grain of cooked rice, and every night I would try to lure the mice out from under the stove and into the wide space of the kitchen floor. If a mouse was hungry enough and I was quick enough, I could catch it by trapping it under one of Madame Han's big straw hats.

. . .

"The way they talk, you'd think Nanking never even existed," my mother said one day after coming back from the consulate, where she was still trying to find my father.

Monsieur Han had a job in a bar serving drinks. He would come home early in the morning and go into the kitchen and take his shirt off and hang it on the back of the chair and sit down and drink some tea before he went to bed. I rarely saw his face, mostly I saw his feet from my place on the floor. They smelled like some kind of cheese I never in my life would want to eat. When Monsieur Han was finished he got up from the chair and sometimes he would accidentally step on my hair as he made his way to the shelf to put back his cup.

Before bed one night, Madame Han came into the kitchen with my mother and sat in the chair and her breasts rested on the table while she said that my mother would have to find money or get a job instead of going to the consulate every day, because she and her husband just could not keep feeding us the way they had been, and that she was sorry, she said, but if she could, she would feed us all sea bass and roast duck. And then she cried and the tears fell to her chest and slid down her breasts.

The next day my mother borrowed a dress and a hat and gloves from Madame Han. Before she left the house she told us to wish her luck. My amah wanted to see what kind of luck my mother would have so she pulled straw from the broom and held out four pieces of different lengths and said to us, "Take one," and we did — me, Poulet, my amah and my mother. I came up with the shortest piece of straw. My mother came up with the second shortest.

"Don't go looking for a job today," my amah said to me, and to my mother she said, "It's okay, you may be lucky. I only wish I had some bear paws to give you for bravery and strength. Take these instead," she said, and gave my mother four crickets she had found out back behind Madame Han's house. I helped my mother put the crickets under her hat and then she kissed her gloved hand and blew us kisses goodbye.

I searched for ho-gat-sen with Poulet. When I found them in the dry dirt she held the blue stones up to the sun and told me she saw the water in the ocean. Standing on top of the hill where

Madame Han's house was, we faced away from the city. All we could see were trees and fields. When we turned around to look back at Saigon we were surprised that so many streets and so many buildings could sneak up behind all that countryside.

My amah came out wearing an apron and put her hands on our shoulders and looked at the fields with us. I could smell flour on her arms. Poulet showed her the ho-gat-sen and my amah put them in her mouth and then spit them back into her hand and showed us how wet, the blue was more like the blue of shallow water and not dark like the blue deep in the middle of the ocean. Walking back to Madame Han's house, my amah spun around in circles and clapped the turtle song for Poulet, and as she did the flour came off and floated up around her.

Because it was Madame Han's birthday we ate noodles and broth for lunch. Madame Han said she wished that for her birthday she could have a heavenly bat. We told her they were really just rats that lived in caverns, feeding off stalactites. But, she said, bat or rat or whatever it was, if she had one she'd live to be two hundred years old and be able to see from here to Shanghai, and even far away she could see the tongues of the Peking ducks hanging upside down in the marketplace.

"The bat's wings fly you above death, that's how you live longer," my amah said to Madame Han.

A storm was coming. Outside the sky was as dark as the inside of a one-thousand-year-old egg.

"When it gets as black as the outside of the egg is when we have to worry," Madame Han said, and then she made us get up and help her bring the clothes in from the line strung between two trees in the back.

The rain started while we were out there, and we ran back inside screaming, holding pants and shirts and dresses in our arms. Inside, wet and laughing, Madame Han said she had nothing for us to dry ourselves with but the clothes we had just brought in, and so I took a dress of Madame Han's and rubbed it over my head, drying my hair. Madame Han came over and touched my hair and said to Poulet, "Run, get me my scissors from the drawer."

Madame Han said I needed something more around my face.

"I can't watch this," my amah said. "If you attract the men on the street, just be careful you don't let them follow you anywhere and just be careful you never talk to them."

Madame Han started by placing a wooden bowl over my head. She said that way I would think I was at a French hair parlor, and the wooden bowl was the dome they would use to let the hair potions do their magic. The bowl smelled like the scallions we had had with our soup.

The sound of the scissors cutting was pleasant. I thought how easy it would be to fall asleep, the sound relaxing me the way staring into a fire or watching waves roll in always made me calm.

Finished, she took the bowl off and took me to her bedroom to look in the mirror.

"Fifteen, that's a good age for this haircut," Madame Han said.

When I looked in the mirror I thought how I could be my older sister, even though I didn't have one. My face looked thinner. My hair cast shadows under my chin, along the sides of my neck, that weren't there before.

Poulet jumped on me piggyback and put her face close to mine and looked at us both in the mirror and said, "Do I look like you?"

"No, you're a baby," Madame Han said to Poulet. "Tian is a young woman."

I still wore the jumper with the let-out hem.

"Try this," Madame Han said, and I tried on a skirt made of silk with pale blue polkadots on it, and I tried on a white silk blouse, too big for me because my breasts were not as big as Madame Han's.

"This is an art," Madame Han said, and she showed me how to roll nylons up into a ball and put them in my brassiere.

When I looked down I had trouble seeing my feet because the brassiere stuck so far out.

The rain pounded down on the roof. There was lightning and then huge cracks of thunder.

"Ooh," Madame Han said, and went to make sure the window was all the way shut. When the lightning struck I looked at myself in the mirror. I looked strange in the electric light, pale, like a ghost of my older sister come back from the dead to warn me of danger.

Then, for a second, I thought it wasn't me standing there but Leandri, just after she had cut her hair short to make all the hair for the Leandri dolls that she gave to the children.

"Let's see how you dance," Madame Han said. Poulet stood on my feet and hugged me by the legs while Madame Han took the lead and the three of us danced around the room, but we weren't singing any song to dance to, we were just dancing to a rhythm in the falling rain, between the bolts of lightning and sounds of thunder.

When my mother walked in the house, she wasn't wearing Madame Han's hat anymore and her hair was all wet, but there was still one cricket sitting on top of her head.

"Is this my daughter?" my mother said when she saw me. "Or is this some other woman come to stay with us, Madame Han?"

"Did you find a job?" I said to my mother. My mother took off the dress she had borrowed from Madame Han and hung it in the closet.

"You walk the streets like that and you know what will happen to you," my mother said. "If your father were here, he would slap you for just walking around in the house dressed like that."

Madame Han stood in the doorway watching my mother.

"If her father were here, he would be out with another woman at some bar in the center of the city," Madame Han said.

My mother stood naked in front of us. Maybe because Madame Han was so big, my mother looked so small. Her breasts were pale and I could see veins under the skin. I wondered if my breasts looked the same.

"I found work in a shop," my mother said. Madame Han went up to my mother and kissed her on the cheek.

"Congratulations, Marcelle, that's wonderful," Madame Han said.

"It was the crickets that did it," my amah said, and then she caught the last cricket under the bowl Madame Han had used to cut my hair.

I zipped up the back of my mother's faded pink skirt for her.

"Have some flour noodle soup," Madame Han said, and so we all went back to the kitchen, where my amah ladled out more soup for us.

"It will be a month until I get paid," my mother told us.

"That's all right, I understand," Madame Han said.

The rain was coming down fast again.

"It'll do this all night," my amah said. When we asked her how she knew, she said it was because the jade bowl on the shelf was darker than usual today, and also a farmer had told her.

We wanted to know what the store sold that my mother was going to work in.

"Undergarments," my mother said. "This is good soup."

That night, before I slept, I took one of the noodles from the soup and tied a string around it and trailed it along under the stove, waiting for a mouse to come. I had caught only two mice the entire time I had been with Madame Han, and I was hungry for another pork bun. I cast the string under the stove, sending the noodle as far back into the darkness as I could. Then I slowly pulled the thread in. It was difficult to see in the dark, the rain clouds covered the moon. I kept pulling and pulling on the thread, but I could not see the noodle. I thought maybe the string had come untied, either that or the noodle had already been devoured.

I lay on my side and kept pulling. The same moment that I realized the noodle was gone, I realized that there was a mouse sniffing my lips and my nose. I could feel his whiskers and I could smell him. He smelled like mouse droppings. I grabbed him as quickly as I could. He was easy to catch, and I thought that maybe he was sick or weak from lack of food, but I soon realized that he was neither — he was quite fat and his fur thick. He did not scream. He wriggled and I felt his pee running down my hand. I held him a long time. I could hear my mother and my amah and Poulet breathing in their sleep. I thought I would kill the mouse in the morning and then hold him dead by the tail and show him to Madame Han. I petted his head with my finger. His wriggling seemed to quiet down. I felt him lick the side of my hand. I petted him for a long time. I wondered which of his relatives I had already killed — maybe his sister or mother or brother or father.

Monsieur Han walked into the kitchen holding a lit kerosene lamp. I held the mouse close to me. Monsieur Han filled a pan with water and set it on the stove. I wondered if he was watching all of us sleeping. I wondered what he was thinking. The water boiled and he poured his tea and then sat down at the table. With the light from the kerosene lamp I could see that the mouse I had caught was black. I heard Monsieur Han drink his tea. I heard him swallow. Monsieur Han never spent longer than five minutes drinking his tea. I closed my eyes and thought how after he left I would keep the mouse for the night under the same wooden bowl that my amah had put the lucky cricket in. All of a sudden I thought I must have been drifting off to sleep because I heard a voice. It was Monsieur Han's. I had never heard him speak before.

"What's that you've got there?" he said.

I opened my eyes. I thought maybe he was talking to someone else, or that maybe Madame Han had walked into the kitchen to join Monsieur Han in drinking his tea.

"A mouse?" he said. I turned my face and looked up at him. I saw a man with many wrinkles around his eyes, a round small nose like a boy's and bloodshot eyes. His hair was black and as straight as chopsticks and greased. It stuck out like it could prick you, like the quills of a porcupine.

"Yes," I said. I held up the mouse to Monsieur Han.

"Oh, it's a fine mouse. A healthy one too. He must be a very good friend," Monsieur Han said, and he petted the mouse with a finger. "What name have you given him?"

Of course I hadn't named the mouse. I was going to kill it in the morning.

"I don't know," I said.

"He's got to have a name. Let's think. Let's give him one," Monsieur Han said. "How about Caesar?"

"Caesar?" I said.

"It sounds good, doesn't it? Caesar? Come here, little Caesar," Monsieur Han said and then he laughed. He stood and rinsed his cup out and put it on the shelf, then he said, "Goodnight Caesar," and he took the kerosene lamp and left the room. I heard him climb the stairs. After a while I let Caesar go. I thought he would run back as fast as he could under the stove. I couldn't tell for sure because it was so dark, but Caesar didn't seem to be running anywhere, instead it seemed he was going to stay by my head all night long. Right before I fell asleep I felt him walking around in my hair.

In the morning he was gone, and I thought how stupid I was — I could have been eating a nice pork bun for my breakfast if I had only held on to that black mouse.

My mother was leaving for her job, and my amah made her keep the lucky cricket in her pocketbook because the first day on a job was always difficult.

"Find out if the man you work for is a horse or a dragon," my amah said as we watched my mother walking down the street, her high heels grinding dirt and stones as she went toward the center of the city.

...

There was work to be done. I cleaned Madame Han's windows with one of her old dresses. The pattern on it was bouquets of flowers, and under the bouquets were names of flowers. Gardenia, rose and baby's breath. When I was done washing the windows, I washed the dress and hung it up to dry on the line in back of the house. It had stopped raining and the sun was starting to come out. The grass looked greener. There were some mushrooms too. For my amah I picked some puffballs and inky caps. "Good, we can see when the next earthquake will be," she said when I gave them to her. She did not save the mushrooms for cooking like I thought she would, she broke them in half and shook their gills and their insides out onto a piece of paper in the middle of the table.

"Come see my horse," Madame Han said when she walked in the room.

She was wearing riding pants that were baggy at the thighs, and as busy as my amah was figuring out the date of the next natural disaster, she looked up from her mushrooms to see what Madame Han was wearing.

"You could store things around the sides of your legs with those pants," my amah said. "Make bags and boxes a thing of the past."

Madame Han took us down to the end of the street and walked us through a meadow and then she took us to a field fenced with bamboo poles. She leaned over the fence and whistled a two-note whistle. We waited.

"There, see him?" she said.

He was roan, that's what Madame Han said.

"Roan? What kind of name is that?" we asked.

"No, that's his color. I call him Yigah, because he's my number-one horse," she said. She whistled her two-note whistle again.

"How many horses do you have?" we asked.

"Just this one. Yigah! Come here!" she said, and then she slipped through the gap in the fence and walked toward him.

"Wait on this side," my amah said to me and Poulet.

We watched Madame Han hold on to the horse's mane and then seat herself on him. The minute she was up, the horse took off through the trees. Madame Han raised her hand in the air. Maybe she was waving to us or maybe she was holding on with one hand because she could. We waited by the fence, leaning over it the way we had seen Madame Han lean over it. We swatted flies off our arms and our faces. My amah braided Poulet's hair. Birds flew above us, catching air pockets and just gliding. I wanted to ride the horse too. I thought if I rode the horse, when I saw my father it would be something to tell him that I did. He would have to think how brave I had been. He would probably tell me I was just like him. He would tell me again about the horses he owned as a child, and how he went riding once and rode right into a tree branch, but didn't fall off, just held on to the branch, his legs dangling in the air, and how he whistled and called for the horse to come back for the longest time, and then finally the horse did come back, and rode right up under him and all he had to do was drop down and the two of them, horse and rider, were off again, and the horse wouldn't listen when my father tried to turn him right or left, and he just kept going in the direction he wanted to go, until the horse led my father right up to a bear in a stream, and my father pulled out his gun and shot the bear clear through the head.

"Let's go inside," my amah said.

"Where did she go?" Poulet said.

"Horses grow wings and take you close to the sun," my amah said. "Either that or she stopped at a bar."

The dress I had used to wash the windows was dry. I tried it on and it fit in the length, but the bust was too big. I took it off. I went up to Madame Han's room. Monsieur Han was snoring in the bed. I opened Madame Han's drawers and took our her nylon stockings and rolled them into balls. I thought if Monsieur Han woke up he would ask me again about the mouse and so I was glad I hadn't killed it.

Downstairs I put on one of Madame Han's bras and stuffed it with the rolled-up nylon stockings, then I put the dress on again.

My amah went back to reading the pieces of crumbled mushroom on the kitchen table. She didn't look up, but she spoke to me.

"When I was a girl I wanted a cuttlebone vest. Cuttlebone is as hard as conch," she said.

"And so?" I said to my amah.

"Nineteen fifty-four," my amah said, reading her mushrooms.

"Nineteen fifty-four?"

"Yes, that's the next earthquake," she said.

"I'll be twenty-two. Will we be here?" I said.

"No. Not here. No one will be here," my amah said, and she took the piece of paper and held it out the window and let the breeze take the mushroom pieces away.

When Madame Han came back her hair was all about her face and she was sweating as if she were the one who had been ridden and not the horse. There was dirt on her face. She was smiling. She ran up the stairs, leaving the door open behind her.

"What a great horse my Yigah is!" she called to us. We followed her up to her room and sat on the bed by the sleeping Monsieur Han's feet and we watched Madame Han take a basin of water and hold her head outside the window and let the water pour down over her hair and her neck.

She had gone all the way through the forest, it must have been far, she said, but they were going so quickly that she didn't want to stop.

"Yigah was a tiger, he flew past the leaves and the branches like they were nothing. I thought he'd be bleeding and cut, but he wasn't at all," she said.

Monsieur Han snored and we laughed and Madame Han walked over to him and placed a kerchief over his nose and mouth. Every time he snored, the kerchief fluttered. Madame Han said there should be a way to harness that energy — turn windmills and set sail boats.

We heard a noise downstairs. It was loud, like somebody moving furniture and crashing into walls. We all ran to the top of the stairs. It was Yigah, coming up the stairs.

"I left the door open!" said Madame Han. "Yigah, no! Go back down, go back to the field!" Madame Han tried to push him back down, but in the narrow stairwell there was no place for him to

turn around and he was not going to go down backwards. Yigah
kept coming up. Madame Han said to let him up and see if he had
enough space to turn around in the bedroom, and if he did then
she would lead him back down the stairs.

Monsieur Han was still fluttering the kerchief over his mouth
and nose with his snoring while Yigah's hooves banged on the
wooden floorboards. The horse nuzzled up against Madame Han's
neck and she petted him and slapped her hand on his side, saying
he was a crazy horse and hadn't they just spent all that time together and wouldn't he be more comfortable in a stall with clean
hay and some feed? The horse seemed to look around Madame
Han's room. He walked over to one of Madame Han's perfume
bottles on the dresser and he sniffed it and knocked it over with
his nose.

"He just wanted to see where you live," I said.

"I think you're right," Madame Han said.

My amah stared at Yigah as if he were not just a field horse but
a horse ridden by one of the Four Heavenly Kings who guarded the
slopes of Paradise.

"Let him stay as long as he likes. Quick, Tian, bring him water.
Poulet, pick him grass," my amah said. "He can tell us the future,"
she said, and she put a chair down close to the horse and she sat in
it and watched him.

If Madame Han tried to leave the room he would whinny and
grab her shoulder in his teeth.

"Really, Yigah, I've got things to do," she would say.

When Monsieur Han woke up, Yigah started to kick at him and
he had to run from the bedroom with his arms covering his head.
Yigah was not going to let Monsieur Han stay in the room and be
anywhere near Madame Han.

When my mother came home, we heard her calling to us.
"Hey, where is everybody?" we heard her say at the bottom of the
stairs.

"Up here," we yelled.

When she walked into the room and saw all of us and the horse, she said, "Oh, Jesus, what happened to Monsieur Han?"

We laughed so hard the horse became worried and walked around us, making sure we were all right. When the horse quieted down, he stuck his head out the window like the house was one big stall and we were his stable mates.

That night we ate our soup in Madame Han's bedroom, keeping the horse company and wondering how we were going to get him out. There was a lot of talk about how, if he got in, there was a way to get him out. There was talk about sawing the house in half and starving the horse.

"No, the horse is here for a reason, he'll leave when he's ready," my amah said.

That night all of us, except Monsieur Han, slept in Madame Han's bedroom. When I woke up during the night the horse was lying down, but his eyes were not closed and he seemed to be looking out the window at the crescent moon. I could not sleep because I was thirsty, so I went down to the kitchen, holding a lit kerosene lamp. I could see it was already very late because Monsieur Han was back and had already had his tea and was now sleeping on the floor by the stove and snoring again.

He slept in the kitchen all the next day. We moved around him while we prepared our morning meal of rice and sauce. Once he woke up and tried to move to the bedroom. Yigah lunged at him and then reared, striking with his forelegs as if the air were a mountain he was trying to climb. Monsieur Han ran back down to the kitchen and resumed his place by the stove. He started to snore the moment he put his head down and we started to giggle and Madame Han told us to hush, but she too was giggling and then Monsieur Han opened his eyes and said, "That horse has to leave by tonight," and then he fell back to sleep.

. . .

I had asked my mother where she was working and she had said it was right next to a store where we had bought our flour. One morning Madame Han said we needed flour and that Poulet and I should take a walk after our meal and buy some supplies.

It was clear in the morning and a little cool and I thought maybe it had rained the night before, because the air seemed so fresh and I could see the city so easily from way up on top of the hill.

As we walked on the path Poulet told me her feet hurt her, so I carried her on my shoulders and told her she would now be our eyes, since she could see the people in the crowds best, and that she should keep an eye peeled for our father.

I bought the flour first and then I tried to find the store my mother worked in. Next door to where we bought the flour was a ladies' undergarment store. I told Poulet to wait outside and I went in.

A bell hanging in the door tinkled when I pushed the door open. There were no windows in the shop and it was difficult to see.

"Hello?" I called, but no one came out from the back. Brassieres hung motionless from the ceiling, suspended in air by strings at their straps. The cups of the brassieres were filled with newspaper.

"Hello?" I called again. I heard a noise behind the counter. I looked over and I saw a man with wire-rim glasses folding panties and brassieres and putting them into boxes. I thought of Mr. Spain folding his shirts and pants and putting them into his suitcase.

"Excuse me!" I said. The man did not look up. I tried to reach over the counter to tap him on the shoulder, but I could not reach, and so I tapped him on the head. He felt his head with his hand as if he thought a water drop had fallen on it. I tapped him on the head again, this time a little harder. He looked up and then he smiled a smile that showed rows of white teeth that seemed as big as the horse's teeth.

"I'm looking for my mother! She works here!" I said loudly. The man shook his head and pointed to his ear. I leaned close to his ear and said even more loudly, "My mother, she works here!"

The man shook his head. "I work here, only me," the man said, very softly, almost whispering.

"No!" I yelled back into his ear. "She started work the other day. Her name's Marcelle," I said, so close to his head that my lips touched his ear.

He smiled again. "No, I'm sorry, no one here but me. Would you like to buy a brassiere?" he said and he came out from behind the counter and started showing me the models hanging in the air, touching each one with a cane. They swung back and forth, out of time with each other, sometimes banging into each other. One lost its newspaper stuffing, and the balled-up newspaper uncurled when it fell to the floor. I could read the headline, something about the Japanese invading Indochina and starting the war. The newspaper was six years old.

I left the shop, grabbed Poulet by the hand and started walking quickly.

"Where's Maman? Where are we going?" Poulet said.

"To the consulate," I said.

It was easy to spot our mother because she was wearing Madame Han's hat. She stood in a long line that went around the corner of the consulate. She stood very close to the back of the person in front of her. I thought if I were the person in front of my mother I would turn around and tell her to please step back, that pushing me wasn't going to make the line move any faster.

Poulet started to call out to her, and I tried to put my hand over Poulet's mouth, but it was too late, Maman had already heard Poulet calling. When she saw us, she looked as if she were going to run, but she didn't, probably because having waited so long on the line, she wasn't going to give up her place. So she just turned her back to us, maybe thinking we wouldn't know her from behind. We went up to her and faced her from the front.

"Hello, Maman," I said.

She did not answer. She turned around so that she had her back to us again.

"I went to the store," I said.

She did not say anything.

"The store next to the flour store," I said.

She turned around and looked at me. "Did Madame Han send you to look for me here?"

"No. We came to see where you worked, to say hello."

"Well, you can see I don't work anywhere, not at any store next to the flour store and not any store next to any other place. So hello and goodbye," she said. The person in front of my mother moved up a place, but my mother did not seem to notice.

"Maman?" She did not answer. I pushed her by the arm so she moved up in the line. At first she did not know why I was pushing her, and then she realized and she moved up very quickly, maybe not believing that she could have forgotten to take every chance she could at getting closer to the consulate and finding our father.

Again she stood very close to the back of the woman in front of her.

"I won't tell anyone," I said.

"I'm not ashamed," my mother said. "I'm looking for my husband and I'm looking for your father."

"Is there any news?" I said. My mother turned around and looked at me.

"No, there is no news. But I was talking to a woman here yesterday who told me they are coming up with a new list, an updated list."

"List of what?" I said.

"The dead," she said.

I didn't see what good it would do to find out every day that our father wasn't dead — I would rather have gone on thinking he was alive and the purpose of going to the consulate was to be able to write to him and to see him again.

"You realize if he's dead, he's probably with that woman who took off her head and brushed her hair," she said.

"What?" I said.

"I said, even in death he will cheat on me," she said.

"What about 'till death do you part'? Marriage ends after death, there can't be cheating then," I said.

"I don't need help standing in line. Why don't you go back and sit with Madame Han, maybe she has some more clothes for you or a new hairstyle she's just dying to try on you," my mother said.

I left. Poulet held my mother's hand and stayed with her, to wait on the line to see the list of the dead.

One of the streets I took home led past the store that sold the brassieres which my mother was supposed to be working in. Through the door I could see that the deaf old man was still behind the counter. When he saw me he waved for me to come back into his shop and he reached up and touched one of the hanging brassieres and set it in motion.

I kept walking. Men whistled and clicked their teeth at me and made hissing sounds and called me doll. Waiting for cars to pass, I stood with a crowd on the street corner. Someone touched my rear end. I grabbed the hand and followed the arm up and saw a man who was smaller than I was. He had no teeth. His pants were too short and they were torn and jagged. He looked like a castaway who had just come from a desert island. He smiled and then he put out his tongue and wiggled it and slid it around to the corners of his mouth.

I quickly let go of him and ran. Cars honked their horns. Drivers leaned their heads out and raised their fists. I ran all the way back to Madame Han's place and I ran straight up the stairs to her bedroom. Yigah was still there, standing in front of the dresser as if he were looking at himself in the mirror. I touched the horse the way I had seen Madame Han do, gently slapping the side of his neck and petting his nose. I looked out the window and saw Madame Han with my amah at the clothesline, hanging up wet dresses and skirts.

I realized I had never even sat on a horse. I took Yigah by the mane, climbed up on the mattress, and then I slung one leg over and pulled myself up onto him. The horse walked a few feet and then stopped in the middle of the room. His back was wide and I thought if I sat on top of him a long time that it would hurt my legs. I tried imagining what it would be like if Yigah started galloping off through the trees. I couldn't imagine how I would keep from falling.

When I heard Madame Han and my amah walk in the downstairs door, I jumped off Yigah by standing on his back and springboarding myself onto the bed. I jumped so hard that I heard something go crack in the wooden frame. I got off the bed very slowly. Hardly breathing, I left the room and went downstairs.

In the kitchen Monsieur Han was sleeping at his place by the stove.

When my amah saw me she said, "Where's Poulet?"

"I left her with Maman," I said.

"At work?"

"Yes. Is there any fresh water?" I said.

"She's at the consulate, isn't she?" my amah said.

Madame Han looked at me too. I did not answer. I sat in a chair and stared down at Monsieur Han. From his clothes came the smell of tobacco. He had worked all night in the bar.

"Well?" Madame Han said.

I looked at her. She was wearing a dress that was low-cut. Her big breasts looked like the heads of babies, like Madame Lin's breasts. I wondered why she and Monsieur Han did not have any children yet.

"There's a new list out. It lists the dead. That's what she's waiting on line to see," I said.

"What about the store?" Madame Han said.

"Oh, the store is there all right. There's a man there with teeth like Yigah's, but he can't hear very well. He has a lot of old newspapers," I said.

"I thought it was undergarments," my amah said.

I nodded. "That too, they seem to go hand in hand."

"So there is no job? She doesn't work there?" Madame Han said.

"She is very good at standing on line. She does it well all on her own," I said.

"Was he on the list?" my amah said.

"No — I don't know. She hasn't seen it yet." I said.

"She's got to get work. I can't just keep feeding you all. Once a week, yes, go to the consulate. But every day?" Madame Han said.

"I'd like to learn how to ride the horse. Can I?" I asked Madame Han.

She did not answer me. She walked back outside to where the wet dresses and skirts hung on the line. She was wearing her riding pants and I wondered if they kept her from falling off when she rode.

. . .

When Monsieur Han woke, he stood and shook dust off his pants and his shirt and he sat at the table and ate rice and sauce. Madame Han moved around the kitchen, taking out a board and cutting onions on it.

"The horse better be out of here by tonight," Monsieur Han said, and he finished his meal and left for his job.

When Maman and Poulet came home, Madame Han was still cutting onions and she was crying. Yigah started to whinny.

"You've cut enough onions for all of Cho Lon," my amah said to Madame Han. Madame Han nodded her head.

"Is that dinner?" Poulet asked.

"I don't know," Madame Han said, crying.

"Here, let me do it," my amah said, and she took the knife from Madame Han and finished cutting the onions.

Madame Han took off her apron, shook it out, folded it and put it in a drawer. My mother sat down. She took the pin out of her hat and set the hat on the table.

"We'll leave in the morning," my mother said.

I could hear my amah stop chopping the onions, just for a second.

"No, you're not leaving," Madame Han said. "You're going to find work, that's all. I've asked my husband. He says you could clean in the bar. You're to go meet him there now."

"All right," my mother said, and she changed her clothes and left the house.

That night we ate onions for dinner.

"We'll have dreams of mourners," my amah said.

Yigah would not leave Madame Han's room. We tried putting a halter on him and leading him down the stairs, but he rose high up into the air and almost hit his head on the ceiling.

"He's not ready yet, he hasn't told us the future," my amah said.

"Yigah, goddamn you," Madame Han said, and she put her face up against the horse's face.

We sweated for hours, pulling on Yigah and pushing him and trying to get the halter on him and trying to blindfold him and trying to cajole him with onion and grass and the promise of hay.

It was still a few hours before Monsieur Han and my mother were supposed to come home from the bar.

"Let's sleep, just for a little bit, and then we'll try again," Madame Han said.

We all slept on Madame Han's bed, and I dreamt I was at a beach, getting ready to walk into the sea.

When we woke up it was because Monsieur Han was in the room saying, "Get up, get out of my bed, finally my bed back. Hah, how lovely, I don't have to sleep on the floor!"

We sat up and looked around the bedroom. Yigah was gone.

"What did you do with him?" Madame Han said to her husband.

"Nothing. You think he'd let me touch him?" Monsieur Han looked at the bed and rubbed his hands together and then he jumped onto the bed yelling, "Yippee!"

The moment he hit the bed we heard a huge cracking sound in the frame and the bed crashed to the floor so hard that I could feel the force of it going up through my rib cage. Oh, no, I thought, this is my fault.

The bedposts, which were standing straight without support, started to sway and then toppled over and rolled across the floorboards.

My amah quickly made me and Poulet go downstairs. From upstairs we heard Madame Han screaming at Monsieur Han for being so foolish, like a child, and jumping on the bed. And then Monsieur Han said, "I can't believe I have to sleep on the floor."

Later, when we were all lying down on the kitchen floor, ready to go back to sleep, we asked my amah if Yigah had foretold the future yet.

"What did you dream about?" my amah said.

I told her I dreamt I was walking into the sea.

MY MOTHER DID NOT SLEEP THAT NIGHT. SHE LEFT THE
house early, wearing Madame Han's dress and hat.

My mother did not sleep for three days. At night she cleaned
the bar and during the day she waited on line at the consulate. On
the fourth day she came back from the bar shivering, her teeth
chattering and with a forehead as hot as a frying pan.

We told her today she must sleep, but she left the house anyway,
heading for the consulate with a blanket around her shoulders and
sweat on her brow.

"Go with her," my amah said to me.

We sat on the consulate steps and I bought my mother tea from
a vendor and she shivered and she told me about how when she
was a child she had a doll who was her height and had all the same
clothes she had, and that her family was so wealthy that they could
afford a maid whose only job was to dress the doll and keep the
clothes in the doll's closet clean and pressed.

"It was a full-time job. God, I hated that doll," my mother said.
And then she said, "Let me just lie down for a minute." She put her
head in my lap and I stroked her hair away from her sweating
face. The sun was out. I could see all the red highlights in my
mother's hair. I could see the wrinkles around her eyes. She slept.
Her breathing was hard. The line was moving forward, but I didn't
want to wake her. I let someone behind us move ahead of us. My
mother started to talk in her sleep and twisted her head from side
to side and ground her teeth.

The rest of the day I let her sleep with her head on my lap and I
kept letting people pass in front of us. When the consulate closed, I
woke her up.

"Maman, it's time to go home." I nudged her. I sat her up.

"Is he there? Is he on the list?"

"No."

We walked home through the dark streets, resting in doorways while my mother caught her breath and wrapped the blanket tighter around her shoulders. While we rested in one doorway, an old woman came out with a broom and threatened to hit us with it if we didn't leave.

"Afraid we'll scare your whores away?" my mother said. The old woman hit my mother on the back with the straw end of the broom. I started running with my mother down the street. She tripped along the way and fell. I tried to get her up, but she said, "No, in a minute." She lay looking into a puddle in the lamplit street. "Look at that," she said. "You can see the moon in there."

As soon as we walked through the door of Madame Han's house my mother fainted, and she would have fallen again if Madame Han and my amah weren't there to help me hold her. We took her up to Madame Han's bedroom and let her sleep on the bed that had crashed to the floor. All night we wiped her body down with wet cloths. Her body was thin and white as rice. The cloths soaked up so much of her fever that they felt as hot as if they had just been boiled.

When Monsieur Han came home, ready for bed, Madame Han told him to sleep on the floor in the kitchen. In the morning the black mouse I had caught days before and that Monsieur Han called Caesar was sitting in Monsieur Han's shirt pocket, sniffing with its nose and blinking its eyes while Monsieur Han snored. With each snore the black mouse rose on his chest and then fell back down.

"She needs to go to the hospital," Madame Han said over our morning meal.

The hospital was in an old school. On the walls were painted the alphabet and rabbits and geese. They gave my mother a bed by a window that looked out at the hills. A nurse hung a clipboard at the foot of my mother's bed.

"The list, let me see the list," my mother said to me in her fever, and she pointed at the clipboard and pushed at me to go get it. Under "Diagnosis," I read "Typhoid."

"Is he on it?" my mother asked.

Under "Prognosis," I read "Poor."

"No, he's not on it," I said.

She developed a pink rash on her chest and her belly, and when my amah came to visit she said it was a rose blooming up inside her and that we should put her bed nearer the window so sunlight could feed it.

When Madame Han came to visit she brought my mother a lavender robe, but my feverish mother thought that it belonged to one of my father's women, and she made me check it for stray hairs that might belong to the woman who took off her head.

Sometimes my mother would look out the window at the hills and say she saw the Chief of the Montagnards there.

"Hurry, go greet him," she would say, "and bring him this rice, tell him I took it from the general while he was sleeping," and my mother would hold out her cupped hand and I would pretend to take rice from her.

"Don't drop even a grain, we want him to get us out of this place," she would say.

One day the sun rose like a red ball and my mother said, "Why are the Japanese raising their flag? Has someone won the game?"

Nurses rubbed my mother's feet and her legs and her arms.

"Get your hands off me," my mother yelled, and then she turned to me and said, "Quick, go to the Great Room and find Leandri, tell her to help," and then my mother fell asleep, her head way back on the pillow while the sunlight shone in through the window, and in her nose I could see her veins and the redness of her nostrils.

I thought if Leandri were here we could walk down the streets of Saigon together and I would watch the men turning around to watch her walk by.

That night, when I went back to Madame Han's house, Yigah the horse was back in Madame Han's bedroom.

"Someone left the door open downstairs again," Madame Han said.

I went upstairs to see Yigah. He was sleeping. The room was warm from him. I went to sleep on Madame Han's bed. I dreamed again of walking into the sea. This time there was a man standing in front of me. He had a beard and a mustache. I did not know who he was. When I told my amah what the man looked like in my dream, she said it was Robert, my mother's brother in France.

When Monsieur Han came home and saw Yigah back in his bedroom, he said he wasn't going to sleep in the kitchen, and that he would rather sleep in the bar — there, he might not have a bed to sleep on either, but at least he could have a table and a drink on the house.

Madame Han said fine, go, leave, Yigah could protect her better than he could, and at least the horse did not snore.

Before Monsieur Han left he went to the kitchen and lifted up the wooden bowl that was turned over on the floor and said, "Come here, Caesar," and he put the black mouse into his pocket and slammed the door shut.

. . .

My mother walked the halls in her sleep. She would go up to others in their hospital beds and pull back their covers and say, "Yeu, is that you?" with her eyes closed.

The nurses told me to tell her to stop, that she had almost given one man a heart attack, and another man was asking them all day who was the angel who had come to him in her sleep — he'd like to make a proposal of marriage.

"Is he rich?" my amah asked the nurses. When she found out he wasn't, she said the next time my mother walked in her sleep, they should head her in the direction of the beds where the rich men were dying.

When I told my mother she was walking and talking in her sleep she said I was lying and she told me to stick out my tongue to see if it was black.

"Just as I thought, black as shoe polish, black as tar, black as night," she said, and then, "I want to go home."

"You can't go yet," I said. "Besides, Yigah is back in Madame Han's bedroom."

"No, not there — home, France. Did I ever tell you about the restaurant that serves baby eels? Oh, and the mussels cooked in wine and tomato? What's my lunch today?" she said.

I lifted the cover on my mother's tray.

"It's cabbage," I said.

My mother smiled. "Oh, there was stuffed cabbage filled with pignoli nuts, bacon and bread," she said.

An old man walked by in his bathrobe, holding his bedpan. My mother grabbed my arm.

"Quick, ask him if he knows your father," and she pointed to the old man. I did not move.

"Go," she said. I walked up to the old man.

"Good morning," I said. He stopped to look at me and he turned his head to the side with difficulty, as if he had not looked anywhere else but straight ahead for a number of years.

"This is my urine," he said, and he lifted up the bedpan. The urine was pink, as if it had been mixed with wine. I went back to my mother.

"No, he hasn't seen him," I said. But my mother's eyes were closed and I do not think she heard me. Beneath her eyelids her eyes were moving back and forth, as if she were reading in her dreams. I sat beside her on the bed and held her hand. I looked out at the hills and I thought Saigon looked pretty, the sun was setting right behind a tall church spire.

Back at Madame Han's, Poulet was sitting on my amah's back and my amah was riding her through the kitchen, neighing like Yigah, and Poulet was pointing her finger in the air and making the sound of a firing bullet.

Madame Han was in her bedroom, sitting on Yigah, wearing her riding pants and hitting the horse with a crop.

"Where's Monsieur Han?" I said.

"He's not staying here anymore, he prefers the tables at the bar to floor in our kitchen," she said.

"My mother is asking everyone at the hospital if they have seen my father," I said.

Madame Han got off Yigah.

"Here, you try him," she said, and she gave me a leg up onto the horse and I sat on him the way I did the day I jumped off him and made the first crack in the bed. Madame Han took Yigah by the bridle and started to lead him down the stairs.

"Come on, my love, that's right, that's the good Yigah," she said, and then she told me to lean back on the horse as he went down the stairs. She led us to the field and there was a cool breeze and we could smell the grass and some flowers that we thought smelled like cherry blossom, but there was no cherry blossom tree nearby.

Once in the field, Madame Han told me to get off and that we would leave Yigah tied to the fence post for the night, but Yigah decided it was time to take me on a moonlight gallop instead. He started off and Madame Han yelled for me to hold on with the insides of my legs, but I could feel myself slipping so I grabbed on to Yigah's mane and I yelled — and then I fell off.

"Where did he take you?" my amah asked when I walked back into the house.

"Two feet from the fence," I said.

That night I dreamed that the man with the beard and the mustache at the beach was eating cabbage he had picked from the waves in the sea.

I woke up when the moon was high, and I could hear Madame Han crying in her bedroom on the cracked-frame bed that rested on the floor.

Poulet laughed in her sleep. My amah slept with her eyes open and one hand raised in the air.

The next morning Madame Han was still crying on her cracked-frame bed. My amah gave me rice and sauce to bring upstairs to her. Madame Han would not eat. She rolled over to look at me and her eyes were puffy and her nose was red and her hair was bent and flattened. The place smelled like a barn. There was hay on the floor and grain in a pile.

"He's sleeping with another woman," she said to me.

"Yigah?" I said. Madame Han rolled back over on her belly and started to cry again.

"Monsieur Han?" I said, and Madame Han cried louder. I could not imagine any woman wanting to sleep with Monsieur Han, with his hair sticking out as straight as chopsticks.

"I don't believe you," I said. Madame Han said it was true. Why else would he say he was sleeping in the bar?

He had taken to keeping Caesar in his shirt pocket and I imagined a scene where he embraced a woman and she saw the mouse and fainted in his arms.

"Please, go to the bar, tell me if he's with another woman," Madame Han said.

"Me?" I said.

Madame Han sat up and grabbed me by the shoulders.

"You must. It means a lot to me."

· · ·

The bar was empty in the early morning. Light came in from the skylight and I thought how for a bar it would make a good home, plenty of space and warmth.

There were hundreds of cigarette butts on the floor and empty liquor bottles stacked up in a corner. On the wall there were tapestries of mountains and trees and I remembered the general and how he had proudly told my mother that the tapestry behind his desk represented his home country of Japan.

"Can I help you?" a man said, standing up from behind the bar.

"I'm looking for Monsieur Han," I said. The man pointed to a door and I walked through it into another room.

All over the floor were men sleeping and snoring, still wearing their clothes, lying on their sides and hugging themselves with their arms. I walked between the men and looked for Monsieur Han.

When I found him he was snoring, and the mouse was running up and down his side and his legs and running around his head.

"Monsieur Han," I whispered, and the mouse ran inside his shirt pocket. Monsieur Han did not wake up.

"Monsieur Han," I said more loudly. I could hear other men around me rolling over.

I pushed my foot up against Monsieur Han's side while I said his name again, this time even louder. Another man woke up and told me to be quiet. I wondered what Leandri would do in a situation like this. I thought she would just go home and tell Madame Han that her husband was not with another woman, but only with a bunch of other skinny men sleeping on the floor in the bar. But then I thought if I did that Madame Han would not believe me, and that the only proof I could give her was the actual Monsieur Han. Leandri would have found some strength in her small bones to carry Monsieur Han home on her shoulders, hitting his back the whole way and telling him to wake up, he had a wife who needed him at home.

"Monsieur Han," I screamed, "wake up!"

Monsieur Han sat up and all the other men who had been sleeping woke up too.

"Madame Han is looking for you," I said in a whisper. Monsieur Han stood, and I thought good, he is going home to his wife now, but then he slapped me hard across my face. I walked backwards a few steps and then I ran out the door, through the bar, across all the cigarette butts, and out into the street, where I noticed my lip was bleeding. I dabbed the blood on both my lips and then I looked at my reflection in a shop window. The blood looked like lipstick, but the hand mark on my face made me look like I had just been slapped by a man twice Monsieur Han's size. I put my hand to my face and held it there as I walked.

Back at Madame Han's place, my amah was getting ready to go see my mother at the hospital.

"Did you find him?" she asked.

"I don't think he's coming home," I said.

"Then tell Madame Han you could not find him," my amah said.

"I found him. He wasn't alone, but he wasn't with a woman," I said. My amah nodded her head and then she left the house.

I walked up to the bedroom. Madame Han was sleeping. On the floor lay her riding pants. I put them on and looked at myself in the mirror. I was too small and the pants hung below my hips.

"You can have them," Madame Han said, startling me. "Did you find him?"

I turned back to look at myself in the mirror again. If I kept the pants, there would be no place for me to wear them except inside the house, since they were so big.

"Yes, he slept at the bar. There is no woman," I said. Madame Han put her head back against the pillow.

"Maybe that's worse, knowing that it's not another woman, just that he doesn't want to be with me," she said. "He didn't used to work in a bar. He worked in an office, and when he came home he would bring me dessert. We would take walks through the city, by the harbor, imagining where we would live if we could live anywhere, imagining what we would be like together when we were older, how we would be able to read each other's minds."

I told Madame Han not to worry, that Monsieur Han worked in a busy place, that I was sure he still wanted to be with her, that in fact he asked how she was and said to send her his love.

"Is that true?" Madame Han said.

"Yes," I said.

"You're a good friend," Madame Han said.

• • •

"The rose is blooming," my amah said when I met her at the hospital. The rash on my mother's chest was more red and raised than ever. My mother's hands were tied to the side of the bed with sheets so she could not scratch herself.

"I need a drink," my mother said to us. My amah put a glass of water to her lips.

"No, a real drink," my mother said. Someone overheard, and he started to laugh. We looked over and saw it was a doctor — the doctor from the ship we had sailed on.

When he saw me he blushed, and then he came over and he bent down and he kissed my mother's hand, which was strapped down with sheets, and then he kissed my amah's hand and then he kissed mine.

"What's this?" he said, picking up the clipboard that hung from the foot of my mother's bed.

"Typhoid?" he said. He felt my mother's forehead. Without looking up, he called out "Nurse!" A nurse came to his side.

"Give her an alcohol bath right away," he said.

"Make it vodka," my mother said. "Don't you dare soak me in rotgut rum."

While my mother was being bathed, the doctor asked me how I was. He wanted to be sure we had enough food. He asked if we had found my father. I told him about my mother losing her job. He said that what she had would take a long time to cure. She needed to stay in the hospital even after the fever stopped. He would put her on morphine for the pain, but that was all he could do for now.

Back at Madame Han's house I discovered that if I filled the legs of the riding pants with other clothes then the pants would stay above my hips. Poulet helped me stuff the pant legs with Madame Han's old brassieres and kitchen rags.

Madame Han came downstairs wearing a black lace dress and high heels. She said she was going to the bar to visit Monsieur Han.

My amah stirred soup in a pot.

"I don't think he'll be back," my amah said. She said a neighbor had pulled bamboo sticks from jars at Cho Lon and had predicted misery for the house of the Hans.

Poulet got a file and started filing her teeth into points, saying she wanted to be a Montagnard girl and could I help her cut her hair into bangs. My amah took the file from her and told her she'd file her tongue down to a stub if she continued to say such things.

"Take her out," my amah said to me.

We walked on the rue Catinat. We thought if Leandri were here she would be on this street, wearing a long top slit high on the sides to the hips and long silk pants, looking into the windows of shops, making men bump into streetlamps because they were watching her instead of watching where they were going.

We walked in the shade of tall tamarinds and rubber trees. Poulet tapped a rubber tree and we chewed the gum. A woman selling fruit-flavored ice on sticks held out four marked beans in a bowl and invited us to a game of chance, but we had no money to play with.

A barber hung his mirror on a tree and set a folding chair on the sidewalk and called to customers by cutting his scissors in the air. In front of a crowd, a dentist fitted a gold tooth.

It was siesta. On the sidewalks, people rolled out their sleeping mats next to roasted chickens and ducks lacquered bright red hanging from their necks off carts. Those in the sun covered their heads with white kerchiefs, those in the shade slept face-up to the sky.

Poulet and I went to the river to watch the houseboat people. Older children splashed in the shallows and younger ones, tied to trees with rope around their waists, watched their siblings play. Men played dice and talked. A hawker in a skiff sounded his gong, and women on boats waved for the skiff to come by them, they wanted to see what the hawker had to sell. Poulet took off her clothes and jumped in the water and splashed with the children, and I yelled for her to come back — the river water was thick with disease. Bamboo leaves floated by with rats on them, ferrying the rats downstream to where human excrement collected in sludge-like piles at a bank on the river known as Hell.

I had to go ankle-deep in the water to pull Poulet out. She splashed me with the green water and it felt heavy, like oil on my arms and legs, and I thought it would never wipe off.

Back at the house, Madame Han sat in her cracked-frame bed on the floor, in her black lace dress and her high-heeled shoes, and she slapped herself in the face over and over again.

"Help me," my amah said. I held one hand and my amah held the other so Madame Han could not keep slapping her face, which was now already so red that the rest of her looked pale. I thought it looked as if her head was on someone else's body.

Later that day, we found out that the neighbor who had read the bamboo sticks at Cho Lon was right — the Han house was falling apart. Monsieur Han was not going to come back and he was not going to give Madame Han any more money.

All that night my amah slept on one side of Madame Han and I slept on the other side, and we each held one of her hands so that she could not hit herself while we slept.

In the morning I went to see the doctor from the ship. We took a walk and I asked him what possibilities there were for my getting a job, and he said there was a job in the prison, they were looking for a translator. I would have to forge my passport so it would say I was already eighteen. The job paid better than what I could get working at a rubber plantation, cutting out imperfections from the long strings of rubber — that was what most girls my age did. He said he could get me the job on one condition, that I accompany him to the movies that night.

"Get me the job first," I said.

THE PRISON WAS NOT FAR FROM THE PLACE WE CALLED Hell. If the wind was blowing the right way you could smell it. When the wind blew the other way you smelled smoke from the banana leaves that were burned at the shore.

My job would be to translate for the French what the Vietnamese prisoners were saying when they were being questioned. The Vietnamese prisoners did not readily provide answers — they would speak only if they were hit or whipped or tortured. The French told me I could have the job if I could get an answer out of a Vietnamese man who had been a prisoner for two weeks.

The room was small. There was only the guard, the man and myself. I stood a few feet away from the man and asked the same question of him over and over again.

"Did you throw the grenade?" I said. The man had stained his pants. "Was it you who threw the grenade?" I said. The guard beat the man's knees with a club and he fell to the floor. I lay down on the floor with the man. I put my head next to his sweating head. In Vietnamese I said to him, "Today is your last day — they will kill you if you keep saying no. Say yes and they will keep you alive to find out more. Only give them one response a day, and, who knows, then there is hope you will be freed by the Vietminh. I have heard they are already so strong they are freeing prisoners in Hanoi and Cambodia."

The man lifted his head and looked at the French. I asked the man again, "Was it you who threw the grenade?"

"Oui," the Vietnamese answered.

· · ·

On his bicycle seat the doctor wheeled a movie projector. He wheeled it into a square and projected Charlie Chaplin on the wall of a building. We drank sugarcane juice squeezed from a hand mill he had brought in the basket of his bicycle. We sat on crates that used to hold bars of soap. Up from them came the smell of roses. My amah, who had come along to chaperon, sat behind me and laughed at Charlie Chaplin, and every once in a while she would say to me, "Tian? Tian? Are you all right?"

"Meet me again tomorrow," the doctor said when the movie was over.

"I'll be too tired from working and I'll have to see my mother," I said.

In the morning I put on Madame Han's clothes and wore a sweater over the dress, to hide the fact that the bosom was too big for me. From the bed Madame Han asked me if I could go to the bar and please speak to Monsieur Han again, I was the only one who could make him change his mind.

"All right," I told her. I kissed her goodbye and I noticed she smelled like onions.

They had killed the Vietnamese man who had confessed to throwing the grenade. The day was very warm and the wind was blowing from the direction of Hell, and the French wore kerchiefs over their mouths, looking like bad guys at a holdup instead of officials in charge of a jail. They offered me a kerchief, and I wore it too. I had brought a picture with me from Madame Han's house. It was a watercolor of a castle on a hilltop. I asked if I could hang it up in the interrogation room. The French nailed it up for me. They congratulated themselves on hiring a woman, they could see I would brighten things up for them.

While I asked the prisoners questions that day I looked at the castle on the hilltop. I could not look at their eyes. I pictured my father in the castle, waving for me to come closer. By the end of the day I had questioned ten men, two of whom were so severely beaten they died. I do not remember any of their faces. I never looked into their eyes.

At the hospital my mother asked me to check the chart again at the foot of her bed.

"Is he on it?" she asked.

The chart still read "Typhoid," but this time it prescribed a dosage of morphine as well.

"No," I said. My mother smiled.

"You always bring me good news," she said, and then she fell back to sleep, still smiling. I opened her robe and looked at the rose-colored rash on her chest. The nurses had rubbed cream on it and the rash shone as if it were wet.

The doctor came by. He wanted to know if he could walk me home. I told him I wasn't leaving for a long while. He brought a radio and set it on my mother's bed. He turned it on and asked me to dance. The other patients, those who could, propped themselves up on their pillows to watch.

"No, I don't want to dance," I said. The patients made a booing sound. The doctor turned the radio off.

"I think I'll have news from Nanking," he said.

"How?" I said.

"A friend of mine is there, another doctor, he knows a lot of people. If I ask him, he can look for your father."

"All right," I said.

On my way back to Madame Han's house I stopped at the bar to look for Monsieur Han. The bar was crowded. Incense burned on every table and long sticks of it were stuck into the walls, in the woodwork. The incense smelled like clove. Men lay down cards on low tables, others threw dice. The smoke from the incense coiled over their heads. A man touched me on my arm and swung me toward him. I thought at first that Monsieur Han had found me. The man smiled and put his drink in my hand.

"Drink, sweetheart," he said. I tried to give him back the drink, but he wouldn't take it. I kept walking, the drink in my hand, looking for a place to put it down, and looking for Monsieur Han.

I asked the man behind the bar if he had seen Monsieur Han.

He hadn't. I walked into the room in the back. I expected to see men sleeping on the floor again, but there were just more low tables and more men playing cards and throwing dice. Only these men were not poor like the men in the main part of the bar, these men had stacks of piasters next to their elbows. A man came up to me and asked who I was and who I was looking for. When I told him, he stepped out into the main part of the bar with me.

"He's gone," he said.

"Gone?" I said. I imagined there really was a woman he had left Madame Han for, and now he was living with her and she was paying his way and he did not need his job anymore.

"He said living at home would endanger everyone," the man said.

"Endanger?" I said.

"Don't you know? He's joined the cause," the man said.

"The cause?" I said.

I walked back to the house, relieved I could tell Madame Han that her husband hadn't left because he didn't love her, he had left because he did love her. When I went into her bedroom, my amah was with her and she was sleeping and my amah put her finger to her lips, telling me to be quiet so I would not wake her. In whispers I told my amah what I had learned in the bar.

"With his skinny body and his funny hair," I said, "do you think he'll make a good soldier?"

My amah did not answer me.

She took the drink out of my hand — I had forgotten I was still holding it. She stood up and went to the window and looked out, and then she closed the shutter and continued to look out through the slats of the shutter. When she spoke it was hard to hear her because her mouth was so close to the wood.

"We might still be in danger. You never know who he told or if he told the wrong person or even if that man in the bar who told you didn't tell a lot of other people and some of them the wrong people. I wish there was a deer in the house, we need some luck," my amah said.

"We could bring the horse up," I said.

"No," my amah said, and then she came over to me and rubbed my temples and I asked is that for good luck and she said no, I was no Buddha, rubbing my temples was supposed to make me relax so I could sleep and work well at my job the next day.

In the morning, while eating my nuoc mam, I told Madame Han about her husband.

"Oh, nonsense, he can't shoot a gun. He's not gone for any cause, except the cause between his legs," she said, and then she said, "Get me out of this dress," and I helped her change her clothes and then she said how the house was in ruins and that she'd need to buy a broom and some soap and get rags. Before I went to work, I gave Madame Han some of the money I had earned.

She held me close to her and told me how thankful she was. I left the house. Walking down the street, I smoothed down my hair, which I realized was wet from Madame Han's tears.

At the prison, the wind was blowing from the city, and it smelled like pavement and exhaust mixed with the smell of cooked duck and burning wood. The French were hungry. They wanted to know what I could cook for them.

They had rice and they had guns.

"Lend me a gun," I said.

"Wait now, you're not a Vietcong girl, are you?" they said.

"Are you hungry?" I asked. They gave me the gun. I went to a tree and sat down a few feet from it and I put one finger in my mouth and moved it up and down, and I whistled at the same time, and the whistle came out warbled and soon a grouse came and sat on a branch of the tree.

"Shoot it now!" the French said. But I held up my hand to signal the French to be quiet, and I waited and I kept on whistling. It was a whistle my father had taught me when I was five. He said when I got older he would teach me how to do the whistle without my finger. I imagined that when I saw my father again I would tell him I was sixteen now and wasn't that old enough to learn to do the whistle without my finger in my mouth?

I didn't shoot until there were twenty grouse on the branches. My father had taught me it's best to shoot when they are in a group, because they let their defenses down and won't spring up and fly away. I shot three in a row. Two fell under the tree, and one I shot in midflight as it was heading over a nearby swamp. The bullets had all gone right through their heads.

I plucked their feathers and stuck bamboo sticks through their bodies and roasted them whole over an outdoor fire I had sent the French to make while I prepared the birds. While we ate, the French told me I could work for them any day, and they asked me where I learned to shoot and I told them my father, and that he was lost up in China. They said they knew people there, they could ask the people to ask where he was.

When I interrogated the prisoners I looked at the picture of the castle on the hilltop and I imagined my father walking down the steps of the castle, walking closer to me.

...

I could not find my mother in the hospital. They had moved all the patients to make room for new ones who had just come in. Three families had been at home when the Vietcong tossed grenades in through their windows. I saw the doctor working on a patient and he looked up at me but he did not smile.

My mother was put in a corner of the hospital. I found her shivering and shaking. I checked her forehead — her fever was back.

"I need my shot, it's been two hours," she said. I told her I would go find a nurse, but she was holding my hand so tightly I had to pry her fingers loose. The nurses were all busy with the victims of the grenades. They were cutting clothes away from bloodied arms and legs and running down the halls with blood on their uniforms from carrying victims to surgery.

My mother asked again for her shot. I told her soon.

"Take me to the window," my mother said. The window near her old bed was now blocked by victims and doctors and nurses and bags of blood hanging from poles and bright lamps.

"I can't," I said.

"Take me!" my mother screamed. I had not expected her to scream.

I began to wheel her bed away from the corner of the room. I had no idea where I was going, but I thought if my mother felt she was moving, then she would think I was taking her over to the window. I moved her from one corner of the room to the next. She rolled her head back and forth on her pillow. There was something white at the edges of her mouth. Other patients who had also been put in the corner of the room yelled at me to stop wheeling her around, they couldn't sleep. I stopped wheeling her. I think she forgot about the window.

"Get this off!" she screamed, and then she wrapped her hands around her neck and it looked like she was trying to take off her head. For someone with a fever she was strong. The more I tried to pull her hands away, the harder she held on.

She stopped screaming and I could hear gurgles coming from her throat as she tried to pull her head off. I wondered if you could strangle yourself with your own hands — would you stop before you could not breathe any longer? Was there something about us that made it impossible to kill ourselves with our own hands? A nurse came running over to help me. She gave my mother a shot. My mother took her hands from her throat and she looked at them.

"Where's my ring?" she said.

"Don't you remember? You sold it for passage aboard the ship to Saigon," I said.

"Someone's stolen it from me," she said.

"No, believe me, you had to sell it," I said.

She smiled. "It was such a beautiful wedding. The dogs were our ring bearers. Yeu had trained them to walk very steadily with the rings balanced on the tops of their noses like schoolgirls balancing books on their heads. We had no cut flowers, instead Yeu had entire trees brought in that were blooming cherry blossom. The aisle was a carpet of petals. The church looked like a forest. Narcissus and branches of apricot trees arched in the doorways and the orange firecracker flower was draped over the windows. All that your amah could do was nod her head and say how prosperous we would be. Your father took my hand and told me 'I do' before the priest had even asked him if he did take me to be his wife. 'I do, I do, I do!' he said, laughing, and the priest laughed too and I cried at my own wedding because I did not think I could contain all of my love for this man and I thought there must be someplace outside of myself to put it or I would burst."

I left my mother while she had her eyes closed and she was still remembering her wedding day. There were marks from her fingers going up her neck that looked like a flame had been licking her there.

. . .

Men drove fish on the river like cowmen driving cattle. They would drag nets weighted with cans and scrap metal from parts of jeeps upstream toward the weir while boys in dugouts banged sticks together and slapped the water with paddles, and slowly the fish were forced to a wall, through a gate and into a floating corral.

The French from the prison watched the driving of the fish and told me to walk with them on the other side of the river, where there was a snub-nosed Bristol that had crashed years ago, and that looking at the snub-nosed Bristol was much more exciting than watching fish get penned.

We had the afternoon off. There were no more prisoners left to interrogate until the French brought the next batch in from Phu Long. We were like children with nothing to do but kill time by the river and look at broken-down things and walk through the water with our pant legs rolled up and talk only about what we saw and not about what we would do or what had happened in the past. We lifted rocks, looking for centipedes. One Frenchman, who was very short, kept finding parts of a jeep. He found a battery and he found a steering wheel. The others said he always found things, and that his nickname was Spare Parts. They said he had a houseful of batteries and steering wheels and doors and bumpers, but he didn't have enough parts to make one jeep that could drive. They said he cooked out of oil pans and drank out of headlight casings. His house chairs were jeep seats and his tables front ends. The other French were named Su-Su, André and Tomtom. Tomtom was the one who knew about planes, so when we came to the Bristol he climbed right into it and started pressing buttons, saying that was how to get the baby off the ground. The plane didn't look to me like it was ever going anywhere again, and if it was going anywhere, it was just going down. It was sinking above its wheels, deep into the mud of the swamp. Tomtom said I should get into it, so he got out and I sat down and pressed the buttons. There were bird droppings on the seat. It looked like the bird had eaten berries. I thought how next year we could come to the plane and we wouldn't be able to sit in the seat because it would be overgrown with weeds and berry bushes and birds' nests.

André was so tall that at the prison little Spare Parts would sometimes stand on a jeep battery to talk to him. Spare Parts was a lieutenant, and André a corporal. Out in the swamp, Spare Parts had found a battery and he stood on it and he called André over to him. André's shoulders stooped over and it made you think what a waste of all that height if he was just going to let his head and chin tuck into his chest like a prehistoric bird.

"Get me a prisoner!" Spare Parts ordered, and then he laughed because he was giving André orders out in the middle of nowhere and could do it just because he had found a battery to stand on and look André in the eye.

Su-Su was named Su-Su because he was easygoing. Sometimes Spare Parts would punch Su-Su in the belly, trip him with his foot and then pull Su-Su's pants up almost to his rib cage because he knew when he did that Su-Su would only curl himself into a ball in a fit of giggles when anyone attacked him.

Tomtom thought this was a good strategy and probably kept Su-Su alive when he was fighting on the front line near Dong Hoi. Tomtom was called Tomtom because he said he was part American Indian. He didn't look it. His eyes were blue and his hair was blond.

Spare Parts found a toothbrush floating in the water, and he lifted it up and showed us how he cleaned his teeth with swamp water, and André called him a crazy Frog, and said if he got malaria we would just let him sweat until Johnny came marching home again.

I found more ho-gat-sen and put them in my pocket for Poulet.

We heard a shot, and then Tomtom came out of the reeds holding up a hedgehog, saying did I know how to cook these.

Outside, we ate the hedgehog grilled. It was getting late. I would have left earlier if it had been a day we had really worked.

André stood up and I looked at his shadow on the ground. It was huge, and with his head all bowed it looked like André was always sad.

"Tian, I have news from Nanking, it's not good," André said.

I was swallowing the meat of the hedgehog. I had cooked it with wild thyme we found by the reeds. A small piece of thyme stuck in my throat. I coughed.

"It's nothing specific, it's just that Nanking has almost no troops left there," André said. "Nationalist troops, I mean."

"Do you have names?" I said.

"No, but it's confirmed," he said. The sun set behind André. I picked up the men's dishes and went to wash them out, but Su-Su took the plates from me and told me he would wash them and that I should go home and bring my little sister the ho-gat-sen.

"We'll see you tomorrow," they said, and waved to me as I walked with the wind blowing from the direction of Hell.

Poulet lined up the ho-gat-sen on the floor like they were racers at a starting line.

"What about dolls?" I said to my amah.

"She doesn't play with them," my amah said. I went to see Madame Han, out by the horse in the field. She was feeding him hay from her hand.

"Do you want to ride him?" she said to me.

"No, he almost killed me the last time," I said.

"Where do you think he is?" Madame Han said. I couldn't tell if she was asking me where my father was or where Monsieur Han was.

"I don't know," I said. I pet the horse and took some hay from Madame Han's hand and fed him.

"He is not going to live long out there," she said. "How is your mother?"

"The morphine is helping, I think."

"Watch out, she'll get hooked on that, it's like opium, it can kill her worse than the typhoid," she said.

The next day at the prison I was told to ask a Vietnamese if he owned a kalim kai cart and if from that cart he had sold poisoned kalim kais to those who were not Vietnamese. A French child had died the night before. "Did you shave the ice and then pour the poison over it and then the fruit syrup and then hand it to the Frenchwoman who in turn gave it to her child?"

The man shook his head no. Su-Su asked me to ask him if he knew that the child had died that night in the hospital — the doctor had said it was from poison. I told the Vietnamese, but he did not know. He said he would never poison a child.

Su-Su pulled out a small glass vial from his pocket. He shook the vial back and forth between his fingers.

"Tell him to open his mouth," Su-Su said. I told the man, but he would not open his mouth. Su-Su then told the man in French to open his mouth, and he slapped his face, trying to get him to open.

In Vietnamese the man told me, "I did not poison anyone."

"What was that?" Su-Su said. "He's a liar. Ask him then why he's so afraid to open his mouth?"

"I don't know what's in that bottle," the man said. "I have never seen that bottle before."

"You know it's poison. You know that because it's your poison and you killed that Frenchwoman's child. Is that entertainment for you people? Killing civilian children? Is it?"

The Vietnamese man did not answer.

"Is it?" Su-Su said again. I was thinking how the man was lucky it was easygoing Su-Su interrogating him and not someone like Spare Parts or André, who would have had him drink the entire vial of poison by now and would have broken both his arms.

"Do you know what happened to that child?" Su-Su said. "He went home and he said he had to go to the bathroom because there were pains in his belly, just little pains at first, and then he fell off the seat in the bathroom from the pain. He was so young he did not understand it, and when his mother asked him what was the matter, he said it felt like there were two tigers fighting in his belly. She took him to the hospital and the doctors made him vomit, but by then it was too late, the poison was already in his blood. His tongue turned black and the insides of his mouth leaked black fluid — as dark as oil. The mother tried to wipe the black off with the hem of her dress.

"'Maman,' the boy said, 'I must have lied about something terrible.' And then he died, and the mother was left standing in the hospital with her dress streaked with the black bile of her dead boy, all because she had wanted to treat him to one of Vietnam's special sweets, a kalim kai."

By the time Su-Su had finished his story he was sitting on one of Spare Parts's batteries. He had his head in his hands. His fingers were very short, like they had been chopped off at the first digit, and for a moment I imagined them to be the dead boy's hands. Su-Su stood up and walked out the door.

"What's going to happen to me?" the Vietnamese man said.

I looked at the painting of the castle. I tried to imagine my father there, but I could not picture him. Maybe he was deep inside the castle, walking its halls with his hands behind his back, thinking of a way to contact us.

"I don't know," I said to the Vietnamese.

Spare Parts and André walked into the room. They told me to leave. I shut the door behind me and I could hear the Vietnamese man gasp. His last words were the ones he spoke to me. There was no time for him to ask that they let him live or to tell them again that he did not poison the boy with his kalim kai cart.

· · ·

At the end of the day the doctor came to the prison.

"Who are you?" Tomtom said.

"I'm the doctor," he said.

"Well, no one's sick here," Tomtom said. The doctor looked at me and smiled. He walked over to where I stood boiling water for tea.

"Hello, Tian," he said.

"You know this man?" Tomtom said.

I did not say anything.

To the doctor I said, "Would you like some tea?" He took the tea and stood in the middle of the room.

Then Spare Parts walked in, and when he saw the doctor he said to Tomtom, "Who is that?"

"A doctor," Tomtom said.

"Who's sick?" Spare Parts said, and stood looking at the doctor.

Next to walk in were André and Su-Su. They both asked the same thing. "Who are you?" they said to the doctor, who was standing in front of me and watching me pour the rest of the water into cups.

"I'm a doctor. I'm the one who told Tian about this job."

"Oh," the men all said, and then they invited the doctor to sit down in a chair.

"Tian, you never told us you had a doctor friend," Tomtom said.

I did not say anything.

"What's your name?" André said. I had never known the doctor's name. I looked at the doctor.

"Carol Dupree," he said. I could see the men trying not to laugh.

"Are you two dating?" André said.

The doctor looked down at the ground. "Ah, I would like very much to take Tian out this evening."

The Frenchmen stared at the doctor.

"Is that all right?" the doctor said.

The Frenchmen were silent. They looked at each other.

"I don't know," Su-Su said, "she's very young. Shouldn't she have a chaperon?"

"Of course," the doctor said. "Ah, maybe one of you gentlemen would be so kind?"

"I'll do it," Su-Su said. At the same time Tomtom and André and Spare Parts said it too.

The doctor laughed. "I'm pleased that Tian has so many fine fellows looking after her. Good, let's all go for dinner this evening."

. . .

Madame Han took all of her clothes out of the closet and laid them on the bed.

"Here, this one leaves the shoulders bare and just wraps around the bosom, I'm sure it'll fit you," she said.

"It's not a ball," I said, "it's just a dinner."

I picked up another dress. It was straight, made of gray silk with small threads of gold. The collar was high.

"How about this one?" I said.

"But the bosom," Madame Han said.

She was right, the dress did not fit me. The darts in the breasts stuck out so far that my amah said Madame Han could curl up in one of the cups and my amah herself could fit in the other and they could both go as my hidden chaperons.

There was nothing else I could wear except my jumper. I did not want to go out to dinner with the doctor and all of the Frenchmen wearing an outfit that fitted Poulet better than it fitted me.

When the doctor came to the door, with all the Frenchmen behind him, I told Madame Han to tell them I could not go.

I ran to the field and petted Yigah and fed him hay. When it became dark, I started to walk back to the house. Coming up the street was a group of men. It was the doctor and the Frenchmen. When they saw me, the doctor handed me a package.

"I would like, um, I would like you to accept this . . ." the doctor was trying to say, but the Frenchmen cut him off, and they were all yelling, "Try it on! It's a dress, come on, hurry up, we're all hungry."

I took the package and ran up to Madame Han's room. I tore it open and pulled out a dress that was the color of lemon, made of silk, with a long, full skirt.

While Madame Han helped me put it on, I asked her how she could have told them and I told her how embarrassed I was and then she spun me around and made me look in the mirror and Poulet walked in and she whistled, and Madame Han kissed my forehead and told me I looked beautiful.

That night we went to Cho Lon and ate Peking duck for dinner. I wrapped some pieces of duck in a napkin when no one was looking and put them into the purse of Madame Han's that I had borrowed for the night. I wanted to bring the duck to my mother.

The Frenchmen asked me to dance before the doctor did, so I danced with them one by one. Tall André, with his head curled into his chest, proved to be the best dancer. He led so smoothly I began to feel I wasn't dancing in a club in Cho Lon, surrounded by other dancers knocking into us, but was dancing in the quiet of the Great Room, on the oriental carpet, the symbols for fire and water and metal and air and earth under our feet and the window looking out over the dark forest and the mountains, where I knew my father was living with the Montagnards.

Dancing with the doctor was difficult. He held me tightly, as if he thought I would float up and away, fly over the heads of everyone in the club and out over the canals and over the Saigon River.

After the dancing I told them I was leaving, and they thought I meant home and they were all going to get in the car and take me to Madame Han's, but I told them no, I wanted to see my mother.

They drove me there and I said goodbye to them.

The inside of the hospital was dark. They had moved my mother's bed again, so I had to go up to each person to see which one was Maman. When I found her she was sleeping on her belly. I lit a lamp. I could see the hair at the nape of her neck was knotted and sweaty.

I shook her by the arm. She moaned and then she turned her face to me. At first I thought I had woken the wrong person and that this wasn't my mother but some old woman who looked like my mother from the back.

There were big black circles under her eyes and her lips were white and her skin looked like wax paper. When she lifted her face for a kiss from me, I could see the skin on her neck was wrinkled, as if it were a loose silk stocking, fallen down around an ankle.

"Maman, I brought you some duck," I said, and I unwrapped the Peking duck from the napkin and fed her pieces.

I thought she would notice my dress, but all she said was "Could you please turn off the lamp?"

I lay down with her on the bed when she finished the duck. I lightly tickled her back and then I could tell she was asleep again and I held her.

Early in the morning the nurses came to wake us up. It was time for my mother's injection and for her legs and arms to be rubbed.

I went outside, expecting to walk back to Madame Han's, but Su-Su and André and Tomtom and Spare Parts and the doctor were all asleep on the steps of the hospital, leaning against each other in such a way that if you took one of the men away, then all the others would fall over one another like a house of cards.

"Gentlemen!" I said, loudly. The doctor woke first and then they all stood up and brushed off their clothes and rubbed their eyes.

"What are you still doing here?" I asked.

"We're waiting to take you home," the doctor said.

They brought me home. My amah was awake, sitting by the window, and when the others left she said to me, "I remember when I wrapped a sheet around your breasts so the Japanese would not know how old you were," and then my amah left the room.

"What is that supposed to mean?" I called to her, but she kept walking.

I took off the lemon-colored dress and hung it in the closet.

IT WAS THE YEAR OF THE OX AND WE STILL LIVED IN Saigon by the Cau Canal and we ate rice buns filled with bits of lamb for dinner because, my amah said, the sheep is opposite the ox and that way our year would be balanced.

Madame Han said she was going to try to find her husband and that she was tired of not knowing whether he was dead or alive, whether he would someday come back or whether he was with the cause forever and the trees and hills of the jungle were his home.

"Because it's the Year of the Ox," the doctor said to me when I asked him why he had brought me a silver pin in the shape of a phoenix. It was a day the doctor did not have to work, and he was wearing a short-sleeve shirt and I noticed what I had never noticed before, that the doctor's arms were freckled and thin, like a woman's.

"Carol," I said to him, "I can't accept this."

"But what about the dress, you accepted that," he said.

"The dress was from the others too, I work with them, I had to accept." I put the pin back in its box and handed it to the doctor. I thought he would leave then, but he stood in the room and looked at the pictures on the wall.

"I know someone who says there is a lieutenant named Yeu at the front line up north. I'll be hearing more from him soon," the doctor said.

I did not believe him. "Who is this man giving you all this information?" I said.

"I can't tell you."

"You have to leave now," I said. The doctor nodded his head and then he left.

There was a lot to do at work. Spare Parts had filled the jail with Vietnamese who had bombarded a rubber plantation with mortar shell. They had killed the French plantation owner, its manager, some French supervisors and even a few of their own, some Vietnamese men whose job it was to tap the trees. Spare Parts said there was still the ringleader to catch, and he was going to make these prisoners tell him who the man was and where he was hiding.

I translated for seven days straight. The men were the strongest I had ever seen. No one divulged anything about the incident or who was involved. The French took turns beating the Vietnamese for their answers. I believed the French were more exhausted by giving the beatings than the Vietnamese receiving the beatings.

I slept on a cot for an hour or two at a time, then the cycle would begin again, and Su-Su would have to wake me by pulling me by the arms up to a sitting position and getting me to walk back into the interrogation room.

I started smoking cigarettes — it helped me stay awake. Every time André or Tomtom saw me with one in my mouth, he took it from me and said I shouldn't smoke, and then he smoked it himself. Spare Parts and Su-Su gave me their cigarettes to smoke. During the translating and asking questions, there were long periods when nothing was said, because Tomtom or Spare Parts or whoever was interrogating the Vietnamese thought that long pauses would make the prisoners so nervous they would answer. During these times I blew smoke out through my nose and practiced blowing rings of it out of my mouth. A few times I fell asleep in the chair, and the cigarette in my hand would fall to the floor.

My amah visited and brought us rice and nuoc mam. We ate it while we interrogated the Vietnamese. Spare Parts said you could see their mouths water when we picked up the chopsticks and ate our meal.

"Maybe this will turn the tide," Spare Parts said. But still, even after we offered them our food if they talked, the Vietnamese stayed silent.

One man the French had beaten so badly couldn't walk but had to drag himself along by his arms. His kneecaps had been slammed so many times with a hammer that they were no longer where they should be, but had floated somewhere around the sides of his legs in pockets of fluid that had swelled so much they looked like pork buns and not knees. Spare Parts would only have to touch the man's knee with his forefinger to make the man scream out in pain.

On the seventh day of translating I slept in the chair and dreamed the man screaming was the Japanese general who had been bitten by his horse, and that my mother and I had to find her cologne quickly for the general's shoulder or else he would beat us with sticks and with whips. When I woke up, I was being carried over Su-Su's shoulders and he was taking me to Madame Han's house. At her house he put me down on the cracked-frame bed on the floor.

Yigah was back, and before I fell asleep I could feel him bend down to me and sniff my hair.

I dreamed I was at the beach again, the man with the beard and the mustache was there, but this time I was facing the shore instead of the water. There was a large building with many columns, and behind the columns were rows of shops. There were steps that lead to the beach. People had tables and chairs on the sand, and table-cloths covered the tables, and they had baskets of food and they ate off plates with silverware and cloth napkins. There were people all over. In the distance I saw a building with the words "Au Bon Marché de Paris" written on it.

"It could not be Paris, with a beach," I said to my amah later, when I told her my dream.

"No, but it's somewhere in France," my amah said. "Tell your mother the next time you see her."

The next time I saw my mother, she had fallen off her bed and she was lying on the floor and she said she did not want to get up, that she had a fever and the floor was cooler, and did I remember how beautiful my father's fingers were? Did I at least remember that? she asked me. "Or do you only remember how there were other women's hairs on the lapels of his clothes? Other women's

perfumes at his collar? Other women's face powder on his face —
making him look smooth, his face made up and mannequin-like?
Other women's discharge at his crotch . . ."

"Maman, get up off the floor," I said.

"Christ, tell me what you remember," she said.

I sat down on the floor with her. I told her I remembered his
long fingers, how they tapered like candles at the ends. I remembered how tall he was, how he could lift me up on his shoulders
and I could see the Forbidden City, the Great Wall, and even India.
I remembered the dogs and how they were always at his side, their
heads right at his legs — when he turned right, they turned right,
when he turned left, they turned left, as if gravity worked side to
side. He was the Earth, and they were the Moon. I remembered
how he let me ride those dogs in the rain. Their fur was hard to
hold on to and the wet fur smelled like an old attic and he made the
dogs run from one end of the garden to the other while I clutched
the fur at their necks, riding each one in turn, the rain falling so
hard I could not see my father's face, only his figure, dark and off to
the side.

I remembered how he came back down from the mountain. He
looked like Christ off the cross. His hair was matted with dirt.
There was dirt everywhere on him. It was trapped in his eyelids, in
the corners of his mouth, and sitting on the curves of his ears,
winding around like dirt on the road that wound its way up to
Chungking. I remembered how he danced with you. We could have
been at a ball and not with the Japanese at Kontum. Even the
Japanese stopped to watch.

My mother was asleep again. She was so thin now, or I was now
so strong that I could lift her by myself. I lifted her up in my arms
like a groom taking his bride across the threshold. She was so light
I thought I could carry her all the way back to Madame Han's
house. Better yet, I could carry her back to China. I would set her
down in front of my father so that when she awoke he would be

there looking at her. I carried her to the window before I carried her to bed. There was some smoke in the distance, over the canal. People were burning incense and setting off fireworks. It was Tet. The sky lit up from a rocket. Saigon was beautiful. Air from the open window brought in the smell of the burning lotus incense and the smell of the charcoal fires burning in clay pots cooking sweet potato and banana.

When I left, I walked by the doctor, who was working on some papers. He had his glasses on the tip of his nose as he looked down. He looked old. I stood in the doorway for a second, I was going to say hello to him. I wondered what he did on Tet. Maybe he would like to walk with me to Le Loi Boulevard, toward the hotel, and see what kind of fireworks they were setting off there. But when he looked up, and I saw the dark circles under his eyes, I left the hospital. I was thankful he did not call out my name.

"Here's a pen, write a letter," my amah said, giving me the label from a can of peaches to write on.

"Dear Robert, we are writing to you because your sister is very ill. She has typhoid. The situation in Indochina is grave. We will be trying to leave here as soon as possible. We will go to your house in Biarritz. I hope all is well. Madame Chao Shu Lan, amah."

I wrote as she spoke, but when I finished the letter, I told her we could not send it. We did not know this man, how could we all go there, and how would my father know to find us there when he came back? "Besides, there's no post, the letter will never get there," I said.

"Give it to Spare Plug, he'll get it there through the French," she said.

"Spare *Parts*," I said. "Anyway, how will we get there?"

"By boat, by plane," my amah said.

"What about Madame Han, where will she go?"

"She'll stay here, she wants to wait for her husband."

"I've never been to France," I said.

"You'll like it, they have tight dresses that show off your cleavage," my amah said.

"Things could get better here. Tomtom said the other day that the French are sending reserves." Just as I said this we heard the roar of motorbikes driving down our street, with Vietnamese teenagers, drunk on wine, yelling out for the French to get the hell out of their country and go back to France where they belonged. We heard bottles breaking. My amah took the letter from me and folded it, then she sealed it with wax from a burning candle.

Madame Han came down in her robe. Her hair was neatly brushed and she wore lipstick and rouge. She wore it all the time now, even in her sleep. Just in case her husband should come back, she wanted to look good for him.

"What the hell is that?" she said, opening the door and looking down the street at the motorbikes driving past.

"It's the Tet celebration, just kids," I said. Madame Han pulled her robe tighter around herself.

"Where's Poulet?" she said.

"Asleep, it's late," I said.

"What are you two still doing up?"

"Placating the water spirits, hanging paper streamers," my amah said, and she took the labels off more cans of peaches, cans of meat and kumquat, and she started hanging the labels in the windows.

"You certainly know how to have a good time," Madame Han said. "I'm going back to bed."

· · ·

Spare Parts said he would try sending the letter, but he did not think it would get to France for a few months, and then, who knew how long before it reached Biarritz?

"What's France like?" I asked him.

"Imagine a beautiful place in Indochina. Imagine it and then take away the awful heat and the jungle and the goddamn fish sauce and rice and replace it with food from the heavens and smells of vineyards and the French language that caresses the palate of your mind with its poetry."

"Oh, come on," André said. "France is all right, but Indochina is beautiful too. Did you see the fireworks over the canals last night? Or have you been up north where the hills are?"

"Yeah, I've been up north to those hills, I've eaten the dirt on those hills," Spare Parts said. "You can have them, I'll take France any day," he said, and then he started to sing "The Marseillaise." André laughed, and Spare Parts stood up and started conducting everyone and made us sing it too. When we got to the end, Spare Parts wanted us to sing it again, but Su-Su told him it was enough, give it a break and sit down, and Spare Parts got mad and he punched Su-Su in the face. Su-Su did not do anything. He felt his face where Spare Parts had hit it and then he walked outside. As he stood there, a car drove by and someone in the car pulled out a machine gun and shot the walls of the prison and then shot Su-Su as he was reaching into his breast pocket to pull out his pack of cigarettes. When we ran outside we saw Su-Su sitting dead against the wall of the prison. He held the cigarettes and his hand was out as if he were offering one to us as we walked by.

· · ·

When we told my mother we were thinking of going to France to stay with her brother she grabbed the sides of her bed and gripped so hard we saw her blue veins rise up under the white skin on her arms.

"And how do you think your father will find us then?" she said in a whisper. I thought if she didn't whisper it, she would scream it.

"This is your idea, isn't it?" she said to my amah.

"Look out the window," my amah said, and she had me wheel my mother's bed to the window that faced the street.

Down below there was a protest going on. The Vietnamese were parading with signs reading, "Out with the French," and they held sticks and stood on the backs of oxen to hold their signs high.

"I am not French, I could stay here for a long time. I could move to Cho Lon, just a few blocks away and live as peacefully as if I were wearing the tiger's claw charm and a peachwood amulet. It's not me who needs to move out of this place," my amah said.

"No one French will be here for very much longer," I said. "My father will not come looking for us in a place that he thinks is too dangerous for us to stay in."

My mother tried to stand up. She put weight on her legs and her legs buckled. We caught her and lifted her up, and she was so light that if we lifted her with any more force she would have flown into the air.

"I can't even stand up yet, how am I supposed to get on a boat or a plane?" she said.

"We'll send for you last. You'll be safe in the hospital, safer than Tian and Poulet are, staying at Madame Han's house."

My mother lay back down on her bed.

"Isn't it time for my injection?" she said. I looked at her chart. Her morphine wasn't due for another two hours.

"It hurts, here," she said, and she pointed to her chest and opened her robe and showed us her rose-colored rash.

"Ayaah," my amah said, and stepped back from the bed.

"What?" we all said.

"It looks like the footprint of Buddha that has marks on the side of his foot made by the tears of the sinful woman," she said.

"Fuck, get out of here," my mother said, and she closed her robe, sat herself up against some pillows and lit a cigarette.

· · ·

Up and down Madame Han's street the French were leaving. They had bought tickets to Marseilles. They loaded their clothes and their suitcases and their cedrela-wood tables onto rows of pedicabs that waited outside their houses and then they told the pedicab drivers to head out toward the quay.

We kept Poulet inside and did not let her out on the street. Yigah stayed in the house too, and Poulet rode him up and down the stairs and through the rooms. Naps she took lying forward on Yigah's neck, holding on to his mane. She ate meals sitting up on Yigah, and when she dropped a crumb on his back she wiped it off. She believed he would someday grow wings, so she was always feeling the horse's sides and telling us to feel his sides — she could feel bumps there where the wings were ready to sprout.

Ho Chi Minh decreed that all homeowners in the third and fourth districts should destroy their houses so that the French could not use them or hide in them. Madame Han lived in the third district.

"Nonsense," Madame Han said when a Ho Chi Minh soldier came to her door with the news. When he returned the next day, telling her she had two weeks left in her house before it was destroyed, she told him she was not destroying the property of her husband and that Ho Chi Minh should concern himself with what was happening on the front line and not what was happening in people's homes.

The soldier who had come to give her the news took an ax and slammed it into the wooden door and split a hole there wide enough for us to fit through.

"This door could have been you," he said.

Right then, Yigah came up from behind Madame Han to see what was going on. He charged at the Vietnamese and ran after him through the door, Poulet on his back, holding on to his mane eating a pork bun, and the Vietnamese screaming, looking over his shoulder, seeing murder in Yigah's rolling eyes.

• • •

From working at the prison, I had saved enough money to buy three tickets aboard a ship to Marseilles and one ticket aboard a plane.

"Buy the tickets now," my amah said. But I thought we would need more money before we set sail for Marseilles. We still hadn't heard from my mother's brother. What if we got to Marseilles and couldn't get to Biarritz from there?

"What if we had to stay in a hotel and buy food?" I said to my amah.

"You wait too long and there won't be any passage by ship or plane, there just won't be any room," my amah said while she made a soup of bindweed and young manioc.

At dinner, Madame Han would not eat.

"I'm afraid if they find out that my husband's wife did not comply, then they'll treat him poorly, wherever he is. They have their ways of letting these things be known," she said. "I'd rather have him back alive than have this house."

After dinner she handed us axes and hammers, and we set to work chopping legs off chairs, splitting the table in half, splitting bowls in half, breaking plates, pulling doors off cupboards, smashing windows.

Yigah ran around the house nervously stomping his feet, rearing at the sound of our hammers and axes hitting the wood.

We took the doors off their hinges. Grasshoppers jumped on the floors. Moths circled the lamps. We took knives to the mattress of the cracked-frame bed. We slit it, doing our work in a cloud of feathers floating by our heads.

We stayed that night in the field. We slept on blankets covered with sheets to keep mosquitoes off us. We woke in a mist. We could see the destroyed house across the way. Yigah was still standing inside, looking out a window whose glass had been smashed.

When I went to work the wind was blowing from Hell. I rounded the corner to the prison and saw the Vietnamese on guard. I did not see Spare Parts or André or Tomtom anywhere close by.

I went to the quay and bought passage for three on board a ship to Marseilles. Then I took a pedicab to the Tan Son Nhut airport. There I bought a ticket for a plane to Marseilles. I went to the hospital and told my mother the boat would leave the next morning.

She laughed. "Have you even heard from my brother?" she said.

"Maman, there's no job left for me, there's no house. I'll get there first, to make sure Robert can meet us."

"Have you ever been on a plane?" my mother said.

"No, of course not," I said.

"I like the turbulence, it's like being rocked," she said.

The doctor came to talk to me. He said my mother had become addicted to the morphine. He said it was too dangerous to take her on a long journey now.

"Leave her here until she's off it," he said, "then we'll send her ahead in a few weeks."

I left the doctor my mother's ticket for the ship.

There was a curfew in place. It was getting dark. I ran back through the streets, praying that I could trust the doctor and that he would make sure my mother got to France to join us. I ran to the field near Madame Han's house. Madame Han had already left. She had gone to a barracks set up by the Vietnamese for those who had destroyed their homes according to Ho Chi Minh's decree. She had left me a letter. I put it in the pocket of my jumper.

"We leave in the morning," I told my amah and Poulet.

We slept our last night in Saigon under a thin sliver of a moon.

I left my amah and Poulet off at a narrow quay near the foot of the boulevard Charner. On the sun-baked gravel strip I kissed them goodbye and told them that I hoped their journey would be more comfortable than the last one. This time they would be sleeping in berths and taking their meals in the ship's restaurant.

My flight to Marseilles was to leave in two hours. I watched the ship set sail amidst the sound of French music coming from a gramophone brought to the quay by river workers. The river was peaceful. Junks piled with rice and sampans carrying fruit and vegetables and caldrons of noodle soup floated by. Three boys floating in a huge round wicker basket used a stick in the water to propel themselves along.

"What do I do now?" I said to myself out loud. I would have liked to say goodbye to Spare Parts, Tomtom and André, but I knew

I would not be able to find them. I did not think I could say goodbye to my mother again. It would have made me cry.

I thought about what my father was doing. I wondered if he carried pictures of us in his pocket. Did he show these pictures to his friends in the army? Or did he only carry a strand of hair from the woman who took off her head?

I went to see the snub-nosed Bristol that André had showed us alongside the swamp by the prison. Walking was hot, sweat broke out on my upper lip, and I remembered how Spare Parts had said France was everything lovely I'd ever seen here in Saigon, only there wasn't the goddamned heat. I would miss the heat, I thought to myself, the constant humidity and high heat were comforting, so strong in their presence they were like another being, a thing that went with you everywhere and provided companionship.

The abandoned airplane was still there. I climbed into the cockpit and sat in the cracked leather seat, covered with stray banana leaves and swamp grass and crawling bugs. I could not see through the windshield for the mud and grime. I took Madame Han's letter out of the pocket of my jumper and I started to read:

Dear Tian,

I wish you the best of luck in France. Perhaps your uncle will be a kindly gentleman who will be able to provide for you better than I have been able to.

Don't worry about your mother. I am sure that she will be fine. It will take some time for the Vietnamese to get the French out of here completely, if they ever do. I am sure that years from now, when you come back to visit, you will see that the French influence has remained.

Someday I will hear from you, and you will tell me to meet you in the lobby of the Hotel Caravelle. I'll be an old woman with a cane and a small ugly dog and I'll sit in the corner in one of those brocaded Louis XIV chairs and I will wait for you because I will have arrived early because old women have so much time on their hands. I will sit the dog on my lap and talk to it and tell it to be still, and I ask it did it know who it was about to meet? A friend of mine who stayed with me when she was a young woman and who helped me out more than she would ever know. Then I will look up and see this beautiful woman wearing a beautiful dress of the latest fashion, making bellboys' and men's heads turn as she walks through the lobby. I will lift my hand and, fearful you will miss me sitting there in the corner, I will lift my hand higher, as high as I think it can go for my old body, and I will wave at you and start to stand with the use of my cane to come forward and greet you.

Tian, I look forward to your visit that day. Start living a wonderful life now and you will have the stories to tell me when you see me again.

Madame Han

When I finished the letter, I took a banana leaf from the floor of the airplane and I wrapped it around the letter and put it back into my pocket. I thought how everything in Indochina was wrapped in banana leaves. I wondered if there were banana trees in France too. I was sweating, sitting in the sunlight. I put my head back and let the sweat drip down my temples so I could feel it running down the sides of my neck.

"Goodbye, Saigon," I said out loud to the sky.

MY MOTHER WAS RIGHT — ON THE AIRPLANE THE turbulence felt like a cradle rocking. Other women clutched their husbands' arms when we hit pockets of air, but I found the motion soothing. I wondered who was flying the plane. I pictured Tomtom and Spare Parts and André at the controls. I imagined swinging open that little door at the front of the plane and seeing them all there, and they would sit me down and show me what the instruments meant, and they would point at stars, naming constellations.

I wondered how long the plane could keep flying without having to stop for more fuel. I thought how wonderful it would be to just stay where I was, being rocked by the turbulence in the darkened plane and not have to land in Marseilles, or any of the other cities along the way that I had never been to. What if my uncle wasn't there to greet me, and if he was there, how would I know what he looked like?

A woman next to me spoke in French. She asked me the time, but I did not have a watch.

I could feel her looking at me even after I had let her know I did not know the time.

"Are you French?" she asked.

"No, half French," I said.

"And the other half Vietnamese?" she said.

"No, Chinese," I said. "My father is Chinese and he is fighting with the Nationalists."

"Why were you in Saigon, then?"

"I don't know. I suppose because it was safer than Shanghai," I said.

"How long were you in Saigon?"

"Oh, a long, long time," I said. And then I remembered, it had only been last year that we had all come to Saigon, and I was about to correct myself and tell the woman I was wrong, that it hadn't been such a long time, but she had already asked for a pillow from the stewardess and she was now sitting back in the seat with her eyes closed.

. . .

We reached Marseilles at night. There were so many lights down below I thought the plane had made a mistake and we were landing in Paris instead.

When we landed, I took down my one bag and followed the other passengers out onto the tarmac. The night was cool. I was wearing the lemon-colored dress the doctor and the French soldiers had given me, and it had no sleeves. It was strange to think that everyone here was French. In the terminal I saw people kissing each other and hugging each other hello. I sat in a chair and waited. I was the only one in the entire airport who looked even slightly oriental. I figured if my uncle was there, he would be able to find me first.

While I waited, men came up to me and offered me cigarettes, and I accepted them. I was getting hungry, but I was afraid to spend what money I had. The men asked me if I needed a taxi or a ride. I told them I was waiting.

The men smiled, and when they left me alone they kissed both my cheeks.

The cigarettes were strong. I went to the bathroom and rinsed my mouth. In the mirror I thought how silly I looked wearing a lemon-colored dress in a place cool enough for coats.

After three hours and no sign of a man who could be my uncle, I stepped into a taxi and told the driver I needed to go to the train station.

I could not believe how few people there were on the streets. Even at night, the Vietnamese were always out on the streets. Some would wear long, flowing ao dais and cuans and take walks or shop. Others would be selling kalim kais or coconut on the sidewalks.

"Where is everyone?" I said to the driver. He looked at me in the rearview mirror and held his hand up in the air as if to say he did not know or it did not matter to him. The car smelled of cheese and I heard the driver unwrap some paper and then he began to eat a sandwich while he kept one hand on the wheel.

I was hungry, and I was thinking how good it would be to have some warm rice with some nuoc mam poured over it and a sweet potato. I looked out at the trees. They were not rubber trees. When the driver finished his sandwich, he uncorked a bottle and drank some wine.

"Cheers," he said to me, and lifted the bottle up and looked at me in the mirror.

It was late at night and only a few people were waiting at the train station. I bought a round-trip ticket to Biarritz. I knew I would have to be back in a few weeks to meet my amah and Poulet when their ship sailed into Marseilles.

I took Madame Han's letter out and smelled the banana leaves I had wrapped it in. I started thinking what I would be doing if I were in Saigon right then, but I realized that there was nothing left there, not Madame Han's house or Spare Parts or Tomtom or André and Su-Su. I wondered what happened to Yigah the horse. Did he find some other family's bedroom to visit and did he give them dreams of the future too?

Gypsies lived in the train station. Gypsy women leaned against pillars and breast-fed their children. The men rolled cigarettes. For belts on their pants they used rope. Their hair was as black as their eyes. When they slept, they lay back on the floor with their hands behind their heads, looking up like the ceiling of the train station was a starlit sky.

. . .

The first thing I smelled when I got off the train in Biarritz was the sea. I could not see it from the platform of the station, but I could smell it.

I walked to the beach first. The sun had been up only a few hours and already people had spread out blankets on the sand. Down the beach, toward where boats were moored, men hauled in nets filled with silver fish. When I faced the shore I saw the building

I had seen in my dream, when Yigah had slept in my room. Behind the columns of the building people shopped, buying peaches and lettuce and fish, and rabbits and chickens hanging from poles.

I looked for my uncle. My mother had talked of Biarritz like it was a small town, but there were so many people on holiday here that it seemed more crowded than the first night of Tet on the streets in Saigon.

I looked at what other girls wore. Some were built like Leandri and wore skirts made of thin cloth, and you could see their hip-bones showing through. I had always wanted to wear an ao dai and cuan pants when I lived in Saigon, but now I wanted to see how I would look in one of those thin skirts.

I looked at all the people on the beach, and I thought if I had to I would sleep on the beach at night and in the mornings I would wade in the shallows.

By eleven o'clock I decided it was time to try and find my uncle, so I asked directions to his street.

At the door of a house that was carved with wooden squares, I knocked and I waited. Carnations grew in window boxes along the street. Small dogs leaned out windows and took turns barking at each other. Finally a man answered the door. He had a beard and a mustache, and he was wearing a striped silk robe. I knew he was my uncle Robert.

"I am Tian, Marcelle's daughter," I said. The man who looked at me was the same man I had seen in my dream. I realized then that he may have dreamt of me also.

"Come in, come in," he said. Once inside, he stood me in the middle of the room and then he walked backwards and said, "Let me look at you!"

"I don't look much like my mother," I said.

He sat down on the sofa and put his head in his hands. "You've come to tell me she's dead, haven't you?" he said.

"Not at all, she's in Saigon, did you get our letter?"

"Oh, thank God," he said, but then he started to cry. I looked at the pictures on his hutch. There were pictures of my mother I had never seen before. She was standing next to her brother at the beach in Biarritz. She was smiling. I thought how when she was that age she didn't even know my father existed.

My uncle wiped his nose on his sleeve. "Look at me, like an old woman crying," he said. "Come." He took my hand and led me to the kitchen. He pulled out cheese and bread and eggs. "Tell me everything," he said while he started to cook.

When I finished telling him, he was crying again. I told him about Yigah the horse and how he lived in the house and wouldn't let Monsieur Han near his own bed. Uncle Robert laughed.

"That's good," he said. "I like those kind of stories."

Uncle Robert's bathrobe had slid open down his chest and I could see gray hairs and a fat belly. When we finished our eggs, he slapped his belly and said, "I'm almost ready for lunch."

We took a walk through town. He showed me the Casino Bellevue and said he had been robbed there a number of times. Surf crashed up on the rocks. I asked if it was always this rough, and he said no, sometimes the sea was like a sleeping dog and you couldn't kick it to get it to stand up or turn out a wave. I asked if it was true that his father walked into the sea to die, and Uncle Robert said it was true, and then he asked how would I like to try fried dough and chocolate. The dough stuck to my teeth and Uncle Robert said what I needed to cure that was some grilled sardines, so we sat at an outdoor café and he ordered me a plate and he ordered himself a plate and he ate the sardines with his fingers and I ate the sardines with my fingers and he said how his sister was lucky to have a daughter who took after the French side of the family and enjoyed all of what France had to offer.

Uncle Robert had eyebrows that looked like they had been combed upward.

"Do you have a wife?" I said.

"Yes, she's visiting friends in Spain," he said.

I told him the story about Mr. Spain, that he was from Italy and not Spain and that he had a pig in his town who lived in the bar and advised the people on how to live their lives.

When I told the story I thought of the last time I saw Mr. Spain, a ball of flame falling into the ocean, still holding his wicker suitcase.

"That's another good story," Uncle Robert said.

We walked all over town, and Uncle Robert said all the boys were looking at me and that he could see he would have to beat them off with sticks.

"Cochon!" he yelled at one man.

"Cochon, really," he said to me. "He was looking at your arms, I saw him. The nerve, with me walking with you too!" Then Uncle Robert began to yell "Cochon!" at everyone, even when no one was looking at me, and I would laugh and my uncle would say, "You see that, he was looking at your ear, the nerve, in front of your uncle." Or he would say, "You see that, he was looking at your pinkie finger, I'll show him," and if it was evening and he had his cane, he would lift it up and shake it, yelling "Cochon!"

He showed me how to gamble at the casino. Every time he lost money he would lift his cane and yell, "Robbers, thieves!" and then he would feel his heart and say, "I have to leave." Walking home, he would buy the fried dough dipped in chocolate.

"I feel much better now," he would say.

On the street he would say, "Ah, breathe with me," and he would inhale deeply and I would inhale deeply and we'd walk to the beach and he'd bend over in the water and cup his hands and lift the water and rinse his face. I thought maybe he did this because he wanted to be close to his father, who had drowned at sea. They had never found his body.

Uncle Robert taught me how to swim. Side by side we would swim along the shoreline. At first, when I would get tired, he'd tow me by my hair, saying it wouldn't hurt, and it didn't. Then, later, I became a stronger swimmer and we would swim for an hour and I would try to put my arms in the water at the same time he put his arms in the water, and I would try to kick at the same speed he was kicking.

When the waves were big he taught me how to hold my arms out and face the shore on my belly, riding the waves straight onto the sand. Some afternoons he slept on the beach and I put pebbles in his navel while he snored. When he stood up the pebbles would fall to the sand and he would say, "What's this? The sky must be falling."

...

Later that month, my amah and Poulet and finally my mother all made it to Uncle Robert's house. They came one evening when it was raining. Uncle Robert and I picked them up at the train. When I hugged them I thought their hair smelled like banana leaves, or maybe it was the rain I smelled. My amah cried and wiped her face and said it was just drops of rain.

When my mother came she stepped off the train wearing a red hat shaped like a saucer. I wondered where she had bought it, and with what money. The hat's netting covered her face, and when I went to kiss her it tickled my lips. I could not see her eyes very well through the netting, but I thought she might have been crying. I had to go collect her bags, and I was thankful for that, because when Uncle Robert hugged my mother, I knew everyone would be crying.

My mother would walk around Uncle Robert's house using his cane, pointing with it out the windows, saying someday my father would be back and we'd see him walking down that street.

One night I heard Uncle Robert talking to my mother in the kitchen, telling her maybe she should begin to consider that her husband was not alive anymore.

"Maybe that is the way to proceed," he said.

"Fuck you," I heard my mother say to him. "That's the attitude I'll take to proceed," she said. I saw my mother pick up the cane and walk upstairs with it. I knew she was going to the window to sit and watch. I heard her cough.

"Get some sleep," my uncle yelled to her from below.

"Fuck you!" my mother yelled.

"And fuck you too!" he yelled.

"Yes, well fuck you back!" she yelled.

It was just as she said this that Uncle Robert's wife walked in the door, having returned from her visit to friends in Spain.

Her name was Laurette. When she saw me, she put her hand on my face. "You must be the beautiful Tian," she said.

Uncle Robert saw his wife and then he yelled up the stairs, "Fuck you twice!"

"Hello, mon cheri," Laurette said to Uncle Robert, and kissed him.

"Fuck you thrice!" my mother yelled.

"Yes, well fuck —"

Uncle Robert tried to say more but Laurette covered his mouth and she yelled up the stairs, "Hey, Marcelle, come down here and say hello. I'm starving, let's eat some ham with butter and bread."

Laurette took my hand and we went to the kitchen and she started to make sandwiches. When my mother came down the stairs she kissed Laurette, and Laurette hugged her and told her how good it was to see her and to see her daughters.

Uncle Robert walked in behind my mother and pulled out a chair for her to sit in, saying, "A chair for Queen Fuck."

Laurette had brought bracelets made of gold that she gave to us after we ate the sandwiches. Mine was a charm bracelet with lanterns and horses and carriages hanging off it.

At night Laurette walked in her sleep down the street in her robe knocking on doors, asking neighbors where she could find a needle and thread. Uncle Robert followed her in his striped silk bathrobe, having heard from a physician that it was harmful to wake a sleepwalker while she was walking.

"She needs tiger's milk before she sleeps," my amah said, and so my amah spent the week trying to find a shop in Biarritz that sold tiger's milk, but all she could find was a shop that had a tiger skin, so she had Uncle Robert buy it. At night Laurette sat drinking milk at the kitchen table with the tiger skin covering her shoulders.

"Will this work?" Laurette asked.

"It depends on the tiger," my amah said.

That night Laurette did not sleepwalk in the streets, she only walked in her sleep inside the house, opening closet doors and bedroom doors, asking out loud, "Where is the glue?"

In the morning my amah said it may have been too old a tiger or a tiger who had died a senseless death and not a tiger who had died roaring.

When my mother was strong enough to walk outside, she went to the post office, looking for ways to find my father.

"There should be some kind of list," she said before she left the house.

Uncle Robert drank coffee and played dominoes in a club where no women were allowed. When he came home he would sleep on the couch, and Poulet would climb onto him and twist his eyebrows so that one pointed up and the other pointed down.

One day my mother came home from the post office saying she met a woman there who had lost her husband during the war too, and what the woman had done, out of desperation, was send a bottle with a message in it out to sea, and that's how the woman found her husband.

"Get to work, children," my mother said to us, and she made us find bottles and write notes and she took us down to Le Basta, where the small boats were tied up, and she rented a boat and I rowed us out to sea until she said, "Stop, this is good," and we threw the corked bottles out over the water with messages on them that read, "If anyone knows the whereabouts of Major General Yeu, please tell him his family is living in Biarritz, France."

Later Laurette took us to the market and we bought pigs' cheeks for dinner, and when we ate them my amah said we would have dreams of mud.

One morning my mother stopped coughing and she didn't

need the cane. She came down the stairs wearing one of Laurette's suits and said she was going to find work.

"Bravo," Uncle Robert said.

"Oh, fuck you," my mother said, and she left the house. When she came back she had a job working for a marchioness. She ran the woman's house, making sure the servants cleaned what they had to clean and cooked what they had to cook.

· · ·

It became too cold to swim, so Uncle Robert took me for walks in the hills and we looked for mushrooms, which Laurette would fix with stews.

I started school and girls called me half-breed and told me to go back to China where I belonged.

I made one friend, named Rebecca. She lived down the street. She took me to a party and we locked ourselves in the bathroom and sat with our backs against the claw-footed bathtub and smoked cigarettes and she told me how she was going to be a model someday, so I told her I knew a woman named Leandri who ate cotton balls dipped in olive oil so that she could fool her stomach into thinking it felt full.

· · ·

At night figs fell on the roof.

"That's the Buddha walking," my amah said.

I dreamt I was my father and I was watching the woman take off her head and start brushing her hair.

In the morning I went to the roof and collected the figs and we ate them with our rolls and coffee.

My mother looked in the mirror and said she was getting old. "From now on, don't walk down the street with me. People will know how old I am if I have a daughter seventeen," she said. My mother took Poulet to her bridge games and her luncheons. I shopped with Laurette, took walks with my uncle and spent time with Rebecca.

We had snow in Biarritz. It fell overnight. Fat flakes fell inches thick. In the morning the temperature rose and we were wearing shorts and throwing snowballs at each other. Everywhere there was the sound of the snow melting and crashing off eaves.

My amah climbed in her bed and said she was sick. We brought her a doctor, but she bit his hand when he tried to feel the glands in her neck.

"I just need to sleep," she said, and slept for four days. She did not eat food or drink water. When she woke up she walked down to the sea and sat in the shallows and rubbed sand on her arms and her legs.

"Where am I?" she said to us.

"The beach," we said.

"In China?" she said.

"No, in France," we said.

She laughed. "I want to go home."

"No, there is no home," we said.

"What's this?" she said, pointing to the hole in her leg.

"It's a hole," we said. She laughed harder and so did we. Tears fell down her face. We held her hands.

When she stood up she looked at me and said, "You were such a cute baby, I remember how lovely the back of your neck was. Let me see it." I moved my hair away for her to see.

Uncle Robert had told me that as you get older you forget things from when you were young. When I asked him what kinds of things, he said from what he could remember it was people's faces he was forgetting.

It had been two years since I had seen my father. I walked through markets thinking maybe I had just passed him and he didn't know who I was and I didn't know who he was. In my dreams he took the form of the Japanese general, or Yigah the horse, or Philippe, a boy from the boys' school in Biarritz, who said he heard that Chinks didn't have hair between their legs and that he'd like for me to lift my skirt so he could see if that was true.

In the morning, still sweaty around the nape of my neck from the bad dreams, I ate my bread and butter and drank my coffee, wondering how much longer dreams like this could last and hoping that one day my mother would come home with news that my father was dead so maybe I could get some sleep.

I stayed home from school because I had a fever. Laurette pulled out a box of photographs she had from the day my mother and father got married.

She handed me a picture of my mother and father standing in a shaft of light coming in through a window while they said their wedding vows. The photograph was yellow around the edges and it looked overexposed. My mother's and father's faces looked as if they had been photographed just as a bright light or a bomb had exploded. If I hadn't recognized my father's long legs and my mother's figure, I would have passed over the photograph, thinking it showed some distant relatives married years ago, when camera quality was poor and couples were wed in modest clothes and quiet company on hilltops near their homes.

"I can't see his face," I said to Laurette, and I handed her back the photograph.

I went to school and stood outside the fence, calling to Rebecca. She had long, chestnut-colored straight hair that she never tied back or braided but always kept loose and when she ran over to me the sun almost made it look red, and I thought I would have liked to have her hair instead of my own black hair, which stayed the same in sunlight as it did in darkness.

"Come with me to Marseilles," I said to Rebecca through the fence.

She turned around to see if the nuns were watching, and since they weren't, she climbed the fence and jumped to the road. I grabbed her hand and we started running, heading for town.

I bought the tickets and we sat on the train. It wasn't until we had gone for miles and Rebecca had lit a cigarette that she turned to me and said, "What's in Marseilles?"

"My father," I said.

Rebecca grabbed my arm. "Really?"

"No. But the consulate's there and maybe they can tell me he's dead."

Rebecca looked out the window at the passing fields and haystacks.

"Look at him," she said, and pointed to a man without a shirt pitching hay.

· · ·

Marseilles was cool, and leaves had already dropped from the trees. The clouds hid the sun.

We waited on line at the consulate for three hours. When we finally reached the window, a small woman helped me. She was so small that I thought I was talking to a child, and I wondered how she could possibly know if my father was dead. As I gave her my father's name, she wrote it down on a piece of paper — *Major General Yeu*. I wished she hadn't written it down, because seeing it in black ink made me think it possible he was alive.

She went over to some shelves and stood on a ladder, to look through files. She brought a thick folder back to me.

"I found him," she said. "He's on the missing persons list."

"Well, then you didn't really find him, did you?" Rebecca said over my shoulder.

"How many on that list end up being dead after all?" I asked the small woman as I noticed how short her fingers were and wondered how she held the fat files with them.

"It's difficult to say," the woman said.

"No," Rebecca said, "it's difficult to hear. Just tell her."

The woman looked up at me. "Only a small number off this list are found alive — maybe ten percent, maybe less," she said.

"How old is that list?" I asked.

"It just came in," she said.

"Then it's safe to say I can think of him as dead," I said.

The woman closed the file and went back to her ladder, and

from where she stood on it she said, "From a report from such a place, yes, it is safe to say that most of them are dead."

On the train back to Biarritz, Rebecca scanned the land for signs of the man she earlier saw pitching hay without his shirt.

"Maybe now he's got his shirt back on because of the cold and I won't recognize him," she said.

"Yes. He'll be hard to find," I said.

. . .

Uncle Robert took me to hunt for mushrooms.

"These will kill you," he said, knocking over a mushroom with his cane, exposing the gills.

. . .

My mother was traveling for the marchioness. She would take planes to northern France and to Paris and come back the next day. When we asked, she said she was sent to search for objects for the marchioness's house. She went to Flanders for curtains and the Loire valley for vases. She begrudged the time spent traveling, saying how it was impossible to check with the consulate on the status of her husband when she was always rushing to and from the airport.

"He's dead," I told her.

She slapped my face. She wore a ring with a green stone and a thick, coiled band, and the ring always turned on her finger, so when she slapped me the stone hit my teeth, making the inside of my mouth bleed.

I spit the blood out onto my mother's silk shirt. She slapped me again and threw me down onto the sofa, where she held me by twisting my hair. Laurette walked in and put her hand on my mother's hand and pulled it up, saying, "Marcelle, let's go, you'll be late for your plane."

That night I slept with the tiger skin instead of blankets. My amah tucked the four legs under me.

I dreamt I could take my head off and my mother was brushing my hair.

"This is wrong," I said to my amah in the morning and gave her back the tiger skin.

"All right. Do you want roast rabbit with garlic mayonnaise for lunch?" my amah said.

"Will I have dreams of the garden?"

"No, but your breath will stink," she said.

. . .

Poulet held on to Uncle Robert's leg and he took walks with her around the house, saying out loud, "Where is Poulet? Has anyone seen that little monkey?"

. . .

I fell down a flight of stairs in school. I heard that when the nuns lifted my head off the ground I was saying, "The Japanese."

My amah put cold tea bags on top of my eyes.

"Will I see China?" I said.

"No, just leaves, but in the morning your eyes won't be swollen," she said.

She fed me noodle soup.

"Will this make me live long?" I asked.

"No, it will fill your belly," she said.

She gave me a necklace made of shells.

"Does this call the dolphins?" I said.

"No. The boys will like it, though," she said.

I lay back in bed.

"I need to be alone," I said.

She turned out the light and left me in the dark.

Rebecca came with chocolates. She sat in a chair next to my bed.

"I'll open it for you," she said, untying the string around the box of chocolates.

"What's happening at school?" I said.

Rebecca took a bite out of each of the chocolates and then put it back in its wrapper.

"We're having lessons about college. The sisters are warning us against dating college boys. I asked why, and Sister Dolores took me into the hall and told me there was a name for girls like me."

"What's the name?" I said.

"I don't know, she never told me," Rebecca said. "I've got to go. Feel better." She left the box of half-eaten chocolates at the foot of my bed.

Laurette came into the room.

"Get up, get dressed," she said.

"No, I'm sick," I said.

"We're going to Sofia's," she said.

"Sofia's?"

. . .

Sofia's was an antiques shop that smelled of dust. The shop was so crowded that to make room for vases and lamps, Sofia stored them in other, larger antiques, like caldrons and wooden chests.

Sofia smelled like a gardenia.

"What can I help you ladies with?" she said. She took a stray hair and tucked it in with the rest of her hair, which had been combed back into a chignon.

"Just let us look around," Laurette said.

"Of course," Sofia said, and she went back to her office. Now the room only smelled of dust and age and mildew.

When I asked Laurette what she was looking for, she said it didn't matter, she just liked coming to Sofia's because being around all the old things made her feel young.

I sat down on an ottoman and watched Laurette lift up boxes and old wooden toys. I did not think there was anything there I wanted to touch. Dust was getting into my nose and making it itch.

"I'll meet you outside," I said to Laurette, and started for the door, but on the way out I stopped.

On the wall there hung an oriental carpet. Symbols for fire, earth, water, air and metal were woven into it. It was not the carpet from the Great Room, it was smaller. I smelled gardenias, and then I realized Sofia was standing next to me.

"There are moth holes in it," she said.

There were not only moth holes. In some places the thread was so worn that there was no wool left, just the weave of the carpet itself.

Laurette said since I was feeling sick, she would buy me the carpet as a gift.

At home I laid the carpet on the living room floor. My amah walked in and saw it, and she went and stood on air and said, "I'll eat my dinner here tonight." She did not move, even long after dinner.

Sitting on fire, I took Poulet on my lap and braided her hair. I started to whistle "Parlez-moi d'amour." Uncle Robert, sitting on the sofa, started to whistle it with me. Then he stood up and asked me to dance. My amah started to sing, so while she sat on air, we danced in circles around her, moving to the rhythm of her song. Curled up with her hands under her head, Poulet fell asleep on earth.

That night I dreamt I was in the Great Room looking out the window, and I could see my father coming down the mountain toward us. My mother stood next to me and she kept straightening her skirt and asking me if her hair looked combed and did she look too old.

CHRISTMAS WAS COMING. SHOP OWNERS WRAPPED OUR packages with colored ribbon instead of string. At the casino, chips were changed from black and red to blue and green. My uncle started winning.

"This always happens when they change the chips," he said.

People were trading holiday meal recipes. Laurette wanted to try boar, my amah venison.

"Eating deer," she said, "will bring good luck."

We settled on duck.

"Cured," my amah said.

"No, roasted," Laurette said.

We settled on roasted. Laurette said this was France and the French roasted their duck on holidays and that was that and my amah said that when Laurette came to China she'd make her try cured.

My mother brought home truffles the marchioness had given her as a Christmas gift.

I sent a card to Madame Han with angels on the front. My mother told me it would never reach her and that I'd have better luck stuffing a Christmas greeting in a wine bottle and sending it off on an outgoing wave at sea.

We ate our duck on Christmas Eve. Uncle Robert added leaves to the wooden table, giving us room for all the dishes. Laurette spread out a lace cloth woven with flowers and lit candles scented with clove.

My mother wore a velvet dress that showed the bones around her collar.

Uncle Robert had us all hold hands when we sat down at the table. He was about to say grace when there was a knock on the door.

I remember looking at the table, thinking how much food we

had and how the knock at the door must be the church, asking for food for the hungry.

We heard footsteps and I expected to see Uncle Robert coming back to finish grace.

Instead, my father walked into the room.

He stood looking at us from the doorway. We looked at him.

"Merry Christmas," he said.

"Good God," Laurette said.

"Papa?" Poulet said.

"Yeu!" my mother said, and she stood up and just as she stood she started to fall, fainting. My father reached her just before she hit the floor. With his arm around her back, and her velvet dress showing the bones around her collar, my mother and father looked as if they were dancing and my father had just dipped my mother backwards.

. . .

It was Christmas Eve of 1950 and my father had found us. There was so much news for him to tell that it wasn't until six the next morning that we finished the last bite of the duck and cleared the table.

Before I went to bed I kissed my father. He smelled like soap or shaving cream. I wondered if he still thought of the woman who took off her head and brushed her hair.

I thought I would sleep the whole day, but I woke a few hours later. I heard my mother sobbing and my father telling her everything would be all right.

"I'm home, I'm home, I'm home," he kept saying to her, until she must have fallen asleep in his arms.

The next day we did not go out. We stayed mostly on the sofa — me, my mother, Poulet and my father. My mother lay next to my father on the sofa and Poulet sat on my father's belly and I sat so my mother's and my father's legs rested on my lap and I listened to my father.

His stories were all about people we did not know. There was a battle where a man lost both his hands and still managed to pull a trigger with his toe, killing ten Communists before he himself died from such a loss of blood. There was a time when my father stayed in the hospital after he had been shot in the arm.

"They served chocolate pudding and read to me at night," he said, smiling.

Then there was the time he lived for months in the mountains with the Montagnards. He ate mice and roots to stay alive.

"How did you cook them?" my amah asked about the mice.

"We didn't, we couldn't start fires," he said. He asked me to rub his feet, and I did, and I wondered what dreams mice gave you.

My father took a job at the consulate in Marseilles. On weekends he stayed with us, and we would pick him up at the train station. We never had trouble finding him in a crowd — he was tall and could be seen over the tops of everyone's head.

My mother, when she could, went with us to the train station. She'd make us get there early, and then she would say, "Maybe he's not coming this weekend." Or she would say, "Do I look all right? How is my lip rouge? Damn that train," she would say.

When my father finally stepped from the train my mother would say, "Thank you, God," under her breath and then she would start to run toward him, and then slow herself down, touch her hand to her hair and just walk.

After a time he bought a Studebaker. When he first drove it from Marseilles he told us he was coming on the train, and my mother nearly beat up a conductor, demanding to know where my father was, saying he must have come on the last train. Then my father drove up to the station platform, honking the horn and dispersing the crowd.

He took us for a drive on the beach. A policeman stopped him, and my father told him how wonderful a Studebaker was and he invited the policeman to drive it himself. So the policeman got behind the wheel and drove us through town, honking the horn and speeding through stop signs, yelling at other drivers to move their cars a little faster or he would fucking arrest them.

One day we drove to a hilltop and had a picnic. My father took a nap under a tree and spoke in his sleep.

"Get it off me," he said, and he pulled at his wrists while he slept.

My mother tried to wake him, kissing him on the lips and smoothing down his hair, but he did not wake up and instead he grabbed my mother by the head, and with his eyes wide open he said to her, "I will kill you."

For a while, my mother believed that what my father had said to her in his sleep was true.

We told her he was just having a dream, but she said, "He was looking into my eyes, not yours. I know he was talking to me."

She figured that while he was away in Marseilles during the week that he was planning her death.

"There's another woman he wants to be with," she said. She looked at herself in the mirror and rubbed cream under her eyes while I sat on her bed.

"Move away so that I don't have to see you when I'm looking at myself in the mirror," she said. "A daughter should know better than to flaunt her beauty in front of her mother."

I moved away. I stood by the door and held on to the wood of the frame. Her dress was too tight around the hips and the breasts.

"Aren't you going to change your dress?" I asked.

"No, why?" she said.

"I don't know. Never mind," I said.

"You think it's too young for me, don't you?" she said.

I shook my head no. I started to go down the stairs. She called after me.

"Wait until you get to be my age, then we'll see how you dress, we'll see how easy it is for you to look beautiful for your husband."

I ran down to the street. Uncle Robert had just started out with his cane on his afternoon walk. I caught up with him. He took my hand without saying a word. We walked that way for a long time.

"I knew a man who took out someone's eye with a cane," I finally said to him as we walked.

"I could do the same," Uncle Robert said, and lifted up his cane.

"Then they came and took out *his* eye," I said.

"Ah, an eye for an eye," Uncle Robert said.

We walked to the beach. It was a warm weekend and people had tables set out on the sand for their afternoon meals.

"His name was Michel Riquelme," I said to Uncle Robert.

He nodded his head. "A friend of the family's?"

"A friend of mine," I said.

"I see," said Uncle Robert and then he held my hand toward the sea and said, "Go test the water, see if it's cold."

ONE WEEKEND MY FATHER TOOK ME TO A PARTY. MY mother didn't want to go.

"I look too old," she said to me. "You go with him instead."

We drove to the party in his Studebaker. He brought along two new German shepherds, Bonnie and Clyde. He joked and said that someday he would lead an irresponsible life, not worry about family and go to America, carry a gun and rob banks to pay for his meals. It was raining, and the rain was pouring down hard.

"Watch this," he said, and he stopped the car, opened the door and sent the dogs out to stand on a sea wall in the pouring rain. The rain came down so fast it made their eyes shut.

"They won't move from there until I tell them to move," he said. My father lit a cigarette and kept watching with the car door open.

"Papa?" I said.

"Aren't they great?" he said, still watching his dogs.

"Papa?" I said again, and tugged on the sleeve of his tuxedo jacket.

"What?" He turned to me, breathing out his cigarette smoke so it floated between us.

"Did you miss me when you were gone?" I asked.

"What? Don't mumble. What did you say?"

"Nothing, let's go," I said.

"Do you see them? Would you do that for me?" he said, pointing to the dogs standing in the pouring rain on the sea wall.

"Would you?" he said. "Go on, let's see." He opened the car door and started to pull me out, but I held on to the door handle.

"Release!" he said, pulling me hard so that I let go. I stood by the car looking down at the ground in the rain.

My father pushed me toward the sea wall, but he slipped and fell to one knee. He did not stand up for a very long time, and when he did, he went back to the car and sat behind the steering wheel.

I got in out of the rain and sat back on the passenger side. My father put his arms all the way around the steering wheel as if he were tired.

"I used to dream about the woman who took off her head. Over the years, in my dreams, it was not just her head she took off, but her arms and her legs, so that finally, when I last dreamed of her recently, there was nothing left of her to dream about except that she was once there, and I woke up happier than I could ever remember being." My father looked at me, and he continued.

"One morning I want to wake up and I want to know I don't have a wife who needs my love, or children who call me Father, or a country that calls me its soldier. Is that possible?" he said and then he looked out at the windshield, blurred with rain.

I leaned over my father, to be close to the open door on his side.

"Bonnie! Clyde!" I yelled as loudly as I could. The dogs jumped off the sea wall and started toward us, but my father yelled "Stop!" and the dogs stopped so quickly it looked as if they had been jerked on a leash from behind.

"I'll call them myself," he said, and then he called the dogs and they jumped into the car and he started to drive again.

I could hear the dogs in the back seat licking the rainwater off their fur. Clyde put his head on my father's shoulder. My father turned and kissed the dog's face as he drove.

"Who is my good dog?" my father said.

. . .

At the party, I danced with every soldier who asked me to dance. They asked me questions, but I would not answer them. I am sure they thought I was dumb. My father introduced me to guests and they said to him, "Isn't she beautiful. How lucky you are." They smiled at me and I looked around the room.

While I was standing with some privates circled around me, my father came up and said to me, "We have to dance."

He took me to the floor and we danced. He was a beautiful dancer. People made room for us and stood by and watched. So close to his chest, I could smell his cologne. It was like lemons. I felt his heartbeat and I felt his breath on my hair. I could tell he was looking around at everyone and smiling. I did not want to trip or miss a step. When the song ended he led me back to the circle of privates.

"Be ready to leave soon," he said to me. I nodded.

Back in the Studebaker I pretended to be asleep while he drove and smoked and drank from the glass of gin that he had taken from the party and set on the dashboard. In the back, Clyde was whimpering in his sleep. I wondered if he was dreaming that he was chasing rabbits for fun or that he was being made to stand out in the rain.

That night my father slept on the sofa downstairs. While he slept I sat on the symbol for water and watched his chest move up and down. He had unbuttoned his shirt and I could see his chest was smooth and hairless and dark, not like Uncle Robert's chest, which was a tangle of gray and black hair. I heard a noise, and when I turned around my mother was standing behind me, in her bathrobe, watching him too.

"He'll kill us both," she said, and she turned away and went back up the stairs.

I did not know if she meant he would kill my mother and me or he would kill my mother and himself.

In the morning Laurette came in waving her hand in front of her face, saying, "Phew, gin," and slapped my father's feet to wake him. He only rolled over into the sofa cushions. I could hear him call his dogs' names.

The dogs heard and came running and jumped on him, pinning his back, licking his ears. I could hear my father laugh into the cushions.

He drank his coffee while walking toward the door, ready to get in the car and drive back to Marseilles. My mother, already made up with lip rouge and eyeliner, ran after him in her bathrobe and stood in the doorway.

"But so soon, you just got home yesterday," she said.

"Bonnie! Clyde! Come on, let's get going," he said, and the dogs ran out the door after him, knocking into my mother's legs as they went.

During the week my mother took off two days to take the train up to Marseilles to surprise my father. She found him in bed with a Frenchwoman. My mother later told us that he called her Minou for short and had introduced her to my mother there in his bedroom, and the woman, my mother said, did not even have the decency to lift up the sheet to her chin when she extended her hand for my mother to shake it and Minou's breasts were out for all of the city to see, my mother said. And then my mother added, "By the way, I did not shake the whore's hand."

When we asked my mother what she did do, she said she went into the kitchen, started some coffee and waited for the two to get dressed.

"It turns out Minou was a girl he dated before we ever got married," my mother said.

"You made them coffee?" Laurette asked.

"Yes. We had rolls too. He has mice. I saw the droppings on the shelves. I told him he'd be better off with a cat than those two dogs."

"That pig!" Laurette said.

"Really, he should have someone in to clean the place," my mother said.

"No, that's not what I mean, how could he do this to you?" Laurette said.

"Oh, well perhaps he loves her, that's how," my mother said.

Laurette made my mother go lie down on the sofa.

"She's in shock," Laurette said to me.

"It's a nice apartment, though, such tall windows in the living room that let out onto the city. God, we'll need yards and yards of material just to make curtains," my mother said.

"You're not making anything for him," Laurette said.

"Not me, of course, we'll have them custom made in the Côte," my mother said. She lay on the sofa, staring up at the ceiling. My amah came in with the tiger skin and laid it over her.

"Get this off me," my mother said. My amah tucked the legs of the skin under my mother.

"Get it off!" my mother yelled. My amah felt my mother's forehead. My mother knocked my amah's hand away and shrieked, "Get it off me, now!"

My amah ran backwards a few feet. My mother got up, threw the tiger skin onto the floor and left the house in her bare feet.

"Let her go," Laurette said.

. . .

She did not come back that night, and she did not come back the next day. Laurette thought maybe she had taken the train back to Marseilles, so we called there, but no one answered the telephone.

Uncle Robert and I went out to look for her. He took his cane and we walked through parks and alleys and we walked the beach, but we did not find her.

Uncle Robert looked out at the sea. "Soon it'll be warm enough to swim again," he said. I walked to the water and leaned over and put my hand in it.

"It's warm enough now," I said.

"No, you'd freeze to death," Uncle Robert said.

I took off my clothes and ran into the water.

"Wait, now Tian, stop that," my uncle said, trying to run after me in the water.

I dove into a wave. The water was so cold it stopped my breath when I surfaced. I shot up from the water and the first thing I noticed was a terrible pain in my head. I saw my uncle screaming at me, but I could not hear him, the waves were breaking too loudly. I thought about my grandfather and how he one day just walked into the sea. I turned around and faced the waves. I started walking. It is difficult to walk on sand when the sea is choppy and the waves are coming one after the other. I held my breath as the waves hit and I tried to stand still. I decided that on the day my grandfather killed himself the water must have been calm, and more like a lake than a sea.

When I finally came out of the water, my uncle ran up to me and hit my backside with his cane.

"Damn you, don't do that to me," he yelled. I put my clothes back on while he continued to tell me how wrong I had been. I tried to comb my salted hair with my fingers.

"We're going home," my uncle said. He grabbed my arm and tried to hurry me through the sand.

At home, I learned that Laurette and my amah had found my mother. She had been at a bar, face-down in her own vomit. She now lay on the sofa, talking and mumbling, shaking her head from side to side. My amah had covered her with the tiger skin again.

I slept on the oriental carpet with my head on fire and my feet on air so that if she woke up in the middle of the night someone would be there to help her to the toilet or bring her a drink of water.

All night she talked in her sleep and her talking became part of my dreams and I dreamt the Japanese had come to Biarritz and they were now in our kitchen and we were giving them coffee and rolls and I could see their long sabers poking into the wooden floor and in my dream I thought that my mother better put on shoes or else she would get cut.

I went to school the next day and Rebecca told me she had heard they found my mother in a bar in a pile of her own vomit. At lunch I left the grounds of the school and went to make a phone call to my father. A woman answered the phone. I hung up. I tried again after looking out the window awhile at people walking down the street. This time my father answered.

"Hello," I said.

"Who's this?" he said.

"Tian," I said. In the background I could hear his dogs barking.

"Shut up!" I heard my father yell to them. I held the phone

away from my ear while he yelled and I thought about hanging up the phone and going back to school, or to the beach to swim in the freezing water again.

"Tian?" my father said.

"Yes, Papa?" I said.

"This is not a good time, call back later," he said. I hung up the phone.

"Fuck you," I said. I walked out onto the street. A man passing by stared at me and then made a kissing noise with his lips.

I did not go to school any more that week. I would get my clothes on in the morning and I would go to the beach or I would sit in the park. I saw Rebecca once, when she was walking home from school. I waved, but I don't think she saw me.

When the weekend came my mother made us go with her to the train station and wait for my father. We asked her, if he were to come, then why wouldn't he have driven his car? When he did not come, she said he would next weekend. I told her I didn't think he was going to come to Biarritz anymore and she told me that what I knew was very little compared to what she knew.

"Wasn't I right? Didn't he come back alive from China?" she said.

I looked at her eyes. There were pouches under them I had never noticed before. I wondered what my amah had to cure pouches like those. I thought maybe tea leaves or rabbit or monkey paws.

My mother woke up the next morning saying it was Rat Day. She took a broom and went all over the house banging on shelves and cupboards, making china bowls and plates shatter, and screaming, "Come out, come out, wherever you are!"

Nothing came out. Laurette woke up and ran to my mother and tried to take the broom away from her. My mother held on.

"Not in my house," Laurette said, but my mother did not listen. All morning she tried to drive out rats that did not exist from inside cupboards and behind walls.

"Banzai!" my mother yelled.

We left my mother in the house. Laurette and Uncle Robert and Poulet, and my amah and I took a drive in the country. Everyone got out of the car to walk in the woods, but my amah stayed put, sitting with her back up against the trunk of a tree, looking up at the sky.

"What are you doing?" we said.

"Watching the sun move," she said.

We found more mushrooms. My uncle turned each one over with his cane.

"Will this one kill you?" we asked. "Will that one?"

My uncle shook his head. He did not know.

We played a game. My amah held up an orange.

"Guess how many seeds," she said. We all guessed and the ones who lost had to help my mother clean up the plates and cups and bowls she had broken trying to find rats to kill.

I had guessed right, so I did not go home to help the others clean the house. Instead I went to Rebecca's house. She wasn't there, but her brother told me about a cocktail party she would be at that night, and he invited me along.

I did not find Rebecca at the party. I looked in all the rooms and she wasn't there. I was about to leave when an American leaning against a wall asked me to dance.

There was no music playing.

"Dance?" I said.

"I know the foxtrot," he said, and he took me up by the arms and started to dance with me in the room, while people drinking drinks and having conversations stopped what they were doing, watched and laughed.

He asked if we could take a walk along the beach and I said yes. In the dark, with just lights from the casino and moonlight shining down on us, I wasn't shy and I looked at his face and I looked at his hands. His nose was long, with a bump on the bridge, and I thought how different it was from my father's straight nose. I imagined years later he would wear glasses and the glasses would rest there on that bump on the bridge of his nose. His hands were broad and the veins on them were raised as if he had twice the blood running through him than any other man.

His name was Paul and he was in France because he wanted to travel, and the only way he knew how to do it without upsetting his parents was to join the air force, which he did after the war was over, and got stationed here.

I asked him what it was like to fly a plane, and he answered the hell if he knew, he was afraid of heights and worked at the consulate stamping passports at a desk.

I stayed late at the beach that night while he told me stories of his family, how his father was a chemist and his mother baked pies. They lived in a two-story house in Illinois. Paul had raised guinea pigs as a child. He had a sister, her name was Pat. He had broken his leg jumping off a stair when he was ten but told everyone he had broken it falling off a motorcycle after hitting a car head-on. He was afraid of snakes and dying and his mother's meat loaf.

After midnight I dove into the sea and he stayed in the water waist-deep, whistling American songs, old ballads and folksongs. His whistling was the most beautiful I had ever heard, and I stopped swimming and I treaded water and I strained to listen above the sound of the small breaking waves and the sound of the casino's betting crowd.

. . .

When I walked back into the house from the beach, my amah was on the carpet, sitting on metal. When I asked her what she was doing she said, "Remember when I had you wear a sheet to cover up your breasts?"

"Yes, I remember," I said.

She did not say anything else, she kept sitting on the symbol for metal.

"I'm going to bed," I said. I started up the stairs. I could hear her telling herself a nursery rhyme: "Yigah, hamah, suh tiao twei . . ." The story of the frog jumping from lily pad to lily pad.

In the morning she went to the pet store and came back with fifteen toads that she called heavenly chickens and she kept them under a bowl on the table. With a knife she cut into the skin above each of their eyes and white juice poured out, which she let drip onto a mirror.

"Let that dry," she said when she was done with the toads. The next morning the white juice had dried to a powder, which she collected in a teaspoon and swallowed with her coffee.

When we asked her what the matter was, she waved her hand as if to push us away.

"I'm fine," she said, "leave me alone," and she sat herself back down on metal.

. . .

I saw Paul again. Every weekend he would come by, sometimes driving a beat-up old Citroën he had borrowed from a friend. He would drive me up to the cliffs and we would sit on the hood of the car with our backs against the windshield and out in front of us our legs, entwined, toes pointing toward the sea. Sometimes the Citroën would not start up again, and while Paul held the steering wheel and ran beside the open door, I ran pushing and laughing from behind, my sandals kicking up dust that dirtied my skirt hem and the bottoms of my legs. After the car started we would jump in, and Paul would yell, saying he was hooting and hollering, and then he would bang the outside of the car with his hand. Closer to the sea, passing corn fields on flat roads, Paul would put his arm around me and smile, then he'd look at the road, or maybe at the setting sun, and then he'd look back at me and smile again.

. . .

My father sent me a telegram. "Come to Marseilles this weekend," it said.

My mother begged me not to go. She got down on her knees

and she held on to my ankles and she cried and her black eyeliner ran in her tears down her face.

"If you go there, then he won't come here," she said to me.

"He won't come anyway, Maman," I said.

She did not slap my face. She did not stand up. Instead she slapped at my ankles and dug into my skin with her nails.

On the train to Marseilles I looked down and saw impressions of half-moons up and down my legs.

· · ·

The dogs jumped on me when I opened the door and my father called them off.

That night he told me he was being transferred to Taiwan and that he wanted me to go with him. "What about Minou?" I said.

"She's coming," he said.

"No, I won't go," I said.

"I command you to go," he said.

My father sat back in his chair, and he turned his head, looking out the window at Marseilles. I saw the profile of his nose that was my nose.

"I want you to come with me," he said.

"What for?" I said.

"Because you're mine," he said.

"What about Maman? Isn't she coming too? She's your wife," I said.

"No, that's going to change," he said.

I got up to leave. It was very late. I wanted to go back to Biarritz. I headed for the door.

My father jumped on me and threw me down. He twisted my arm behind my back. My face was on the floor and I could see dog hairs on the wooden boards.

"You're not leaving," he said. "You're my child. No one can ever take that away from me. Not even some goddamned war or Communist regime. They may have taken my home and my country, but I'm the only one who can take you."

I struggled, tried to lift my free arm and hit him, but he got hold of that arm too. I heard the dogs whining.

"Be quiet," I heard him say to them, and they quieted.

I remembered that when I was a girl he had taught me how to put my finger in my mouth and move my finger up and down to whistle to the birds, and I remembered he had said that when I was older he would teach me how to do the whistle without my finger. I started to laugh.

"Is it funny?" he said. I laughed harder. He made me stand up and he took me by the collar to the open window.

Buttons on my shirt had ripped. My brassiere was showing for all the city of Marseilles to see.

"Teach me to whistle now," I said, but I was laughing so hard I couldn't be understood. He leaned me out over the window ledge. I thought to myself, my mother had been right, he was going to kill me.

He was crying, but he did not let me go. Sobbing, he told me I was his daughter and that I was going with him wherever he said I should go and that if I didn't obey he would push me out the window. I could feel his tears wetting my shoulder. I was cold.

"Papa, let me go," I said. He did not answer. He did not loosen his grip. We stayed that way until the sun rose slowly over the city. Church bells rang. Street cleaners started sweeping. My father was falling asleep.

I was able to turn around and get loose. He had slumped to the floor. He mumbled. I got up to leave. Before I closed the door, I turned around and saw that his dogs were standing over him, licking his ears. He was trying to push them away.

THE DAY I MARRIED PAUL I WORE A SILVER SUIT. POULET said I looked like I was a bride from the moon. My mother wasn't there. The marchioness had moved to New York, and my mother's job was now there too. I wanted to invite Madame Han to the wedding, but there was no way to find her in Vietnam. I did not invite my father. The last I heard he had gone to Taiwan, Minou with him and the two dogs.

My amah and Poulet stayed in Biarritz.

Paul and I moved to New York and we lived in a place by the river. Mornings I would walk there and see whores lined up on the docks waiting for men in business suits to drive by. I would walk into the abandoned buildings on the piers. Above me fallen beams resting at angles looked as though they could fall again and hit me on the head. Our first winter the river froze in great chunks of ice. They looked so strong I thought I could stand on one and float for miles.

Paul said I talked in my sleep — he did not know the language. He said it could have been Chinese or Vietnamese. He wanted to tape record what I said so he could play it back to me in the morning.

"Don't," I said.

The marchioness my mother worked for died. My mother came to live with us. She took a job in the afternoons working in an expensive French linen shop. We decided that when Poulet finished school, we would have her sent from France with our amah so she could live with us and we all would be together.

My mother still talked about my father. He had written through a lawyer in Taiwan, saying he wanted a divorce. My mother wrote him back, saying she never would give him one. Minou, his mistress, would never be able to marry him.

In the mornings my mother watched soap operas on television. She would sit in her bathrobe and smoke and cry over the drama on the screen. At dinner she would tell Paul and me what had happened on the shows that day.

"Listen, this is important," she would say, and she would barely finish her meal before she lit up a cigarette and started to tell us stories of loves lost and lives destroyed.

I went to a doctor to have my toes straightened so that it wouldn't hurt when I walked. Before the doctor could operate, he took an x-ray of my foot and said there was a piece of metal inside It turned out to be shrapnel. The doctor couldn't believe I had lived with it for so many years without knowing how it got there. I took the long, curved piece of metal home.

"What was it?" my husband said.

"I think it was part of an airplane," I said. I was hoping it was from the snub-nosed Bristol that André and Tomtom and Su-Su had shown me in the swamp in Saigon. I had always liked that plane.

My mother turned the metal over in her hand. "This is from the Japanese," she said.

"No, I don't think so," I said.

"The Japanese, believe me," she said, and then she went back to watching her television.

There was a blizzard in New York and children on our street made forts of snow and tunneled inside them, jumping up every now and then to throw grenades at each other made out of snow. During commercials my mother went to the window and watched the children playing.

My amah wrote, telling me that my father was flying to New York. I told her I would not see him. My mother thought it meant he was coming back to live with her and that he had grown tired of Minou.

The day his plane was due to arrive, she curled her hair using empty frozen orange juice containers because we had no money for curlers. In the morning she could not sit still and she paced throughout the house with the orange juice containers jiggling as she walked and smelling of oranges. When my father called the house, I had Paul tell him I was not at home, but my mother grabbed the phone from Paul and told my father that she would see him and to please come by as soon as possible. Before my mother could finish what she had to say, my father hung up on her. She kept saying "Hello? Hello?" into the receiver. Paul took the phone from her and hung it up. My mother tore out the orange juice containers from her hair and threw them at the wall. Then she came running at me and she tried to slap me. I caught her hand before she could. I held on to her wrist.

"Stop it, Maman," I said. She looked down. At the side of her foot an orange juice container had come to rest. She picked it up. She touched her curled hair. She held the container up to me so I could see.

"These worked well," she said, and then she started to cry. I held her a long time while she cried. Outside we could hear the children playing battle games in their snow forts, yelling, "Ka-bang! Boom!"

MY FATHER DIED IN 1967, THE YEAR OF THE SHEEP. His liver had failed. We received pictures of his military funeral in Taiwan.

"What a shame," my mother said. "I was just about to give him his divorce."

She cried, but she did not cry as much as she did on the day she thought he was coming to New York to be with her again.

The pictures from Taiwan included some shots of him shortly before his death receiving an award from a Madagascan representative. He had gained weight and his cheeks and his chin looked fat, but his nose was the same.

"He was a good-looking man, your father," my mother said, and she smiled and then she gave me back the photos and put on her hat and went to work at her linen shop uptown.

She did not come home that night. We called the linen shop, but there was no answer. We went to the police. They asked what she looked like.

"Dark hair, red in the light," I said. The policeman looked at me.

"Brown," he said, and typed it on a piece of paper.

I touched my collarbone. "This, her collarbone, is quite pronounced, it's unusual," I said. The policeman looked at Paul. Paul held his hand out at the level of his chin.

"She's about this tall," Paul said.

"Five foot five," the policeman said, and typed it on the piece of paper.

That night Paul and I borrowed a car and drove around the streets of New York looking for her.

"The last time she got lost we found her in a bar," I said.

"You don't think she's in a bar," Paul said.

"I don't know," I said. We drove by her uptown subway stop

and I went down the stairs to look, calling her as I went, listening to "Maman" echo in the empty station.

We drove to a bar near the linen shop. Paul went in while I waited in the car. On the street there was a German shepherd running in traffic. It must have been lost. Cars honked and the dog froze, blinking in front of the headlights. I got out of the car and ran to the dog, whistling so it would come to me. It did not come, instead it ran the other way, heading for the river.

When we finally got to the linen shop the lights were out. On the entire block this was the only store that was dark — all the others had lights on in their windows. Something was wrong. We had to double-park, so Paul stayed with the car, I banged on the door of the shop and yelled, putting my mouth up against the door. I pushed on the door and it opened. I found the light switches but they did not work.

In the light coming in from the street I could see displays of sheets folded like huge Chinese fans hanging from the ceiling. I made my way back to the counter. I felt around. The cash register had been emptied and a pocketbook — my mother's — was also empty.

"Maman!" I yelled. I went to the back of the shop. A door was open slightly and it led down to what must have been the boiler room. I went down the stairs. It was so dark I could not see any shapes and I could not tell how big the room was. When I got to the bottom of the stairs, I was surprised that I had already reached the flat floor.

I heard someone moaning in the dark. I screamed. When I stopped screaming I could still hear moaning. I reached out and started walking. When I bumped into someone sitting in a chair, I checked to see if it was my mother by feeling for her collarbone, the way a blind person would feel the nose and mouth and skull of a stranger.

I pulled a gag from out of her mouth and untied the rope that was around her wrists. It was difficult for her to speak because her mouth was dry. She swallowed, she made a sound with her throat, and then at last she spoke.

"Am I free now?" she asked, rubbing her wrists.

"Yes, Maman," I said, "you are free."

"Then let's go," she said.

Heading up the stairs in the dark, my mother and I collided, sending each other off balance. I reached out to steady her by the hands and at the same time she reached out to hold mine.

"Shall we dance?" she said.